Books by Ivan Scott

Redhead in a Blue Convertible

The Redhead and the Ghostwriter

A Redhead in Tottenham

The Redhead Who Loves Hemingway

A Redhead in Brooklyn

The Redhead and the Fountain Pen

Ivan Scott

Copyright © 2024 Ivan Scott
All rights reserved.
ISBN: 9798340741813

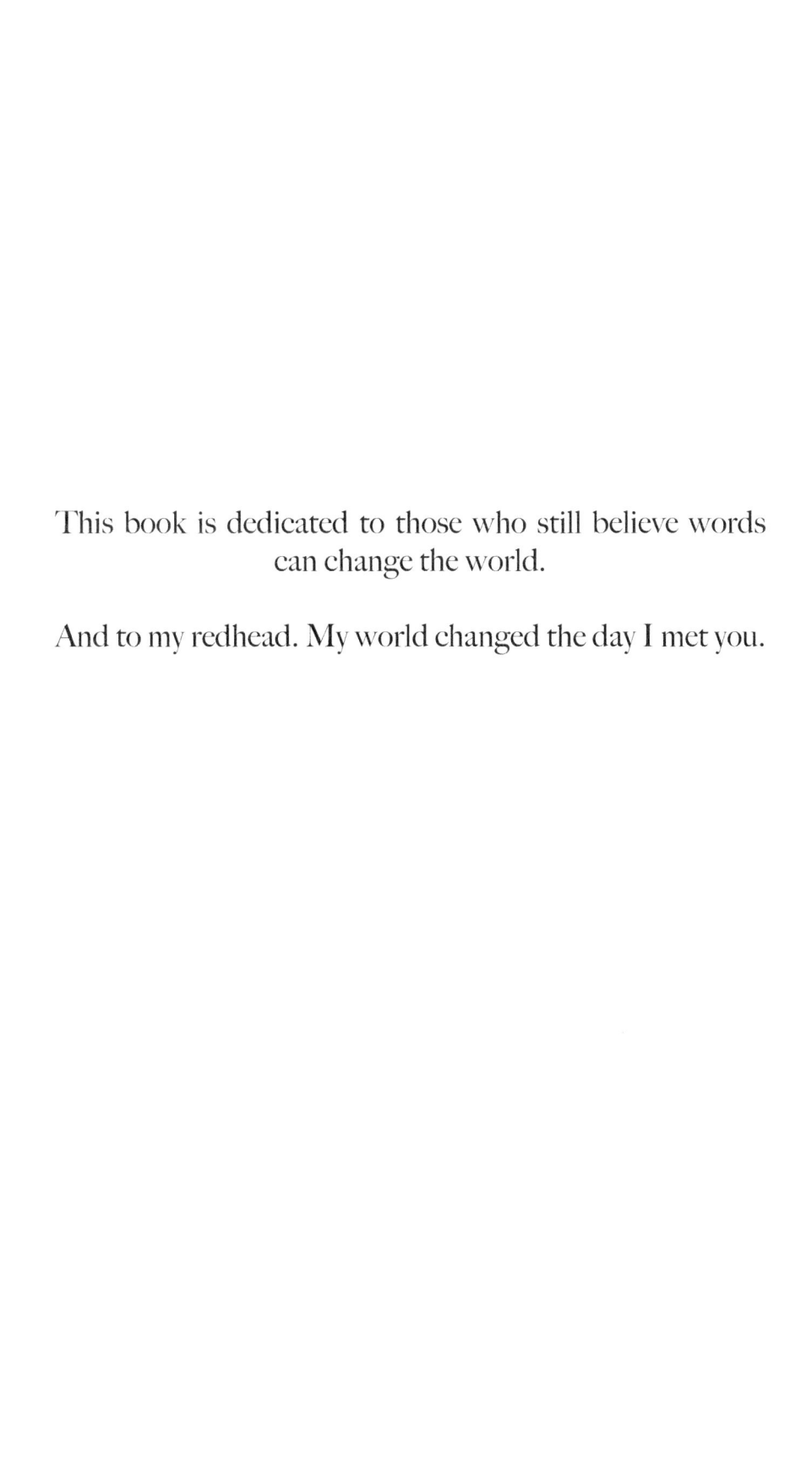

This book is dedicated to those who still believe words can change the world.

And to my redhead. My world changed the day I met you.

one

Catherine.

A name in a letter found in a used copy of *The Great Gatsby* on a dusty bookshelf. I don't know who she is, but I know what happened. And I can't get her out of my head.

Finding her letter in a place I'd never thought I'd be makes me believe someone is pulling the cosmic strings of life. And each string pulls us to where we need to be, at the exact time we need to be there. In life, there are times when we never give a second thought to a minuscule moment flashing by. But it's in those fleeting seconds we become what destiny has waiting for us.

So, one of those minuscule moments came my way earlier today. It was lunchtime, so I ventured out of my new home in the scenic town of Blue Ridge, Georgia see what this sleepy town was all about.

As I walked around the streets, I found the older brick buildings looked renovated and lively. The best part about the town was the wide awnings over the sidewalks, which shielded me from the suffocating July heat.

My new boss, Tara Sutton, told me the best cheeseburgers in the world were at a place called Juniors. When I asked where Juniors was, she said, "On the corner of Maple and Main." As I thought about living in small-town America, where else would it be?

When I arrived at the intersection, I instinctively sniffed for the sweet smell of charred meat. As I walked further, I didn't smell burgers but inhaled a memory from the past. It was the sweet, inky smell of old books. I stopped, closed my eyes, and swore I was in heaven.

The intoxicating scent brings me back to the days when I was nine years old and my mom brought me to a library for the first time. No matter how many years pass, the smell of coffee and hardwoods brings me back to that day standing next to her. Those were days when things weren't as complicated.

I looked around to find where the smell came from. When I turned, I saw my reflection in a glass storefront with the words "Blue Ridge Books" staring back at me. Okay, I can put my stomach on hold for a bit. Let's put my mind to work instead.

I've always had a thing for books. And to be honest, that love has heightened as I've encountered the social media world. Since I'm not a big fan of social media, the last thing I want to do when I finish my day is spend time on the laptop reading about people I've never met.

Besides, I told myself I need to read more books. Take more walks. I need to look someone in the eye, speak to them, soak in their reaction, and let them see me too. Since I need to get my life in order, I shouldn't be wasting time with my nose pressed to a screen reading about other people's lives.

The Redhead and the Fountain Pen

Tucked into the corner of the bookstore were tables and chairs. Behind them a glass counter with sweets resting inside. The odor of blueberry muffins, sugar cookies, and chocolate fudge lured me in that direction.

I ordered a large, gooey oatmeal cookie and a glass of lemonade. The man at the counter told me it would be out in a minute, so I said thank you, then turned and walked to the bookshelves. As I moved forward, my eyes widened when they came to my favorite book.

"Hello, Mr. Gatsby," I said, then pulled it from the shelf. "You're coming with me."

I pulled the book off the shelf and looked inside. As the pages flipped from back to front, a powder blue envelope slipped out and dropped at my feet. I reached down and pulled it from the floor. "Someone forgot to mail this," I said.

The first thing calling out to me was the January postmark. I read the name, Jacob Elster, who lived in Brooklyn, in the middle, and in the upper left corner was a street address, but no name. "Wow, you have had some travels, my friend."

I flipped the envelope over and noticed the ripped flap, so I reached inside and pulled out a folded piece of paper. As I straightened it out, I gazed at an elegant script splashed in purple ink soaked into the crisp ivory paper. The handwriting was beautiful. The words were not.

Dear Jacob:

You might not understand what this is, since it's not on social media, but let me clue you in. This is a letter. I figured I'd explain the concept.

I didn't appreciate what happened on the bridge. Why did you have to be a jackass and tell me how stupid I am to chase my dream? You should have walked away, instead of pulling my heart out and stomping all over it.

There were nights I wished you would leave me an encouraging note. Or asked how practice went. Anything to show you cared. But none of that happened, and after a while, I stopped asking. No worries, I became stronger knowing I had to do this by myself.

As I walked across the bridge, I said goodbye to Brooklyn and hello to a new world. With every step toward Manhattan, the confidence in my abilities and perseverance makes me believe I can do anything. This is my destiny. I make no apologies for who I am, and never will.

Your coldness has only strengthened my resolve. On Friday, I will march over to Geffen Hall and put on the audition of my life. And I won't care where you are, or if I ever see you again.

Goodbye, Jacob.

Catherine

I couldn't take my eyes off the thick purple ink and how the words weaved a tapestry of hurt, but also resolve. She writes as if she will make her dreams a reality, no matter what stands in her way.

As I wondered what Catherine might be doing at this moment, a shadow approached. "Good afternoon. You must be Coach Dawson."

I turned to see a reddish-gray-haired woman with glasses on a chain around her neck standing in front of me. One hand held a plate with what looked like an oatmeal cookie on it and in the other she grasped a tall paper cup. "Here's your order."

"Thanks. Yes, I'm Coach Dawson," I said with a genuine

smile, then I tucked the envelope back into the book. "How'd you know that?" I asked, then took the items from her.

"I'm Irish, so my intelligence is just below that of the almighty. And the gap ain't much," she said with a wry grin and a trace of Irish accent. As she looked me over, the grin vanished. "So, you're the new softball coach? You don't look like much to me."

Her verbal jab left me enamored instead of insulted because I like women with a little sass. My smile went from genuine to flirtatious. "Well, opinions vary."

The woman's wrinkled face, hard a few seconds before, softened, and a grin formed. "Now that's what I like. A man with stones."

"I like a woman with stones too." When she furrowed her brow and stared at me, I thought about what I said. "What I meant was…Well, forget it. You get the idea."

The grin returned. "Welcome to Blue Ridge. I'm Scarlett McKeegan. I own the joint."

"Scarlett McKeegan? I knew I'd meet a nice Jewish girl one of these days."

Scarlett giggled, then told me, "Confidence. A crooked smile. And a sense of humor. I like you already," she said with a twinkle in her eye. When someone from the back called her name, she turned, told the person she'd be right over, then looked back at me. "I have a feeling you'll be back."

Her green eyes bore into me as if I was in the middle of some Jedi Mind Warp trick. I nodded. "Um, yeah. I'll be back."

She grinned, then looked at the book in my hands. "Oh, *Gatsby*. Nice pull. Tell ya what. Since this is your first time in my bookstore, that one is on me."

"Really?"

"Yeah. What can I say? I'm a sucker for a crooked smile. See ya around, Coach," she said, then handed me my order.

I watched her vanish, then walked out of the bookstore to find a cheeseburger. The ice-cold lemonade would help with the hot day. The cookie I would save for dessert.

✒

As the sun dipped below the mountains, I sat on the deck and watched the last hours of sunlight on this summer evening. I turned on the deck lights, then took a seat on the couch next to my copy of *Gatsby*.

I opened the book, then pulled out the powder blue envelope and read Catherine's letter again. As I digested her words, I looked up to see an old friend walk over and pull up a chair. He sat, reached inside his jacket pocket, and pulled out his flask. "Hello, old sport," he grinned, then looked at the book. "I see you got to read about lost love today."

"Oh yeah," I told him. "What can I say, Scott? Your story never gets old."

"I wasn't talking about my book," he said, then sipped from the flask. "A letter written in January travels 800 miles to Blue Ridge and finds itself in your favorite book in July. What are the odds?"

I squinted. "How do you know about the letter?"

"I know a lot of things," he said with a sly grin. "Being a ghost has its perks."

I exhaled. "Yeah, what are the odds?"

"I'm glad you asked. The odds of having another sip from my silent partner here are pretty good," he said, shaking the flask. As far as you go, wanna make the odds even better?"

"Nah. I'm good."

He frowned. "I hate drinking alone."

"You know there has to be someone, somewhere in the world, having a brown water drink at this very moment. So technically, you're not alone."

He raised his flask in salute. "Bless you, Mark," he said, then took another sip.

"What are you doing here?"

"I've been drunk for about a week now, and thought it might sober me up to sit in a library."

"We're on the deck of my cabin."

Scott looked around. "I'm sure there are books around here somewhere." Then he looked down at his tan and white lace-up Oxfords, removed a smudge on the tip, then looked at me. "I wanted to check on you, old sport."

"I'm good. It's nice to be in a new place so I can shake off old memories."

He nodded. "It's good to climb up your thumb sometimes."

Scott spoke in 20s slang often, but some of his phrases went over my head. "I'm sorry?"

"It means to get away. It was the best thing for you." He took another sip, then asked, "What did you think about the letter?"

"There's something intriguing about this girl. I liked reading that she has courage and perseverance. Those things have always resonated with me."

"Look, I'm no gumshoe, but I have a feeling you are about to enter the best time of your life. Keep moving forward and everything will work out." He smiled, then brought his wrist closer to his face. After studying his watch for a few seconds, he told me, "Mind if I get back to New York? I'm on deadline."

"You writing another book?"

"Nah. I have to get home to Zelda. She doesn't like it when I come home late. And when I stumble home, she gets saucy." He stood, looked me over, then said, "You remind me of Gatsby."

"Yeah? I've been looking toward Atlanta like Gatsby did when he gazed at the green light at the end of Daisy's dock. Now I know how he felt."

"I have a feeling about you, old sport. As long as you keep looking for the green light, you'll be okay."

"What's so important about looking for the green light?"

As I looked into the navy blue sky, the only things answering me were the crickets. "Why does he always bail when things are getting good?"

I stood and walked to the railing to take in the peaceful colors of the sunset descending into the mountains. As I stared, my mind asked questions about what the next few months held, and how I was going to handle things. But the longer I stared, the longer the silence confirmed there were no answers. I was on my own to find whatever waited for me.

As the world came back into focus, I walked back to the couch, picked up the letter, and gave it a closer look. As I held the paper in my hands, I asked myself, "What happened on the bridge?

The Redhead and the Fountain Pen

And what was she auditioning for? Who is Catherine and what she's doing now? Is there a way I could help her?"

I stood, then picked up the book, and walked back into my cabin. The first thing I saw was my unzipped backpack with folders sticking out of it. The folders contained player bios, practice and training plans, and game strategies.

As I pondered what lay inside, thoughts of the mystery girl faded into thoughts of a bunch of mystery girls who needed my help more than she did. I have other things to focus on, like my new job, as well as my new life. That trumps any fantasies I have of saving the damsel in distress. It's noble, I'll give you that. But it's also pointless.

The last time I cared about something dear to me, it tossed me aside like yesterday's trash. With the way things are going, I don't need to add some mystery girl to the long list of garbage collectors. Besides, as I mentioned earlier, I don't like getting into the business of strangers, no matter how intriguing it might be.

I'm going to let the mystery stay a mystery. But I will say a prayer that Catherine's broken heart healed, and her audition went well.

two

Have you ever had the feeling you're an actor following a script? Well, today, that's me.

I mentioned Catherine and how I planned on forgetting about her. Getting the team ready for the season, plus being the new coach at Blue Ridge Prep, has me busy. Now is not the time to have any distractions.

Well, all that lasted for about a day.

I spent the morning reading player bios, and when I finished, I scooped up the papers and placed them in a folder. Lo-and-behold, Catherine's letter fell off my desk. Funny. I don't remember putting it there. I shook my head, picked it up, and tossed it back to where it came from.

So, fast forward to this morning. I scanned my desk for an insurance form to send to the parents. As I thumbed through the mess of papers on my desk, I found a folder and opened it to see if the form was inside. It wasn't, but the envelope was. Again, I don't remember putting it there, so I dismissed it as being absent-minded. I get that way during the season.

I picked it out of the folder and dropped it in the wastebasket.

Since it was trash day, it would disappear into the abyss of the trash bin, then I'd roll it to the curb, and that would be that.

But the strings of destiny begged to differ.

When I got home tonight, I ate dinner, then walked to my desk so I could resume analyzing the player bios. The first thing I saw was the wastebasket with trash in it. Someone forgot to take it down before he left this morning. Oops.

When I looked into the basket, the envelope with the familiar handwriting lay on top. Cue the spooky music.

I spent most of the evening on my deck, drinking brown water, and looking into the night. I thought about how I like to howl at the moon, as all people do when their tragic past is still fresh in their memory. As I slipped back to the present, I thought it foolish to wish for the impossible. After downing the rest of my watered-down drink, I thought about the envelope and how it kept popping back into my life. Was someone pulling the cosmic strings I wrote about earlier? But why?

The moon glowed, dripping its silvery beams into the mountains below. The sight made me wonder if Catherine was howling at the same moon, not knowing someone was thinking about her. Someone who also hurt.

As much as I denied it, I needed to do something.

I looked at the empty glass. It must have been the brown water cranking the wheel, but my mind opened like a budding rose. When it came to full bloom, I was no longer a realist but a romantic. My vow not to get involved with strangers melted away like the ice in my glass, and now there was no turning back. I decided the girls could wait for one more night since there was one girl who needed me right now. How could I say no?

As I thought about what to do next, another sobering reality hit me. Was I about to fall face-first into my own...what do they call it? A RomCom? No, it can't be. There is no way I would let that happen. But as I thought about the situation, I went through each point to see if I was safe.

After visiting a few websites, I found what I was looking for. It seems The Hallmark Channel is the gold standard for these kinds of movies. Especially Christmas movies. Oh, it gets worse. There's also something called a RomCom-A-Thon. That's scary.

I found another website listing elements all RomComs must have, so I compared the list to what I'm doing now.

#1 - Two lovable leads. Okay, Catherine seems lovable. I love her passion and strong will. And that woman from the bookstore. Scarlett? She said she likes me. I know that might be semantics, but I have to give that a check mark. Okay, no worries. That's only one.

#2 - A Meet Cute. I have no idea what this meant, so I had to look it up. It's a first meeting where something unique happens that brings the pair together.

I guess finding Catherine's letter might qualify as a meet-cute. I don't know how cute it was, finding a letter where she gets her heart broken, but okay. After a judge's ruling, I'm two for two.

#3 - A unique and troublesome situation. I'm in Blue Ridge. She's in New York. She broke up with her boyfriend and has a broken heart. My heart is being held together with duct tape and Elmer's. Both sound like a troublesome situation, so that's three.

#4 - A good sidekick. Whoo Hoo! I'm saved because...Wait. There's that Scarlett woman from the bookstore. She seems like she'd be fun to hang out with.

The Redhead and the Fountain Pen

There were more listed, but I stopped since I was four for four. I tried to deny the obvious, but it was there, plain as day. I'm smack dab in the middle of a RomCom. Oh goodie...

Now, if I could only look like Ryan Paevey or Cameron Mathison (I had to look them up so don't get any ideas about me knowing jack about RomComs). Okay, following the RomCom Playbook, the script calls for me to find her. Since I'm stuck in Blue Ridge with a full-time job and can't leave, I'll do the next best thing and send her a letter. Besides, a letter is a lot cheaper than a plane ticket.

I figured it wouldn't be too difficult. But, as I wadded up page after page and tossed it across the room into the wastebasket, I was getting nowhere. At this point, if I had to write out a grocery list, I would have screwed that up too.

I made it more difficult by having another splash of brown water. As I sipped, I counted the balls of paper on the floor, instead of inside the wastebasket. As the number climbed, I was no closer to writing a coherent sentence.

"It's not as easy as it looks," a voice said.

I looked across my desk and there was F. Scott, sitting in my leather chair, flask in his hand. "I would ask if you wanted a drink to help with the creative process, but I'm certain another drink will help you in the pass-out process."

"Oh, you're funny. Did you stay up all night rehearsing that one?"

He took another sip then said, "I have my moments. So, you want to write to that Jane, huh?"

I was about to answer, then stopped. I squinted and asked,

"How do you know I was writing to her?"

Scott smiled. "Being a ghost has its perks. It's amazing how easy it is to slip in and out of places when you're invisible." He took a swig from the flask, then asked, "Why are you doing this? Don't you have a football team to coach?"

"It's softball, and yes, I do."

He grinned. "So, why are you doing it?"

I found one of the crumpled-up pieces of paper on my desk, tossed it toward the wastebasket, then sat back in my chair. "I don't know. There's something about that letter that won't let me walk away."

Scott rose, then walked over, picked up the paper, and pried it apart. He read the words, scrunched up his nose like he'd sniffed spoiled milk, then shook his head. "Yuck. If that gal reads this, you won't have to worry about walking away. She'll do it for you." He crumpled up the paper and said under his breath, "More like run away."

I gave him a fake laugh. "I told you, I'm working on it."

"Are you sure you want to do this? You don't know who she is. She could be a real pill."

"Or be in real trouble."

"You love helping the damsel in distress, don't you?"

I thought about Catherine's letter, then smiled. "Everyone needs a hobby."

Scott shook his head and laughed. "That's a lot of bunk." After another sip, he leaned forward. "My advice is to drink. A lot. That way, when you make a fool of yourself writing to a Jane you've never met, then you'll have an excuse. Oh, and you won't care about the consequences. Well, until you wake up the next morning. At least that will take your mind off your hangover."

"Thanks for the vote of confidence."

Scott smiled. "I see what's going on here, old sport."

"You do? Tell me so we'll both know."

"You pull a book off the shelf in a place you shouldn't have been. Then a letter falls out. After repeated attempts to discard it, the envelope magically reappears, causing you to track down the girl who wrote it."

"What do you know about the letter reappearing?"

Scott threw up his hands. "Aw, who can remember?"

"Did you–" I began, then stopped. "Aw, you wouldn't tell me anyway."

"Can't you see the magic in this?"

"The word I'd use is tragic. You're only a letter off though."

Scott grinned. "I hate to tell you this, but what we have here is a full-fledged Romantic Comedy unfolding before our eyes."

As Scott laughed, I replied, "Oh, no. Not you too."

He sat back and nodded like he'd been given a case of bourbon.

As Scott laughed, I told him, "I'm not in a Romantic Comedy."

"I might have been born last night, but I wasn't born yesterday. I know a little something about attraction. And I see it all over your face."

"Scott, you've been dead since 1940. Your compass is off."

He took a sip from his flask, then nodded. "Tell me something.

What are you doing now?"

I looked at the floor, then back to him. "I'm trying out a new fountain pen?"

"Nice try. But I don't see it. Then again, by the time I finish what's inside my silent partner here," he said, shaking the flask in front of him, "I won't be able to see much anyway."

"Great. I'm writing to someone I've never met, speaking to a ghost who's hittin' the sauce and I'm reliving ninth-grade English. And I thought life would be simpler by moving away from Atlanta."

"With the sunshine and the great bursts of leaves growing on the trees, just as things grow in fast movies, I had that familiar conviction that life was beginning over again with the summer."

"I know where you got that one, my friend."

"Thanks. For a minute, I thought you'd forgotten me and were reading Hemingway's books. Damn, that son of a bitch could write."

I looked at the mess of papers on my desk, then told him, "I wish I could write like he did." When Scott raised an eyebrow, I added, "Well, after you, of course."

He laughed, which eased the tension. "Papa Hem once told me he writes ninety-one pages of shit for every one page of a masterpiece. Judging by the mess on the floor, you heard that speech too."

I looked at the mess on the floor, then told him, "I'm trying not to repeat the past."

"Can't repeat the past? Of course, you can. I've got faith in you." Then he took another sip from the flask.

"Thanks for the vote of confidence. Are you going to help me or not?"

While I rubbed my eyes, he asked, "Having trouble putting pen to paper?" Then he focused on my hand. "Or rather, fountain pen to paper? By the way, nice pen. These days, you don't see too many of those."

As I looked at the blue fountain pen in my fingers, I smiled, then told him, "Thanks. Call me old school, but this is the only pen I write with."

Scott took a long pull from his flask, then sat back. "Well, now that you've made me wistful for the old days, let me help. I used to be a talented writer myself."

I nodded. "Used to be?"

He shook his head. "I haven't written anything in decades. As president of my fan club, you should know this," then he laughed and took another sip. After he swallowed, he asked, "What do you have so far?"

I looked down at the paper. "Okay. Here it goes. Dear Catherine." After that, the rest of the page was blank. I looked up and told him, "Well, that's about as far as I've gotten."

Scott shook his head, then exhaled. "My heart is all a flutter."

"Gee, thanks. Now, unless I need to get the paddles and shock your heart back to normal, tell me what should I write?"

He stood and walked over to the desk. "Okay. Writing 101. All good writing is swimming underwater and holding your breath."

I scribbled his words down.

"Oh, don't be a sap," he said with a laugh. "Don't write. Just listen and learn."

I nodded, then placed my pen next to the paper on the desk.

"It means, old sport, that you dive deep into the water, and you don't come up until you're finished. You put everything you have into focusing on the message you want the person to understand. Once you've crafted your message, and you've conveyed the feeling you want the reader to have, then come up for air."

I looked at him and squinted.

He laughed. "Don't worry if it doesn't make sense. You'll figure it out. Give me a shout if you get stuck." He rose, then walked into the darkened part of the room and vanished.

After a few more attempts, which was difficult because of my blurry eyes, I dropped my fountain pen. "I'll pick this up tomorrow when I'm sober."

Oh well. Catherine could wait another day, especially since help was on the way.

three

I began the morning with a walk around the trails close to my cabin. It was the perfect distraction to overcome my writer's block.

Once I returned to my office, I resumed what I crashed and burned doing last night.

I began with a clear head and an optimism Scott would appreciate. Seeing the mountains in the distance calmed me, and it was what I needed as the creativity gushed out of me. I'm not saying I re-created *The Great Gatsby*, but I thought I hit the bullseye for what I wanted to communicate.

Okay, here it goes.

Dear Catherine:

My name is Mark, and I found your letter in a copy of The Great Gatsby while I was in a used bookstore in Blue Ridge, Georgia. I wasn't sure what was in the envelope, so I opened it and read about what happened on the bridge.

Apologies for invading your privacy, but I wanted to tell you how sorry I am about this. I know what you are feeling and am sorry you are having a tough time. I'd be happy to help you get through it since there is strength in numbers.

Peace be with you, Catherine. I hope what happened with Jacob is a distant memory, and you did well at your audition.

Mark

I folded the letter, placed it in the envelope, and sealed it. After adding her address to the middle and mine to the upper left, I walked to the mailbox and placed it inside. Before I closed the lid, I gave the envelope a long look. "Have a safe trip, my friend."

Earlier this afternoon, I had lunch with my new boss, Tara Sutton.

I remember the day I got her voicemail. She asked if I had time to speak with her about the open position at Blue Ridge Prep for a softball coach. At first, I wasn't interested, since I wanted to get as far away from coaching as I could. But she was charmingly persistent in a way that made me like her immediately. Within the first minutes of our phone conversation, I knew we'd be good friends.

We sat inside the Blue Ridge Cafe, reminiscing about our first meeting. "Remember what we talked about when you offered me the job?"

Tara smiled and nodded. "Oh, yeah. I practiced my entire speech in the car on the way there, and as soon as you walked in, I forgot every word."

"Whatever you said must have worked," I told her.

"Well, we're all glad you're here." She took a sip of tea, then placed her glass down and asked, "So, how does the softball team look this year?"

I exhaled, then shrugged. "I hope people are patient. I'm a hard worker. Not a miracle worker."

After lunch, I drove to Blue Ridge Prep to get my office set up. Once I got everything organized, I walked out of the athletic building and around the campus.

I wondered what the tuition for a place like this would run. I'm sure the parents were paying through the nose to have their kids attend a place like this. Then I asked myself, paying through the nose? Who came up with that one? Why would anyone use their nose to pay their bills? Do you jerk your arm up and down and the money tumbles out like a slot machine? Or do you have to sneeze it out? And would the person you are paying accept such a payment? Are there handkerchiefs involved? Sorry, I needed the humor.

As I walked around, taking in the sight of the ivy-covered Gothic-style buildings, I passed the batting cage. I heard the ping of a metal bat connecting with a ball, so I walked closer and saw two girls inside. I stayed away from view as I listened to their exchange.

The blonde swung her bat, sending a line drive ricocheting off the protective net in front of the pitcher. "Nice one, Josie," the pitcher told her.

"Thanks, Anna. By the way, do you know who our new coach is?"

Anna stopped and tossed the ball into her glove. "Nah. Whoever it is, they have to be better than last year."

Josie lowered her bat, then looked out to Anna. "Was it the coach, or were we that bad?"

Anna looked down and shook her head. "I used to think it

was the coach. But lately, I think we drove him to drink."

Josie shrugged. "I don't know. After last year, I was close to not coming back."

"You were going to quit?" Anna asked. "You're our captain and our best player. Why would you do that?"

"Nobody cares about us. Why keep playing when the only people watching are your parents and the other team? What's the point?" She shook her head. "They should have closed us down when they had the chance," she said, staring at the artificial turf of the batting cage floor.

"We both have college recruiters looking at us. We can't stop now. Josie, if you quit, then they were right about us. If we give up, then we aren't worthy of being on anyone's softball team."

I took Josie's comment and filed it away. What worries me is when the captain wants to jump ship, the rest of the players usually follow. Now I knew what I was walking into.

Between sending letters to a girl I don't know, and now this, I should have stayed in Atlanta and gotten a job collecting trash. I'd be a little smelly, that's for sure, but I'd sleep better at night.

four

It's been a few days, so I thought I would check-in. Still no letter from Catherine. I know it has been a week, and the normal letter from Atlanta to New York takes three days. (Yes, I looked it up... And no, I'm not obsessed). Do you think it might take longer to get there since the post office in Blue Ridge might not be as fast as the one in Atlanta? Call it a hunch...

I must confess I thought about my letter more than a few times this week. When did she get it? What did she think? What if she moved and never got it? Then, of course, I shifted from the letter to who she was. What was her dream? And why did her ex run off with someone else? The questions kept coming with no answers.

One question answered earlier is what my softball team looks like. We had our first practice today, and there is a lot of work to do to get ready for the season. That means I need to put away my thoughts about the post office. It's time to get my nose on the grindstone to get ready for the biggest challenge I've ever faced as a coach.

I've always wondered. Has anyone ever put their nose to a grindstone? Is that how they did nose jobs in prehistoric days? Isn't there another way to work harder? I don't know. It sounds like too much pain and not enough of a reward.

Back to the team. They are polite, eager, and desperate to be successful. However, since the last coach didn't care, it takes a while for a team to believe in a leader again. I assured them this was a new day and what happened last year was over. But I saw in their eyes they were not ready to trust me yet. I have to earn it.

With that, I am going to put something on the stove, watch video of our practices, and put a plan together for our first game. I'll be back later tonight.

Guess what? After dinner, I walked out to the mailbox. When I dug my hand inside and pulled out the letters, there was a powder blue envelope wedged between the others. The color and shape were the same as I remembered from the one that fell out of the book, so it must be from New York. My smile grew.

I hurried into the cabin, tossed the other envelopes on the marble counter top, then sat in my favorite chair. My heartbeat accelerated as I tore the envelope open. But as I read the words on the paper, the excitement faded into disappointment.

Whoever Catherine is, she wasn't too happy to hear from me. Her reply was brief, so this won't take long.

Dear Mark:

I received your letter and although I appreciate your words, it's best to keep out of my affairs.

I fell on my ass during the audition. Then last month, I found out my ex is engaged.

Having someone I've never met reminding me of my inadequacies is something I don't need right now. I would appreciate you leaving me and this matter alone.

Sincerely –

Catherine

Gee, that went well. Give me a second to jump into the lake so I can put out the flames engulfing me at the moment...

I don't fault Catherine and understand her feelings. I'm sure some of the venom from her letter came from me asking about her ex and, of course, the audition. Way to rub that salt into her wounds, Mark.

I guess this wasn't the best idea I've had, but at the time I thought it was the right thing to do. Then again, I've questioned my decisions over the last few months, so this goes to show I can't do anything right.

No matter if it was well-intended, I've upset someone and have to take responsibility for my actions. That won't be too difficult since she told me to leave things alone. The good thing is, since we are 900 miles apart, I won't have to worry about bumping into her on the street anytime soon.

I'll say a prayer for her, and as long as God doesn't snitch on me, I won't get another spanking for meddling in her affairs.

Whew. I'm glad my brief foray into the fantasy world is over and I can get back to reality. I have my own matters to sort out, and at the top of the list is rebuilding the Blue Ridge Prep softball team. Now that my focus is completely on them, there is no telling what we can do.

five

Today we opened the season against Ellijay South. Although we played better than I expected, they beat us 10-9.

After the game I walked over to help the student managers pack up the equipment. As I stuffed shin guards into a canvas bag, I looked down to the end of the dugout and saw our starting pitcher, Anna, sitting by herself with her head bowed and torso shaking. The team looked at me, so I walked over and sat beside her. "Hey, Anna. What's up?"

Through the sniffles, she said, "You can pitch someone else next time. The old coach never believed in me, so I guess he was right." I leaned back against the wall of the dugout, waiting for her to speak. Anna took a towel and wiped her face. "I'm sorry, Coach."

"Sorry? What are you sorry for?"

"Losing the game."

"Losing the game?" I laughed to ease the tension. "Last time I checked, and I check every game, there are nine other players on the field. We all have room to improve. Even me. We'll get better and you will too. By the way, do me a favor."

The Redhead and the Fountain Pen

She looked over at me and sniffled. "Yes, coach?"

"When you are on the mound against Union County on Monday, throw more rise balls when you're ahead in the count."

Her eyes lit up, and a tear rolled out of the sparkle. "You're pitching me against Union County? I thought you were coming over to say you were cutting me?"

I shook my head. "Cutting you? Anna, you're the best pitcher we have. If I didn't think you could do the job, I wouldn't have put you on the field. I expect you to be at the top of your game on Monday. Understand? Oh, and one more thing. If you want to cry, do it on the way home. Lesson number one: never let anyone see you cry in public. You be cocky and arrogant, even if you've lost. Bawl your eyes out in the car on the way home if you want to. But never in the dugout. Okay?"

Anna stood, wiped her cheeks, and smiled. She gave me a mock salute. "Yes, sir."

"Now get out of here. I'm sure you have homework."

She laughed, then trotted out of the dugout.

✒

Tonight, I'm going to make dinner, watch video of our game, then have the best night's sleep I've had in weeks. Kind of boring, I know. But after the last few days with all the ups and downs of Catherine's letter, and worrying about our first game, I'd love some boredom.

Before I sign off for the night, I thought you'd appreciate this. When I was eating dinner earlier, I heard the mail truck pass by. It stopped, then I heard the engine rev, and a few seconds later, grew silent. I had to remind myself I didn't have to worry about what was in the mailbox any longer. I'm sure there was nothing important in there anyway, so I'll check it tomorrow.

✒

So much for boredom.

When I walked to the mailbox after work today, there was a powder blue envelope on top of the stack. I did a double-take. "What the hell?" Then it hit me. God snitched. Thanks, big guy.

It took a while for me to summon the courage to open it. What could the letter contain? A pen pal restraining order? My envelopes can't go within five hundred feet of her mailbox?

Then I thought, well, she has no reason to scold me a second time. Once was enough. But what if she's still upset? What if she wants to get a few extra shots in for kicks? With the way things are going in my life, anything was possible.

I patted the letter down a few times, held it to the light, and put it to my ear. When I didn't hear ticking, there was nothing left to stall the inevitable.

I walked out to the deck, and as I sliced the seal open, I pulled my face back and winced. When nothing exploded, I unfolded the letter, and my eyes scanned the paper. The only surprise came from her words.

Dear Mark:

I want to apologize for my previous letter. I was having a bad day and your letter came at the wrong time.

After I had time to reflect, I realized your letter for what it was. Kind words to help me through a tough time. Thank you.

I am also grateful to know you found my book. It belonged to my father and is special to me. I'm glad it's no longer lost.

The Redhead and the Fountain Pen

I hope your offer of friendship didn't have a statute of limitations, and if so, could I change my vote to a yes? In my defense, I am a natural redhead. And sometimes, we can be saucy. Is there a preemptive Redhead Apology Clause I can invoke here? haha

If I could slide that in before the statute of limitations runs out, I have a question. Favorite movie - Gone With the Wind or An Affair to Remember? Mine is GWTW, since I have always had a crush on Clark Gable, but Cary Grant is a close second. Sorry, I sound like an old grandma, and I assure you I'm not, but I like classic movies. Do you like classic movies too? If not, no problem. I thought that was a nice icebreaker question.

Speaking of movies, my friends tease me about watching RomComs. I know it's the same story over and over, and things look bleak in the last fifteen minutes but always have resolution in the last five. Sorry, but I love sappy endings. I know men don't watch those kinds of movies, but I thought mentioning it might be a nice way for you to get to know something about me.

In your letter, you wrote there were reasons you are in the position you are in, so I hope we can share our stories since they sound similar.

Let me know what you think.

Your new friend (Well, hoping to be after my last letter) -

Catherine

Wow, so I'm not such a jackass after all? I guess you never know what a new day will bring. I made a new friend, and also someone who might help me find where I am going since I don't have a clue.

After reading her letter, I read it again, shaking my head with a smile. This is a breath of fresh air from the social media world. I don't know what she looks like, where she's from, or who she is. All

I have are her words, splashed in purple ink on thick white paper. I like it much more than an antiseptic font in a text, email, or social media page.

I couldn't see her face but imagined her eyes scanning each word of her letter as she read it over before folding it up and placing it in the envelope. My finger traced along the paper, knowing her fingers did the same. She not only touched the paper, but she also touched me with her words.

Here's what I came back with...

Dear Catherine:

I was excited to get your letter. Well, the second letter...haha. No worries. I apologize for the intrusion and am happy you reconsidered. It's great to meet you.

The odds of finding your letter were astronomical, so one of these days, I'll have to tell you what happened. I guess it was serendipity (Since I have a thing for Kate Beckinsale, it's one of the few RomComs I've watched). It's nice to know I've made a new friend. And a redhead too? I better start reading books on the side if I am going to keep up with you!

To answer your question, yes, I've seen both Gone With the Wind and An Affair To Remember. Both movies are iconic for their endings. One of my all-time favorite lines from GWTW is, "I've always had a weakness for lost causes once they're really lost."

I lean toward An Affair To Remember. I loved the scene after the death of Nickie's grandmother. He's standing in her house after the funeral, and he hears a piano in the distance like a ghost is playing and then a woman singing. He knows it's Deborah Kerr. Even though she rejected him, and he will never see her again, he puts his hand on the chair she sat in, hoping to feel her one last time. The look on his face, knowing the woman he loves is gone forever, is unforgettable. I'm like you with classic movies. They don't make them like that any longer.

RomComs, huh? Don't tell anyone this, but I have to confess I liked You've Got Mail. Tom Hanks and Meg Ryan were great together.

Here's a question - Favorite book and why? Mine is The Great Gatsby. Good thing that is my favorite book or I wouldn't have found your letter. I like Fitzgerald and that book is my favorite because Gatsby faced terrible odds but fought back, even though he knew He'd never win. Something about that resonates with me.

Since we are now writing letters, do you have a favorite pen? I have a few fountain pens I like to write with and am using one to write this letter. What do you like to write with? Who knows, one day, I could have some fun and pull out the crayons, and write to you that way. After a few brown water drinks, which is what I call Irish Whiskey, anything is possible...haha

I will continue praying for you, and hope your pain passes.

Your new friend-
Mark
PS - By the way, instead of writing goodbye, or see you later, how about we end our letters with, "I look forward to our next correspondence?"

After I sealed the envelope, I walked out of my cabin and headed to the mailbox. Waiting for me was an old friend. "Not bad," he said, nodding at the envelope.

Scott opened the lid for me, and once I slid the letter inside, he closed it, then pulled up the red flag.

"You think so?" I asked.

He nodded. "Someone was listening to my advice. Say, if

you two end up walking down the middle aisle in church, you'll have me to thank."

"Middle aisle?"

He shook his head. "Why would you walk down the middle aisle of a church, ya rube?"

I squinted, then it hit me. "Tell ya what, I wouldn't worry about that. The only time I'll be walking anywhere in a church is to pray our softball team doesn't get destroyed this season."

"I saw that grin when you read her last letter. I'm sure that won't be the only prayer you'll be saying."

"What do you mean by that?"

"Gotta get a wiggle on. There's a gin joint calling my name. See ya." Before I uttered another word, Scott dissolved into the wind.

I turned and walked back to my cabin. After reaching the steps, I stopped and looked up. "A summer storm is coming."

I felt the first breeze roll over me, then into the trees, rustling the leaves in the darkness. After a flash of lightning in the distance, I felt the first raindrops of the storm.

Once I was on the porch, I turned and walked to the safety of the railing to see the storm. As my hands gripped the wood rail, I caught sight of the mailbox when another lightning strike illuminated the sky. It was then, I no longer saw a storm. But a glow. Then a tingle in my stomach for what the days ahead brought.

Is this the beginning of what I'm destined to become?

six

I gave the girls the weekend off so we both could recharge and get ready for the region games we have coming up this week.

With nothing scheduled for the first time in days, I took the time to walk over to Blue Ridge Books to see Scarlett. I had a craving for another of her gooey oatmeal cookies. Plus, it was nice to get out of my cabin and wanted someone to talk to. Scott doesn't count.

As I walked onto the creaky, bronzed wood floor, the pleasant smell of the old bookstore suffocated me once again. Within seconds, Scarlett appeared with a plate covered in oatmeal cookies in one hand, and a tall Styrofoam cup in the other. "I knew you'd be back."

"How did you–"

"Remember what I told you about the intelligence of the Irish?" She said, then led me to the table close to a window that looked out to the mountains.

When I sat, she placed the plate and cup in front of me, then reached over and pulled out a chair for herself. I sat, then asked, "Do you greet all newbies this way?"

"Only the ones who will lead our Lady Lions back from the dead."

"That's going to be a problem," I told her.

"Why?"

"I left my crucifix back in Atlanta," I joked. "You need one if you're going to perform a resurrection. That and a few gallons of Holy Water."

Scarlett gave me a wry grin, then pointed. "There's that smile I like." As I took a sip of lemonade, she asked, "I'm curious. Why did you want to come here?"

"Why not?" I asked.

"You were the head coach at Atlanta Catholic for the last fifteen years. You won nine state championships and the last three in a row. And you resign for no reason?"

"How did you know about that?"

"I signed up for your fan club newsletter," she teased, then touched me on the wrist. "I still haven't received my membership card, so could you check on that for me?" She asked with a wink.

"Yeah. I'll get my membership team on it." I paused, then reloaded. "Again, how do you know all this about me?"

"I want to make sure someone takes good care of our girls this time, so I did my homework. Tara and I go way back, so I told her I'd help." She paused, then her flirty grin vanished. "Our girls need a savior, and then you show up. Why did you take the job?"

I wasn't ready to trust her with the truth, so I gave her a safe reply. "I grew tired of Atlanta traffic. Everything is 45 minutes away. Even when you want to go across the street."

"As mum used to say, stop acting the maggot."

"What does that mean?"

"It's Irish for someone fooling around. Everyone has an

opinion on why you're here."

"What have you heard?"

"Oh, there are several theories. The guys at the firehouse say they fired you for writing English papers for your players to keep them eligible."

"I tried doing that, but since I have dyslexia, they all flunked English that semester. The teacher knew something was up when everyone spelled laugh with two fs."

She squinted, unsure if I was joking. "The woman who owns the dress shop told me you tried to raise money for new equipment by trying to sell the team bus on eBay."

I shook my head. "The team bus? That's outrageous. It was the school president's BMW. I had a buyer lined up before she walked into the parking lot and busted me. Made it kind of tough to close the deal."

This time, Scarlett laughed as she understood where I was going with my replies. She leaned back, then folded her arms across her chest and grinned. "I'd like to think there was a woman involved. She must have broken your heart, and you came here to get away from it. Sorry, it's the romantic in me."

"You've seen too many movies."

She squinted as she looked me over. "I'll figure it out."

"You're sure of yourself, aren't you?"

"You told me you like a lass with stones. If we keep this banter going, you'll end up in your own little RomCom. And I'm available to play your leading lady."

I shook my head, then took a long sip of lemonade to move the conversation out of danger. "Enough of the rumors. What does the community think about me?"

"Since last year's team was awful because of the coach being a drunk, everyone is happy you're here. It got so bad, some girls wanted to quit during the season and they almost canceled the remaining games."

"How many coaches did Tara contact about the job?"

"You were her number one choice," she assured me. "But when you turned her down, she contacted every coach she knew, but nobody returned her calls. There was talk of shutting the program down since the girls didn't want to play, and nobody wanted to coach them. Then you changed your mind, rode into town, and gave us new hope."

"Aw, Scarlett, What can I tell you? I got bored with winning all the time."

Scarlett smiled and shook her head. "Okay, Coach. I'll let it go for now. But one of these days, you'll tell me the real reason you left." She looked me up and down. "Do you go to church?"

"I'm more of a Creaster."

"Creaster? What's that? Worshiping pressed pants?"

I laughed. "Nah. A Creaster is someone who goes to church only on Christmas and Easter. I believe in God, pray every day, and when I get time, I'll sit in the pew and meditate. I also like to light a candle when I have an intention." When I detected a smile, I asked, "Did I pass?"

"You're clear." As I breathed a sigh of relief, she added, "For now." She smiled, then stood. "I meant to ask earlier. Why *The Great Gatsby?*"

I picked at a piece of cookie. As I stared at the crumbs littering the plate, I shrugged, then told her, "I don't know. There's something about someone who knows they're doomed, but keeps fighting on in hopes of finding a miracle."

"What does that mean?"

The Redhead and the Fountain Pen

I waved her comment away. "Aw, nothing."

Scarlett gave me a sweet smile. "Well. A man of mystery too. You keep impressing the hell out of me, Coach Dawson."

"Great. Remember that when softball season begins."

When I got home tonight, I felt my heart pounding into my chest as I walked to the mailbox.

When I reached inside and pulled out a stack of envelopes, I looked down, hoping there would be a power blue one in the stack. When nothing but ivory looked back at me, I shook my head. I need to relax a little on this newfound pen pal thing.

seven

After a good practice today, I sat with the team in the locker room to discuss the game plan for Blairsville. Because of the scorching August heat, I had a few of the parents stock the room with plenty of Gatorade and snacks, so they had a surprise to come back to.

After we finished, I got the girls together in the middle of the room. Then I asked for our captain, Josie, to come up to the front. I took off my state championship ring and handed it to her. She looked at me and shook her head. "Coach? What's this?"

"Slide it on your finger."

"What? Um, I can't. I don't deserve to–"

"Put it on."

When she looked at her teammates, then back at me, I nodded. She slid the ring on her finger and looked at it. I told her, "The first step in achieving anything is to visualize what the reward looks like."

Josie smiled, then held her hand up so the girls could see the diamonds. "Thanks, Coach."

"No, Josie. Thank you. And I thank all you girls."

"What for?" She asked with wide eyes.

The Redhead and the Fountain Pen

"This team is going to shock the world this year. And when they do, I'm going to have a front-row seat to something amazing that will live forever. These things don't happen every day, so you have to savor every moment." As the girls stared at the ring with open mouths, I told them, "Every great story has a beginning. This is ours."

Then I called each player up to the front and had them put the ring on their finger. "All you need is someone to believe in you. We are in this together, and no matter what happens, I will support you, win or lose."

The team cycled through so each girl wore the ring. When the last girl slid my ring off her finger and handed it back to me, I told them goodbye and would see them tomorrow.

I walked back to my office and turned my laptop on so I could complete the batting order and who would be playing where. A few minutes later, I heard music, cheering, clapping, and the slamming of metal lockers. I wasn't sure what was going on, so I walked back to the locker room.

Inside, the girls were jumping up and down, going crazy. I loved their enthusiasm, so I watched from the door and let them continue. As I watched, someone interrupted the party.

"Excuse me. I can hear this racket down the hall. Can you keep it quiet?"

I turned. Not recognizing the heavyset man, I asked, "I'm sorry. You are?"

"I'm Glen Morgan, the science teacher," he asserted over the loud music. "I'm trying to grade papers. Can you tell your girls to keep it down?"

Someone turned the music down, then they all looked at Morgan. Then at me, with raised eyebrows and stone faces.

I turned and faced him. "Look, this isn't the library."

The rotund man with television screen-sized glasses and curly gray hair straightened his back. "Oh. You must be the new softball coach. After last season, I was expecting a priest."

"No, you should have been expecting a softball coach." I paused, sizing him up, and added, "When was the last time anyone cheered this loud at a science fair?"

"Now, see here–"

"No, you see here. You are interrupting a team meeting. Unless we have a uniform that fits you, which I doubt, please leave."

Morgan huffed, then shook his head and walked away.

I turned back to the team. Their faces froze in amazement.

Josie walked to the front of the group. She looked at the girls, then back at me. "Coach, nobody ever stood up for us before. Thank you."

The other girls nodded and expressed their gratitude. When they finished, I told them, "You're welcome. From this day forward, if you give everything you have, both on the field and inside the classroom, you'll never have to fight another battle alone. We'll take everyone on together."

As the girls smiled, I asked, "Who are we?"

They looked at each other, not sure of the answer. Finally, Josie spoke up. "Blue Ridge Prep Lions?"

I nodded. "And what do lions have?"

Again, they didn't speak, so I helped them. "Lions have courage and pride. And starting today, you will have both for the rest of your lives. Now, I ask you again. Who are we?"

"Lions," they yelled.

"And what do lions have?"

"Courage. Pride," they yelled louder.

"That's right," I told them.

Someone walked over and turned the music up again, this time louder than before. The team jumped up and down, their cheering echoing off the lockers. Then they looked at me and waved me into the circle. I jumped in the middle of the madness, and we all began whooping it up. As they cheered louder, I yelled, "I can't hear you!"

The cheering became screaming and stomping. A few of the girls pounded their lockers, while others threw towels around the room. It was bedlam.

Round One was over. Lions 1, Last Year 0.

Was that the thing the girls needed to have a little confidence going into the game tomorrow against Blairsville? They finished second in the region last year, we'll have our work cut out for us.

We'll see what happens.

eight

I watched our girls warming up before the game today. The sound of silence made the loudest noise.

When the umpires told us it was game time, the girls walked back to the dugout and went through the motions of getting ready to play. I looked at them, and when I sensed their anxiety, called them over. As they waited for me to speak, I looked at all of them, and said, "When you step on the field, you will fear no one. Make them fear you."

It had the desired effect as we crushed Blairsville 10-1.

After the game, Tara found me by the bleachers and congratulated me. When I told her all the credit goes to the girls, she shook her head. "It takes someone who tells them they can do it."

I thanked her and also told her about the Morgan incident when the girls were making too much noise. Tara told me not to worry about it. She confessed she had to stifle a laugh when Morgan told her about the uniform jab I gave him. I like her a lot.

In the locker room after the game, I praised the girls for their hard work in pre-season practice and how proud I was of them. I told them, "Ladies, I loved watching you play today.

As I retreated down the hall to my office, I heard the now familiar sound of screaming and pounding on their lockers. I hope I'll get to hear that many more times this season.

✒

When I got home, I reached inside the mailbox, and, since I was on a roll today, there was a letter from Catherine. I still don't know who this woman is, but seeing her envelope and the purple ink makes me smile.

Dear Mark -

My gratitude for your kind words. I'm doing better every day and having someone to communicate with is the best medicine.

Interesting take on GWTW and Affair. I see your point on both. I side with GWTW and told you about my crush on Clark Gable. Even though I didn't agree with her methods, I loved Scarlett's strength. She did whatever she could to keep her home.

The sad thing is when she realized who she was in love with, it was too late and all the tears, pleading, and apologies couldn't bring back the man she loved. Even though the boy didn't get the girl, there was a glimmer of hope in the end.

Speaking of stories, you wanted to know my favorite book? Great question - I have a few. In non-fiction, there was a book about Charlotte Bronte titled, A Fiery Heart, which I love since I'm a big Charlotte Bronte fan.

My favorite fiction book, big surprise, is The Great Gatsby! I am not making that up either. When I read that in your letter, I did a double-take. I guess great minds think alike, huh?

I'm relieved you found my book, since I thought it was lost forever. The book isn't a first edition or anything like that, but my father gave it to me. It was his favorite book, so when I read your letter, well, the second time, I was happy you found it.

I left the book at my ex's apartment. After we broke up, I asked for it back, but he kept putting me off. Then he told me he lost it. I guess he sold it to a used bookstore, and that's how it ended up in Georgia. Crazy, huh? Now I know the book is in a good home. Please take care of it for me.

I'm happy to have someone to discuss Fitzgerald with. The thing I find fascinating about that book is we go through the same things in life now as Fitzgerald wrote about back then. I'm amazed at his other books where he described growing older and how life changes us.

One of my favorite quotes comes from Chapter 8. Gatsby tells Nick, "Well, there I was, way off my ambitions, getting deeper in love every minute, and all the sudden, I didn't care." He'd give up everything for Daisy. That's a line that always gets me.

Why is Fitzgerald your favorite? When you read his words, how do you feel?

I guess this is the part where we exchange Facebook or Instagram profiles or do a Zoom call. Would it be okay to continue sending letters? I know it might be time consuming, plus we don't even know each other's last name, but it's worked so far, so if you're good with it, I am too. Does that sound silly?

I'm an old-fashioned woman who enjoys pen and paper. I loved reading that you like to use a fountain pen since I'm a fountain pen fan as well! Can you tell I used a fountain pen on this letter? Nothing like hearing the scrape of a fountain pen nib on nice paper. Speaking of paper, I recently bought a box of paper, and I used it for the first time when I wrote to you last week. I hope it improves the quality of my writing.

Isn't there something wonderful about a sheet of thick paper that makes you want to write forever? Writing letters is more personal, and seeing someone's written words goes way beyond the sterile cold of an email, text, or anything on social media. Yeah, I know, that's crazy. What do you think?

Well, I guess we have come to the end of this letter. And since we have, here is your question. Do you believe in ghosts?

Oh, and do you have a favorite soft drink? I am a Diet Coke addict an have to start my morning with a cold one. I guess it's just like someone needing their coffee in the morning so don't judge me too harshly...haha

Good night, Mark. Thanks for the letter and the charming conversation. I look forward to our next correspondence.

Catherine

PS - Did I write the last part correctly? I thought your suggestion of ending our letters that way was nice.

This is what I came back with:

Dear Catherine -

Wow! A thought-provoking question to end our last conversation. It made me think about it long after I put your letter away and tried to go to sleep, which I couldn't since the wheels were turning. I woke up a grumpy bugger because of that, so thanks a lot...I'm teasing ya! We'll get to the answer later in this letter.

How are things in New York? Glad to read you are doing better. And to answer your question, letters are fine since I don't have time for social media. I don't think I'd be into it even if I had the time.

I'd rather see handwriting, since, as you wrote, it is more personal. In the world today, things are impersonal with most of our interactions. When I read a handwritten letter, it's as if that person is standing in the same room with me. I'm good with no social media, zoom calls, or even last names if you are.

May I ask what you do? What was the audition? If you'd rather not write about it, I understand. Is what you are doing now what you want to do forever? Is it your passion?

I coach a girls' softball team and found I have a passion for teaching and helping kids to become their best. When I realized that's what I wanted to do, it was like the weight of the world lifted off my shoulders and I found my calling.

    To answer your question, I believe in ghosts. Have you seen *The Ghost and Mrs. Muir*? Since you are a classic movie buff, I'm sure you have, but if not, it's about a woman who buys a house, and it's haunted by a man who used to live there. They fall in love and then have to figure out how to end up together. I won't spoil the ending for you, but I'm sure you'd enjoy it.

    So that begs the question, what happens to those who aren't alive any longer? What if ghosts had an attachment to a place? Why would they want to leave? Nobody has ever proven to me ghosts don't exist, so I'd have to say yes, I believe in them. Well, until proven otherwise.

    To answer your Fitzgerald question, when I read his work, especially *The Great Gatsby*, the words bring me back a hundred years, since that's when he wrote it. The themes are alike. I liked how he described people having undeniable hope for the things they love and believe in. And, of course, how we deal with the realities of life after the moment ends. Win or lose, we keep moving forward, knowing we have to live.

    I loved the quote you mentioned from Chapter 8! I agree, when it's love, you toss aside everything else for that person. I think Fitz got that one right. My favorite quote is at the end of the story when Fitz leaves the reader with a glimmer of hope. "And as I sat there brooding on the old, unknown world, I thought of Gatsby's wonder when he first picked out the green light at the end of Daisy's dock. He had come a long way to this blue lawn, and his dream must have seemed so close that he could hardly fail to grasp it. He did not know that it was already behind him, somewhere back in that vast obscurity beyond the city, where the dark fields of the republic rolled on under the night. Gatsby believed in the green light, the orgiastic future that year by year recedes before us. It eluded us then, but that's no matter—tomorrow we will run faster, stretch out our arms farther. . . . And one fine morning——So we beat on, boats against the current, borne back ceaselessly into the past."

The Redhead and the Fountain Pen

The thing I love the most about that book is the optimistic message at the end. It was a message of life. Fitzgerald nailed it. He wrote that we all won't make it, since time catches up with us, but we press on anyway, and that's the noble way to live.

Okay, question for you - If you could meet one person, living or dead, (Yes, ghosts count too), who would it be and what would you talk about?

It's close, but I'd love to talk to F. Scott Fitzgerald to ask him about his writing.

By the way, I didn't dare write about how F. Scott's ghost visits me. If I tried to explain it to her, she would think I'm nuts. Well, I am nuts, but she doesn't have to know that yet. After I get to know Catherine better, I might tell her about that. Okay, back to the letter.

Speaking of Mr. Fitzgerald, I would like to get your book back to you, since I'm sure it has sentimental value. I'm not sure I want to send it in the mail, or even overnight it, since I would hate it if it got lost. I would be happy to hold on to it until I can figure out a way to get it to you. It's come this far, right? No use getting it lost now.

Well, it's late and I better get going. I'll keep praying for you and know you are one day closer to getting to where you want to be.

We will continue this correspondence later.
Mark

PS- Oh, to answer your question, I love lemonade in the spring and summer, and hot chocolate in the fall and winter. If we ever cross paths, I will know what to order for you...haha

Speaking of correspondence, how long will this continue? I

guess only time will tell. In the meantime, I will stay safe in my cabin, having the thought of a new friend to keep me company. I don't care what she looks like, how old she is, or where she lives.

By the way, curiosity got the better of me, so I Googled her street address to see where she lives and what her building looks like. I know that's a bit stalker-ish, but what the heck, I'm sure I'll never meet her, so it's a moot point. Besides, nobody knows I did it. Well, almost nobody.

"Well, old sport. Looking at property in Manhattan I see. Are you looking to rent or buy?"

I closed the lid on my laptop. "Neither. Just seeing where all my letters were going," I replied as my crimson cheeks gave me away."

"That's a load of bushwa. So, you two discussed fountain pens? How sweet is that?" He joked. "What's next? Discussing pencils and erasers?"

I shrugged. "It's no big deal."

"No big deal? I'll remember you said that."

"Scott, it's nothing. Really."

He shook his head. "Really?" Then, in a mocking tone, he cooed, "The scrape of a fountain pen on paper. Oh boy. My heart is all a flutter," he giggled.

"All right. You've had your fun," I told him.

"By the way. Thanks for bringing my name up. You'd be surprised how quickly people forget you."

"What can I say? She's a *Gatsby* fan."

Scott squinted. "Does she have a sister?"

nine

As I turned onto Tullamore Mountain Road after a long day in the office, I looked forward to checking the mailbox. I was not disappointed.

> *Dear Mark -*
>
> *I enjoyed your last letter. Your words are a welcomed distraction, so thank you, my friend!*
>
> *Before we begin, I wanted to ask if you could hold on to the book for me. I would love to have it back, but it was a miracle you found it, so I wouldn't want it to get lost in the mail. We'll figure out some way to return it, so give it a good home until then, okay?*
>
> *Let me begin things with a joke. What do the movies Titanic and The Sixth Sense have in common? Answer later (I have to keep you interested so you'll read my letter. No peeking to the end).*
>
> *You asked what I did. I'm a music teacher at a school in Manhattan and also give violin and viola lessons to children. It's a great gig since I give back to the kids as someone did for me years ago. Pay it forward, right? It covers my bills until I can get a break doing what I want to do. I play the viola, not the violin, since there is a difference, and I like to be different.*

Hmm...The passion we discussed. I hope you don't mind, but I am not comfortable writing to you about it. Well, for now, at least. My ex knew about it, and since we went our separate ways, I am superstitious about telling anyone. Who knows, I could tell you and then I would never get another letter. Hey, it's happened before...haha Give me a little time and I will explain it all. Losing things I care about has been a theme lately, so I hope you understand.

What I can write is I followed my heart and wouldn't allow myself to compromise the things I've wanted ever since I was a little girl. I knew one day I would have to look back on my window of opportunity and if I didn't take a chance, I'd regret it. Well, I have no regrets, and as long as that's the case, I can live with the outcome. No matter how much it hurts.

To answer your question - the person I'd most like to meet, living or dead. And since ghosts count, I considered that as well. Oooh, this was a solid question, Mark!

While I was on the subway, I thought about who that might be and I almost missed my stop. I mentioned Charlotte Bronte earlier since she is one of my favorite writers, so I would love to ask her questions about her work.

Also, I would love to meet Midori Goto, since she is my hero. She was a child prodigy, and at fourteen, she performed Leonard Bernstein's Serenade, conducted by its namesake. She broke the E string on her violin. The E String is the furthest on the right, in case you were wondering...

She borrowed another violin, broke a second string, then finished the performance with a third violin. She received a standing ovation. The next day in The New York Times, the front page had the headline, "Girl, 14, Conquers Tanglewood with 3 Violins." Talk about having courage, huh?

Okay, answer to the joke: What do the movies Titanic and The Sixth Sense have in common? Icy Dead People...Get it? Sorry, that was silly. One of my students told me that one, so you always have to have someone to blame, right?

What is it you love about coaching? Do you ever wonder how or why you got that gift? What woke it up and made you chase it down? It has to be something in our DNA, and one day we find it. Thoughts?

Question - If you had to lose one of your senses (sight, touch, taste, smell, or hearing), which would it be and why? For me, it would be the sense of smell. The one I would not want to lose is hearing since I love music. Can't wait to hear your thoughts!

Have a great day, Mark. I look forward to your answers! We will continue this correspondence later...

Catherine

PS - I wanted to ask you for a favor. Do you know who Roy Williams is? He was the head basketball coach at the University of North Carolina, but he retired a while ago. My Dad loved him and passed on many of his messages about hard work and sacrifice to me over the years. Since you both are coaches and preach the same things to your team, would you mind if I started calling you Roy? Roy is awesome, so this would be a compliment of the highest regard. By the way, I graduated from North Carolina, so I'm kinda partial. Please tell me you aren't a Duke fan...

Wow. I'm digging this new girl! And I now have a nickname to boot. Not bad for a guy who recently lost pretty much everything only a few months ago...

Who would have thought this would have happened? All from one book pulled from a shelf, and a letter that fell out of it and refused to be forgotten. Crazy, huh? What did I tell you about the cosmic forces pulling and pushing us to where they want us to go?

Back to my *Gatsby* theme, it's boats against the current, right? Is Catherine helping me row until I get back to the shore? I only hope the boat doesn't sink.

Dear Catherine:

Icy dead people? Oh boy. I saw what you did there...

Let's begin in New York. How are you? Are you feeling more human these days? Every passing day is one day closer to you overcoming your hurt. I'm still praying for you, so I hope that helps.

Wow, a Carolina girl, huh? And yes, I am flattered by the Roy Williams reference. Roy is one of my favorite coaches too. I model a lot of how I handle my players with his examples. I also read his book, Hard Work, and loved it.

I graduated from Georgia Tech, so you can take a breath. I'm not a Duke fan...haha

After graduation, I became a grad assistant for the women's softball team. Then they hired me as a full-time assistant, but I was so far down the list, I was responsible for cleaning out the dugout after games. Oh, and I had the most important job of checking to make sure we had enough softballs for batting practice.

I was just happy to be there and didn't care what I did as long as I was helping the team and learning how to be a leader. We appreciate things more when we begin at the bottom and work our way up.

You asked why I love coaching. It's seeing young people, fresh-faced and not yet tainted by the real world. You see these kids, full of hope and craving success. It's my job to show them how to get there, by making the team the most important thing, rather than themselves. You teach them that when the team wins, we all win. But success comes at a price. You have to sacrifice if you want to be successful. It's the same in anything we do, and that's what I want them to learn.

I also have to teach them about losing, which, unfortunately, is a part of life. But in losing, we learn what it takes to be successful. Everyone loses. But instead of becoming discouraged, I teach my players to get off the floor, work their butts off, and go at it again.

The Redhead and the Fountain Pen

That one moment you see someone sacrificing everything for a goal they didn't think they could reach. And then, BOOM, they achieve what they didn't think they were good enough to do. That's what I get up in the morning for.

By the way, no worries about telling me what you want to do. I'm sure you'll let me know when you are ready.

I loved your question, and I have to tell you it was a tough choice. Losing the sense of touch would be the one I would miss the most. I know the touch of another's hand or a kiss, or when someone puts their head on your shoulder are things I would regret not being able to experience.

I figured you wouldn't want to lose your hearing. Since music is your thing, that's a simple decision, right?

Okay, today's question - Since you mentioned music, what is your favorite song to listen to? Since you play the viola, do you have a favorite song to perform?

My favorite song is September by Daughtry. I like it because the song is about all those times when we were young, and the days were special, but we didn't know it. And now that we have grown older, and time passed in the blink of an eye, we still have the memories.

I have taken up enough of your time, so I will sign off for now. We will continue this correspondence later. Hope you have a great week, Cat!

Roy

PS - Since I am Roy, are you okay with being Cat? I figure it suits you.

I folded the letter and placed it in the envelope. As I looked at it, I thought about the woman who would read it in a few days, and what her face would look like when it happened. Those were my last thoughts before I fell asleep.

ten

I guess I made an impression on my team today. Wait, I just remembered. I don't do impressions. Sorry, I couldn't resist that line. I'll explain in a minute.

Our cross-county rivals, Fannin Central, beat us today, 4-2. But it was the first time we went the full seven innings with them in four years. In Georgia, if a team is trailing by ten or more runs in the fourth inning, the game is called, so this was a pleasant surprise the team hasn't seen in years.

Throw in the fact Fannin Central is the second-ranked team in the state, so it's something for us to build on.

Anna couldn't pitch after a line drive hit her foot in the third inning. The only other pitcher on the roster is a freshman named Susie Morris, so I had no choice but to put her in the game.

She threw everything at them and didn't look like a freshman. We would have won today if we could have gotten her more runs, and I told her that after the game. I also told her she'd get another chance against Central one day. Susie nodded and told me, "I'll be ready."

Okay, the part about the impression. For the first time in my career, I got thrown out of a game. But I had a good reason.

The Redhead and the Fountain Pen

In the bottom of the fourth inning, with Josie on second base, our catcher, Rebecca Church, hit a ball into the outfield. Josie took off as soon as the ball landed in the outfield. She rounded third and headed for home, but the throw beat her to the plate. The catcher swiped at her, but Josie slid around the tag. From where I was standing in the third base coaching box, the catcher never touched her, and Josie's hand brushed over the corner of the plate.

The umpire, seeing the ball arriving ahead of Josie, anticipated the out before the play concluded, and called her out even before she slid. A dull roar from our fans let the umpire know he missed the call.

Then it got worse.

Josie popped up from the ground. She walked over to the umpire and asked, "Excuse me, sir. Where did she tag me?"

She was polite and nonthreatening, but the umpire pointed to the parking lot and yelled, "You're out of here."

Josie threw up her hands and, with an astonishing smile, looked around. "I only asked where she tagged me."

The umpire took out a tiny notebook and pen and wrote something into it. I rushed to the scene and got in front of Josie to shield her away from further trouble. I told the umpire, "All she did was ask you where the catcher tagged her."

"I'm reporting her to the Georgia High School Association about this," he told me, then turned his back and walked away.

Sometimes, I let things go. And other times, I don't. With my team, I go for the latter. As he bent over and brushed the dirt off the plate, I said, "While you're at it, why don't you brush that chip off your shoulder?"

He rose and said, "Go back to your dugout now," then he put his mask on.

"Where did my runner get tagged? That's all I'm asking, and then I'll go back to the dugout."

He jerked off his mask. "Coach, your team has been the worst in the region for years, so you won't get the benefit of the doubt from me. And if you coach them to be better base runners, this wouldn't have happened."

As my spine tingled and the blood rushed to my face, I knew this would not end well. "If someone coached you to be a better umpire, you wouldn't have missed the call."

Oh boy.

His eyes widened, then he got in close and poked me in the chest with his mask. "You've got five seconds to get your ass back to the dugout."

Not wanting him to have the last word, I slapped his mask off my chest and out of his hand. Then I got in his face. "I'd tell you the same thing, but after seeing your ass, you'd have to make two trips. And don't you ever touch me again."

"You're out of here," he yelled and pointed to the parking lot.

I pointed to the parking lot and yelled louder. "Why don't you waddle your fat ass out there first so I'll know which way to go."

Our fans roared. The other umpire saw what was happening, so she trotted over to get between us. I leaned in and asked, "Are you afraid of a 17-year-old girl?"

Josie told me, "Coach, I'm eighteen."

I shot her a glare. "I got this."

Josie smiled and backed away. "He's all yours, Coach."

I returned to the umpire. "What did she ask you?"

"You'll read it in my report," he said, turning away. Then he got his notebook out again and began writing.

"Great. And once you're finished, how about you take your

report and shove it up your ass?"

The umpire never turned around. I walked around and got in his face. "My players have more heart and character than you've ever had in your life. And I guarantee they are more of an athlete than you ever were. You never had the guts to play the game in the first place."

As the umpire continued writing, I finished by telling him, "Make sure to put that in your report too, you coward," then I turned and walked back to the dugout. As I walked, the applause grew and when I looked over, the entire team stood in front of the dugout applauding, too.

Josie's father met me at the fence. "You need help, Coach?"

"Yeah." I reached into my back pocket and pulled out the lineup card and handed it to him. "Here's the lineup. Do the best you can."

Before I left, I gathered the team around. "Look, I won't be able to finish this one with you, so play your game, have fun, and don't worry about the outcome."

I walked out of the dugout and waiting for me was Josie. "I'm sorry, Coach."

I smiled. "For what?"

"I let the team down. Are you mad?"

"Yes, I'm mad."

Josie frowned.

"Next time, if you are going to get thrown out, make sure you get your money's worth," I said, then winked.

Josie's frown turned upside down. Then she laughed.

"Don't worry about it, Josie. You handled yourself much better than I did."

"But I wasn't as funny as you were."

"Thanks. We'll take 'em all on together. Nobody is ever going to disrespect us ever again."

Josie and I bumped knuckles. "Right, Coach."

"Let me get going since I am going to have to call Tara and see how we can get out of this mess."

"You were telling the truth, weren't you?" She asked, with hopeful eyes.

I stopped and turned to her. "About what?"

"That first day. Telling us you'd fight for us."

"I wouldn't lie about a thing like that."

She smiled, gave me a meaningful nod, then we walked our separate ways.

When I got back to my office, I called Tara and explained what happened. She laughed when I told her about what I suggested the umpire do with his report. Tara is good friends with the head of the GHSA umpire association, and she'd explain our side of the story. Before we hung up, she told me not to worry about it since she'd take care of it.

An hour later, after I finished the game plan for the upcoming game with Jasper County, I left my office and walked to my car. I looked forward to getting home and having a drama-free evening after all the fireworks earlier.

As I walked by the softball field, I heard a commotion. At first, I thought it was the grounds crew cleaning up the field. But as I looked closer, I was wrong.

There were my girls, practicing the drills we worked on all season. Even though the game ended an hour earlier, and we lost, they were working as hard as when the game began.

Josie returned to the field and acted like the captain she is. She led the team through drills, cheering them on as they moved from one drill to the next. I couldn't hold back my grin.

I walked into the dugout and onto the field. I was about to say something when they stopped and Josie looked at me. "Excuse me, Coach? Remember what you said about practices and meetings? Since this is a player's only practice and you don't have a uniform, you need to leave. We have work to do."

I raised my eyebrows, then threw up my hands and nodded. "I apologize for the interruption."

I took a few steps toward the dugout. As I got to the opening, I heard Josie ask, "Coach?"

I stopped and turned to her. "Yeah?"

She looked around at the girls, then back at me. "We wanted to say thank you for what you did for us today."

The rest of the team stood in their spots and tapped their hearts in silent appreciation. I looked at each of them and smiled. "No ladies. Thank you."

Josie nodded, then looked at the team and asked, "Who are we?"

"Lions," they all shouted.

"And what do lions have?" She asked.

"Courage. Pride," they said in unison, shouting louder.

My eyes watered, but I covered it well. I looked at each girl, then said, "Don't you forget this."

I turned and walked off the field, through the dugout, and into the parking lot. When I was far enough away, I wiped my eyes.

I have a feeling I'll fall in love with this team before the season is over.

✒

In the mailbox was my weekly correspondence from Catherine. Ah, how I look forward to seeing that purple ink. What does she have for me today? Well, let's open the envelope and find out.

Dear Roy -

Oh, a music question? I know there was something I liked about you! I don't think I can wait until the end of this letter to give you an answer, so I will begin our correspondence with that.

My favorite song to play is Clair de Lune, by Claude Debussy. Have you ever heard of it? It's beautiful and one I always wanted to learn. After months of failure, I learned how to play it. Once the music flowed from my viola, I felt invigorated, as all the hours of hard work paid off.

One of my favorite songs to hear is, believe it or not, the Elvis song, Can't Help Falling In Love. Not only is it a beautiful song, but it means something to me.

One night, Mom and I were watching a documentary on music icons and there was a scene of Elvis performing the song. I looked over at her, and she had tears in her eyes. I never said a word, letting her have her dignity, for whatever stirred that emotion within her.

Many years later, I found out it was the first song my mom and dad danced to at their wedding. He's been gone a long time, but the song brought back memories for her. After Mom passed, the song brings that night back to life.

I know the song September and it is beautiful. Sad but beautiful. One of these days, I'll learn how to play it. I already know how to play the Elvis song, so I'll have to put both on a thumb drive for you.

How is your new job going? Are you liking it? How is your team doing?

Okay, question of the day. Favorite cookie? And as a special bonus question, what do you like to drink with it?

I cannot go a week without a glass of milk and Oreo cookies. Although chocolate chip cookies, when they come out of the oven and are all gooey and sugary sweet, are a close second but give me an Oreo and milk every time.

I look forward to your answers and what's new in your life.

The Redhead and the Fountain Pen

We will continue our correspondence later.
Have a great day!
Cat
PS - Believe it or not, nobody has called me Cat before. I guess since I'm a dog person. Feel free to use it.

Well, that was a nice way to end my day, especially after what happened earlier this afternoon. It's comforting to know someone cares about what's going on in your life.

As I looked at the letter again, I thought about how writing letters is unique and mysterious. Anytime you combine those elements, you cannot wait for what happens next. Besides, it's safe, and I need that right now.

Okay, here was my reply.

Good evening, Catherine, or Cat, as now I have clearance to use...

Well, at least it's evening here, but by the time you get this letter, it may or may not be. I don't know, you can adjust my words to fit whatever time it is. Or, wait to keep reading the rest of this letter after, say, six o'clock. That should work. Sorry, I didn't think it was possible to ramble in a letter, but after a judge's ruling, that was an official ramble. I apologize!

Okay, to your question, which gave me a sweet tooth. My favorite cookie is oatmeal. I know it's not the norm since everyone loves chocolate chip and, of course, Oreos. Me? I love both, but there is a side of me, like you, that likes to be different, and oatmeal cookies do it for me. I like mine with milk too, so we agree on that.

How are you? Are you healing? And are you getting closer to your dream? Sorry, I have to ask, or I wouldn't be your friend. I know you wrote you aren't ready to answer that yet, but I was curious. One day, I hope you will trust me with your secret.

Okay, question time - If you had to leave the United States and could never return, where would you go, and why?

I have always had a thing for England and would enjoy visiting London and seeing its history. And Scotland, Ireland, and Australia. I'm sure it has something to do with the accents...

Well, I am off to bed, so we will continue this correspondence later. I look forward to your reply.

Have a great day, Cat!
Roy

After I sealed the envelope, I looked at the letter. What am I getting myself into? Is this what falling for someone is like? Since I've never been in love before, I have no idea if I am doing it right. But the mystery is too alluring to ignore.

Where is Scott when I need him?

eleven

Good news! I got a text from Tara telling me the GHSA cleared Josie and me so we will be at the game on Friday. I won't go into the details, but I'm glad that's over so I can begin the game plan for East Gilmer High.

Being sprung from exile gave me fresh energy. It was a beautiful day, and I didn't feel like being stuck behind a desk, so I packed up my laptop and drove into town. It was time to drop in on a new friend.

As I walked in, Scarlett walked over and greeted me. "Hello, Coach. What brings you by? Did you get paroled from softball prison?"

"Something like that." Then it hit me. "Wait. How did you know about–?"

"I know everything that happens in this town. I even know what color of boxer shorts you're wearing."

"You do?"

"Aw, Coach. Don't you know redheads have superpowers?"

Catherine came to mind. "Yeah, you might be onto something there."

"By the way," she said with a devilish grin, "Did anyone tell you what a nice ass you have?"

I raised my eyebrows, then had to deal with two cheeks engulfed in heat. "Um, well..."

"I've meant to tell you I hate to see you go, but love to watch you leave." Then she raised her eyebrows and grinned.

"Thanks. I think."

Scarlett laughed. "Hot damn. Score one for the old Irish broad." As I shook my head, she told me, "Speaking of arses, telling the ump to shove the report up his arse was brilliant."

"Again, how did you know about that?"

She gave me a raised eyebrow and cocked her head.

I looked at her, then said, "Yeah, yeah, I know. It's an Irish thing. Forget I asked." I paused, then said, "I refuse to let anyone mess with my girls."

"If you keep doing things like that, the people in this town will think you shit ice cream."

I nodded and thought about her words. "Let me ask you about that. How would someone know if a person shit ice cream?"

Scarlett shook her head. "I don't know. I hope whoever it is, they don't invite me over for dessert."

After we finished laughing, I asked, "Do you think there are toppings involved?"

"I'd think at the least there'd be sprinkles. But I'd be real careful if there are Hershey kisses," she said, then laughed harder and snorted.

Her snort made me snort too. "Oh boy. This has gotten out of hand, Scarlett. Are we that deranged?"

She finished laughing, then snorted again. When she got control of herself, she nodded. "Yeah. But why would you want to live life any other way?"

"I couldn't agree more."

"Glad to hear it. You wanna have a little pop? I hear Bushmills calling us."

"Irish Whiskey?" I asked. "Well, now that you mentioned it, I'm sure the brown water is never too far away for you. Especially in this place."

"My grandparents told me it's against the law in Ireland not to have a bottle of whiskey at least a hundred feet from you at all times. So they send me a bottle every month just so I don't end up in prohibition jail."

"I hate to tell you this, Scarlett, but we're in America. You'll be okay."

She walked over to a cabinet, opened the bottom drawer, and pulled out a bottle of brown liquid. "What are you? Rand-McNally?" She asked with a smile.

I laughed, then took a seat at my favorite table overlooking the mountains. While I waited, I looked out the window at the various colors splashed into the trees, teasing me that autumn was arriving soon. No wonder this was my favorite place.

Scarlett walked over, sat the bottle and two glasses filled with ice on the table in front of me. After filling the glasses, she raised hers. "To our Lions. May they make the state tournament this season."

We clinked glasses and sipped our whiskey. The expected sting was a surprising sweetness as the cold, brown water plummeted to my stomach with warm tingles. "I just fell in love with your grandparents." I smiled and took another sip. "I hope the team can keep the momentum going. Who knows, with a few breaks, we could make it into the postseason."

Scarlett smiled. "That's the first time anyone has mentioned the postseason with our girls in a long time."

"Well, they are a special team. With all the hard work they've put in this season, they deserve it. I'd hate it if they fell short of making it to the state tournament."

"Is that why you coach the way you do?"

"What are you talking about?"

"Do you always fight for those you care about?"

I thought about it for a few seconds, then told her, "Yeah. I guess so."

She took another sip, then said, "I never took you for a tough guy."

I squinted my eyes. "What made you think that?"

"Aw, that wavy blonde hair and blue eyes. I thought you'd be more of a lover than a fighter."

"Well, these days, I'm more of a fighter."

Scarlett raised an eyebrow. "Why didn't you fight to stay in Atlanta? Was something, or rather, someone, there you had to get away from?"

I gave her a suspicious smile but didn't answer.

She continued the questioning. "Everybody who comes here is running from something. Why else would you leave Atlanta?"

"My health. I came here for the waters."

"Waters? There are no waters here."

"I must have taken a wrong turn. See what happens when you don't use Waze?"

Scarlett cocked her head and gave me a mischievous grin. "I've seen *Casablanca*, so don't con me."

She busted me on the *Casablanca* line, but I continued to be evasive. "What makes you think I'm running from something?"

"Oh, Coach. Give this old lass some credit. As I mentioned the first time we met, the intelligence of the Irish is second only to God."

We laughed, then she hit me between the eyes. "I'll bet it was a woman, and she broke your heart. You didn't want to keep running into her ghost everywhere you went, so you came here. Should I continue?"

"Oh, Scarlett. I didn't know there was a RomCom-athon this week."

She raised her eyebrows. "How do you know about RomCom-athons?"

I grinned. "The intelligence of a softball coach is only second to God. Well, third behind God and the Irish. But give me a little something for the effort."

She shook her head. "Since you are Blue Ridge's most eligible bachelor, you need to put that girl behind you. Live in the now."

I sat up in my chair. "I guess I'm not as smart as I should be."

"Being an eligible bachelor in Blue Ridge does wonders for a man's social calendar. Too bad I'm taken," she smiled.

Scarlett reached for the bottle. As I looked at her fingers, I asked, "No man in your life?"

Without looking at me, she said, "That's the second thing about the Irish. We know how to keep a secret." After Scarlett winked, she added, "By the way, I host the Blue Ridge Book Club here in the store, and we'd love it if you came by sometime."

"Me? Why me? I'm not an author."

"Neither are any of the women in our group, ya chucklehead," she joked. "We get together, knock back some sauce, and discuss our favorite books. Since you are a Fitzgerald fan, I'm sure you'd be able to talk about his work. *The Great Gatsby* comes to mind."

"Sure. What is on the list for the ladies this month?"

"It's one of those Ali Hazelwood books."

"Never heard of her."

"Of course you haven't. She writes RomComs. You need to broaden your horizons."

"Oh great. A room full of ladies hopped up on Irish Whiskey reading RomComs. I better bring extra security."

Scarlett threw her head back and laughed. "I'll beat them off for you."

"You will?"

"Sure. You know I want you all for myself."

🖋

Fresh from today's mailbox is Catherine's letter.

Dear Roy:

How are ya? What's going on in Georgia?

I liked your question. My grandparents were born in Iceland, and that's where my parents came to the United States from. If I ever had to leave the country, that's where I'd go.

Iceland is a gorgeous place, and you have to see the Northern Lights once before you die. You'd swear that is what Heaven looks like. Well, if you think Heaven is a little chilly...

I have news, but let me explain. It's time to let you in on the secret.

I moved to New York because my dream is to play viola with the New York Philharmonic. My ex didn't support me and thought I was nothing but a dreamer and should give up because it would never happen.

When I didn't make the cut, he laughed and said, "I told you so." That was the final straw and led to the conversation on the Brooklyn Bridge that you read about in the letter you found in The Great Gatsby book.

So, fast forward to this afternoon. I got an email from the personnel manager of the New York Philharmonic, and there is another audition coming up. She liked me from the last audition and hoped I would be back, since I was one of the last performers who didn't make it.

Is this the time I finally break through? Could this be God's way of telling me there was a reason I didn't make it last time, but now is my time? I am freaking out and need some words of advice.

What do you think? And please be kind since I'm a little fragile at the moment. By the way, have you ever seen the movie, A Christmas Story? If so, imagine I said fragile like Ralphie's father...

As soon as she wrote that, I heard the word from the movie and I got a slight teehee. Okay, back to the letter.

I have to send my application in by September 29th, which is good, so I have time to practice. But also bad, since the waiting is the hardest part. Sorry, I sound like a Tom Petty song.

The audition begins on November 13th. If I make it through the first round, the semi-finals are the next day, and then the finals are the day after. I don't know if I'll get that far, but I'm working my butt off to get there.

I've been practicing three times a day. I wake up around five a.m. to practice before I have to go to work. Then when I get home, I will play for an hour, have dinner, take a little time for myself, then practice again before bed. My father once told me, "Either you find a way, or you find an excuse."

Despite this being a crazy week, I still thought of a question for you. What is the most embarrassing thing you have ever worn?

I once wore a dog costume when I was doing charity work for the Chapel Hill Humane Society. I was the Hop Along Hound. The costume came with a dog head, floppy ears, and that silly dog face that made me look like Astro from The Jetsons.

The kids loved it, except for this smart-ass teenager. (Sorry, I hope you were okay with the language). He pulled my tail and said, "You aren't the Hop Along Hound." So, I did the proverbial mascot dog dance, then leaned down and whispered, "Get away from me before I lift my leg and pee all over your head."

The boy screamed and ran off.

Then some punks gathered around and smarted off. One asked, "Have you been spayed or neutered?" Which got a laugh out of his buddies.

I leaned over and quipped, "You look familiar. Didn't we go to the same doctor?"

The gang laughed, and the guy got embarrassed and disappeared. That was a long day, but nobody knew who I was.

So, back to the crisis at hand. Can you say a prayer for me tonight? And tomorrow? And, if you aren't busy, the next day?

I was looking for inspiration earlier and pulled out my copy of The Great Gatsby. One of my favorite lines is, "I thought my opportunity had passed, but now it's standing across from me, begging for me to do something about it."

You know what's funny about that book? When Fitzgerald wrote it, the book wasn't highly regarded. It was a good book, but it wasn't what it is today. A hundred years later, it is a classic and stirs passion in those who read it. Fitzgerald died in 1940, never believing he was one of the prominent writers of the world. And now, the book is an icon and there have been movies made about it. He died never knowing his work lives on today. Not a bad way to give back to the world.

I wish I could tell him what the story means to me. I would also tell him millions of people loved the story and his work.

The theme of the book was the unshakable hope that Gatsby had. He was the underdog throughout the entire story, yet he clung to the belief he could overcome the odds and achieve the things dear to him. I identify with that so much. My dream eluded me before, but it doesn't matter. I will fight for my dream until it becomes a reality. Or die trying.

The Redhead and the Fountain Pen

Thanks for helping me try to make it a reality, Roy!

So, now that I've revealed my past, I'd like to hear yours. What happened to you?

We will continue our correspondence later. Have a great day!

Cat

Her secret intrigued me, and now I knew what she was all about. Her words penetrated the paper, and I shared her worry. But also her passion and determination. In the words alone, I felt something for her. It wasn't love or lust, or anything like that. It was more admiration and awe. And when you know nothing about someone, except their battle through adversity, you can't help but admire their courage.

What do I write to calm her? If I were there, I would hug her and tell her everything will work out. As I thought about it, I wondered how she'd feel as we embraced. What she would smell like. The scent of her hair. The feeling of her arms on my back. Those thoughts stayed with me for the rest of the evening.

Because I'm not sure where to begin, I allowed my coaching instincts to take over. I will convince her to summon the heart I know she has to overcome her adversity. And if she believes in herself, and the gifts she possesses, there's nothing that can stop her.

Then I thought about the second part of her letter. She wanted to know about my past. As much as I didn't have the heart to tell anyone about it, let alone Catherine, I had to dig deep and tell her. After all, she dared to tell me where she's come from.

After an hour of staring at the blank paper, my brain ached from life coming at me from all sides. Between the team, what's going on with Catherine, and not falling into a past I would rather not think about again, I needed a break.

I went out to the deck, sipped the brown water, and opened my favorite book so I could lose myself for a while.

As I poured my second glass, a voice asked, "You think you could pour me a roadie?"

My head snapped up. "Scott? Is that you?"

"Well, it sure as hell ain't William Faulkner. You thought I drank a lot? That son of a bitch was born with a bottle in his hand. And I guarantee it wasn't mother's milk in it."

"What are you doing here?"

"For one, my flask is empty, and knowing you like the brown water, I figured you'd take care of me." He walked over to my bar and poured brown alcohol into his flask. When it was full, he put the cap back on.

"What's the second?" I asked.

"I hear your girl has a crush on me."

"You heard that?"

"I'm a ghost. It's amazing what we're able to pull off. By the way, could you give her a message from me?"

"Anything."

"Tell her how much I appreciate her kind words. When I wrote the book, the only people who read it were me and my editor, Max Perkins."

"Oh, I don't believe that."

"Zelda told me she read it, but I saw it on the floor holding back a door in our apartment. Gee, tough crowd, you know?"

"Oh, come on."

"You know how much dough I made from that book?"

I thought about it, then told him, "Millions?"

"Try two grand. Well, it made millions after I was gone, but my break came when war broke out. They shipped a bunch of my books overseas to the troops. For whatever reason, they loved it and it ended up back on the bestseller list. Someone got a barney mugging for my book to be on that list," he said with a laugh, then unscrewed the cap and took a swig from the flask.

"I have an idea of what that means," I assured him.

He twisted the cap back on it, then walked over and sat. "The book made a comeback because of that bit of good fortune. In the eighties, they banned it at some college in South Carolina. I laughed because they banned my book, but left all the other questionable books out there. Selective enforcement. You gotta love America."

"Banned? I didn't know that."

"Oh yeah. You know your book is a pile of crap when it's not even on bookshelves, then they decide to ban what few copies are gathering dust in someone's basement. Talk about using a sledgehammer to smash a gnat," he said with a smile. "What the hell. I had my moment, I suppose," then bowed his head.

As I stared at him, I saw the real Scott. His face was a sheet of introspection. I knew what to do. "Ya know, Fitz, I love the book."

He raised his chin. "Yeah?"

"Yes, I do. A hundred years later, people are still talking about it. Millions of people love it. I'd say you did well, my friend."

Scott nodded. A small, victorious grin came to him. "Funny. I lived as a failure and died as an author. All things considered, not a bad way to be remembered." He paused, then asked, "What's going on with your girl?"

"I'm glad you asked. You know I needed you the other night."

"What for? I know I'm a ghost, and Halloween is next month, but I don't do haunted houses."

"Oh, that's funny," I replied. "Look, I need your help. I'm getting overwhelmed by this letter thing."

"What's the problem?"

"I'm having all these feelings and don't know what to do with them."

"Do you need to do anything with them?" He asked. "You're writing letters. Everything is fine. Try not to overthink it."

I thought about his words. "Yeah. I suppose. But I've never been in love before. Am I doing it right?"

Scott's face exploded in laughter. "Doing it right?" He asked as the laughter continued. "Well now, falling in love. I didn't think you had it in ya."

"Yeah, I'm trying to figure it out myself." I paused, then asked, "Look, you fell in love with Zelda. Tell me, what's the secret? What's my next move?"

"There's no playbook for falling in love, Mark. To break it into terms even you could understand, all you have to do is step up to the plate, take your swings, and if you're lucky, you'll knock it out of the park. Make sense?"

I smiled and nodded. "Yeah. I see what you mean. Okay, I get it."

"So, where are we with your bat girl?" He joked.

"Catherine's dream is to play for the New York Philharmonic. I researched everything about the Philharmonic, so I understand what she's up against." I paused, then leaned back and exhaled. As I looked up at the sky, I admitted, "My brain is like oatmeal right now."

"You're a good egg, Mark. You'll figure it out. You know, my boy Gatsby had the same problem your girl has. Those damn dreams. Sometimes, the dream feels so close, all we have to do is reach out and grasp it. We're so sure it's there, then we open our hands to find nothing but empty palms looking back at us."

The Redhead and the Fountain Pen

"What do you think will happen?"

"I'm a ghost, not a fortune teller," he smiled. "All you can do is be there for her. Win or lose, be her rock." He rose, then told me, "I hope when she opens her hand, her dream is resting there. God be with you both, old sport."

I was about to ask a question, but all that was looking back at me was the cool September sky. Instead of wanting to turn in for the night, I had an urge to be the rock. And to summon the courage to reveal, for the first time, why I ended up in Blue Ridge.

twelve

Dear Cat -

Your last letter was amazing. Playing viola for the New York Philharmonic? And I thought your dream was to be the shift manager at McDonald's in Times Square...muhaha

You have some lofty goals, my friend. Let's see what we can do to help you get through this!

Here are a few things I thought about before I played or coached in a big game.

First, enjoy the moment. How many times will this opportunity come? Walk into it fearlessly. You don't walk into a fight on tiptoes. You walk into it with your fists clenched. Then you yell like a crazy person, get in a fighter's stance, and yell, "Where's the bully who thinks they can beat me?"

Second, this is your time. You earned the right to be there, doing what you're called to do. I don't know everything about how it all works, but I am certain they don't hand out auditions by walking past Geffen Hall. (By the way, I hope you're impressed. I researched where you are auditioning). Believe in your greatness because it begins with you, and when others see how much confidence you have, it shows.

Third, breathe and find peace. Tell yourself you deserve to be there, that spot is yours, and you feel bad for the ones you are going to beat out for it. Don't worry about who shows up to the audition. They should worry about you. Cat, you got this girl!

Between now and the audition, write to me as much as you like and I will be here to help you. No worries!

I loved your Fitzgerald reference. Yes, our dreams can elude us, but the important thing is we keep fighting for them. Stretching the limits of your talent and perseverance so one day, all the hard work will pay off.

I'm amazed you have the same thoughts as I do about the Gatsby book. I also liked the movie and thought it was well done. If Fitzgerald was here, he would tell you thanks for the kind words. He'd say something like he lived as a failure and died as a writer. Somehow, he knows he's loved.

I enjoyed reading about your dreams and am happy to be along for the ride. I tell my players all the time that the only things you can control are effort and attitude. Focus on both at all times, and your dreams will become reality.

Okay, to answer your question. Hmm, I am embarrassed to write about this, but what the heck?

For Halloween one year, my ex and I dressed as each other for a Halloween party. She wore one of my jerseys, a whistle around her neck, a clipboard, everything. You can guess where this is going…

She dressed me up in one of her dresses, a wig, tights, gloves, sunglasses, and high-heeled boots that made me look like a tall building. The funny thing was the women at the party were jealous of me. "Man, you have the hips for that dress," and, "Rock those hot boots, girl."

I looked rather fetching, and I was happy I could pull that look off. But as I thought about it, I'm not sure if I should have been…

Good thing there was plenty of brown water at the party, so after a while, I didn't care. But it made walking around a bit of a challenge. How do you do that? What do you do when you get a draft up your dress?

My dress was clinging to my tights, and the ex told me, "For Christ's sake, wear some Spanx, will ya?" I don't even know what Spanx are. And I thought I had problems when my boxer shorts bunch up...

And now to answer your other question. Since you had the courage to share what happened to you, here it goes.

I was the head softball coach at Atlanta Catholic School for fifteen years. We won nine state championships, so the program was rolling. We had the parents and community behind us, and we were the most successful of all the athletic programs at ACS. This rankled some people. The athletic director was at the top of the list since he wanted the spotlight for himself. He was a former football player, so he wanted his sport to be king at our school.

He wasn't a fan of girls' sports. Although he disguised it, he told me on more than one occasion that softball was something that should lurk in the shadows. He didn't want anything to get in the way of the more important sports, like football. When we began winning, the praise came to the softball team, not the other sports, and that was something he couldn't stomach any longer.

A few days after winning the state championship, he called me into his office and said he was getting rid of me. When I asked why, he said he'd had enough of me and the softball team.

I reminded him we were the most successful program at the school, so why would he fire me? He snarled. "I'm moving the sports programs in a different direction. It's time for a change."

I told him I would fight this, and he replied that I had a choice. I could either resign and leave without incident, or he would alter the transcripts of some players who had scholarships. Then he would go public with allegations of widespread corruption in the program.

As insurance, he would go into the other players' official files and add bits of false information. Suspensions for drug use, demerits and detentions, and anything else he could think of, so it appeared the students were out of control. And I was the one covering up their deeds so they could stay eligible. It was all *lies, but it would be my word against his.*

The AD held all the power at the school, so it was like a mouse fighting an elephant. I had no choice. Either stay and risk my players losing everything they worked for, or I could take the train and leave so they would be safe. I chose to fall on the sword. And now, here I am.

I told him, "I'll walk out of here and never say a word. As long as you promise to leave my girls alone." When he nodded, I walked out of the door, packed up my office, and never went back. That was the worst hour of my life, saying goodbye to everything we had built, and never coaching the girls again. I still hurt over that.

I lost the only thing I ever cared about. Not only was it coaching at a place I loved, but I lost the players I saw grow into women. I lost my team and I'll never get them or that time in my life back.

I thought about never coaching again, but when a job came open in Blue Ridge, and they needed a coach or they might fold the program, I thought I could help. I guess leaving Atlanta was the best thing that ever happened to me. Even if I didn't believe it at the time. But with so many things in life, what you think is awful turns out to be the best thing that can ever happen to you.

I guess that's why I work so hard, to prove to the world that no matter what some jackass does to me, or tries to do to my team, I can overcome it. I want to live up to the words I preach every day to my team that if they believe in themselves, and do what's right, they can achieve anything.

You and I come from the same past, huh? We loved something more than ourselves, and it broke our hearts. We gave everything up to become who we are, no matter how much it hurts. We'll never look back and regret the past. It's a neat feeling, isn't it?

You're the only one I've told about this. Since you are in New York, and we don't know the same people, my secret is safe with you.

Now that we have that out of the way, let's lighten the moment. Here's tonight's question: What's the funniest prank you have ever pulled off?

I was having a long week and needed a laugh, so I went to the store and bought a twelve-pack of vanilla pudding and a jar of mayonnaise. I cleaned out the jar, keeping the label dry and glued so everyone knew what kind of jar it was.

Then I filled it with the pudding, and drove to Buckhead (The ritzy shopping area in town). I found a park bench by a busy street and began eating the pudding out of the jar.

The looks from people were hilarious. One lady stopped, gave me the stink eye, and said, "Oh, you're sick."

I laughed, then smiled at her, spooned out a huge glob with my spoon, and put it in my mouth. The look on her face was priceless.

Okay, to recap.

1. You are not to worry.

2. You can do this.

3. Walking around in high-heeled boots all night while consuming brown water was a bad idea.

4. Go to the store and buy as much vanilla pudding as you can, and a large mayonnaise jar.

5. Never give up your dreams. Fight harder in the face of adversity.

Well, I better get going. I have to watch a video on our next opponent so I can come up with a game plan.

We will continue our correspondence later.

Good night, Cat.

Roy

PS - When I face a challenge, and things look bleak, I've always recited the David and Goliath scripture. I'm not a real religious person, but this scripture calms me, and I hope it has the same effect on you. "David put his hand in the bag and took out a stone and slung it. And it struck the Philistine on the head. And he fell to the ground. Amen."

The Redhead and the Fountain Pen

I wished there was more I could do, and as I thought about it, an idea materialized. A letter is nice, but what if I made her a card with inspirational words on it? Hmm, I like where this is going.

I found a thick piece of white paper and cut it down so it was about the size of a greeting card. Then I pulled out a cup holder full of crayons I had stashed in my desk (Don't ask) and went to work creating it.

I pulled out a few crayons to see which one would look best. After narrowing it down to Scarlett, Sienna, and Razzmatazz, I finally settled on Cherry, since that looked more vibrant than the others. Sorry, I'm a little OCD with these kinds of things.

I drew a heart in the middle of the paper, colored it in, then took a blue crayon (Don't ask what color of blue I decided on) and added musical notes around the heart. I had to research how to draw musical notes, but I think they came out okay. Inside the heart, I used a purple crayon to write the words, "Courage, perseverance, and peace," and at the bottom of the paper in black, I wrote, "You got this, Cat."

I placed it in the envelope, along with a note.

I told you one day I'd write to you in crayon.

Tomorrow, it all goes north. I'm going to overnight the letter and card so she will get it immediately. It's a small gesture, but those mean the most. I hope it does for her.

✒

I drove to the FedEx store today and, before dropping it in the box, gave it a last look. I was envious both items would be in Catherine's hands. Her eyes would look at it, and I hoped they would sparkle.

I rubbed the envelope for luck, then dropped it in the box.

thirteen

Things are going well, and the team is playing out of their minds. We've won seven in a row and are now 15-6. Was the incident from a few weeks ago the thing that got us going?

It's funny how a little confidence can go a long way. Tara told me this time last year, the team won only two games and their season was over, although there was still a month and a half left to play.

Today, they play with a swagger, and when they take the field, they don't tiptoe on it like they are afraid. They act as if they own the place.

Last week, I had to start Susie, the freshman pitcher I told you about earlier, since Anna's is still not 100%. She allowed three straight hits to begin the game, and I thought we were in trouble. Then she got the next three outs in a row, the last on a strikeout. She trotted back to the dugout, grinned, then told me, "I had 'em the whole way."

It's official. I've fallen in love with these girls.

🖋

The purple ink is back! One thing I look forward to over the last few weeks is those envelopes with a New York postmark. Here is today's letter:

> Dear Roy:
> Thank you so much for your kind words and encouragement.
> I also have to tell you how moved I was to get the drawing of the heart. It's taped to the inside of my viola case and every time I open it to practice, it reminds me of how lucky I am to have someone who believes in me. I'll treasure it always.
> Oh, and just so you know, I am crazy about the color purple, so seeing the words, courage, perseverance and peace made my heart beat faster. That was perfect!
> I wanted to tell you how sad I was to read about what happened. My heart goes out to you. I cannot believe someone would put themselves over a group of girls who sacrificed themselves for their school. Someone took away the thing that made you great and gave you fulfillment. I am so sorry to read that, Mark.
> From reading your letters, I know coaching is dear to you, and to have someone take it away for their agenda is criminal. I pray you will heal, and one day you'll look back on that time in your life with wisdom instead of hurt.
> I debated whether I should have sent my last letter. It's difficult opening up to someone, especially with my dream. Someone I cared a great deal about abandoned me because of it, so whatever happens with the audition, I hope you'll be kind.
> I don't want you to think I am a Debbie Downer since I am happy-go-lucky, always smiling, so people never know I stress over anything. I try to be a powerful woman, but, as you know, there are times we all worry about the things we can't control.
> Thank you for giving me the extra strength to face what's coming. I've already begun following your suggestions. I've worked on my breathing and it

has been an enormous help. The David and Goliath quote is hanging over my desk, so when I look up, I read it and it helps when I worry about what lies ahead.

Oh my God, you didn't dress up like your ex! Are there pictures? I would love to see those hips of yours! And hot boots? I have several pairs myself (You need them in New York. Not only for fashion because you freeze your bottom off up here), so maybe I can find a pair of mine that will fit you if you are ever here for Halloween! You are so silly!

And the vanilla pudding? Roy, I have to say if we ever met, we would be bad influences on each other. I have that twisted sense of humor as well.

A few years ago, I was visiting friends in Charlotte, and the party spiraled late into the night. Don't ask me why or where I came up with this idea, but after several alcoholic beverages, we trotted down to the local McDonald's. I taped a sign on the drive-thru menu reading, "Speaker volume too low. Please shout out your order." Then we took a seat on a bench close to the drive-thru and after a few of the exchanges, I laughed so hard, I almost peed my pants.

I once asked one of my friends if she would dress up as the Grim Reaper at my funeral. All she has to do is stand in the back of the church, twirl her sickle and not say a word. She said she would do it for a hundred bucks, so I have it in my will for the executor to pay her after they drag my casket out of the church.

I can be quite twisted when I want to have a good laugh. I guess you and I are a lot alike. We are both smartasses. It beats being a dumbass...

Here is the question of the evening - If you could speak another language, what would it be?

For me, I can speak Icelandic.

I wrote earlier that my parents were from Iceland and met at the University of North Carolina, so that's how I ended up there. Dad told me his parents moved back to Iceland many years later, and we would visit them from time to time, so that's where I learned the language.

It's a beautiful language and one you don't hear too much about. I *would write to you in Icelandic but think you'd rather hear it than read it since you lose some of the beauty if it's not spoken. And chances are, you wouldn't be able to read it...haha*

Well, I better get back to preparing for my audition. With your encouraging words and support, I know I'll ace it this time.

I look forward to continuing our correspondence later!
Cat

My reply:

Dear Cat:
I knew there was something I liked about you. I have the same twisted sense of humor, so when I read about your pranks, I teeheed, then bowed in reverence.

The last prank I pulled was a hoot. My old apartment (By the way, why do they call them apartments when they are all stuck together) was close to several bars and restaurants. My bedroom window was on the fourth floor overlooking the street where people would park and then walk to the square to have dinner or get a drink.

One night I walked down to a row of shrubs on the sidewalk and concealed a walkie-talkie inside the branches. Then I walked back to my apartment, cracked the window, and waited.

This huge dude and his girlfriend walked by, so I said into the walkie-talkie, "Hey, meathead. Yeah, I'm talking to you. Do they sell men's clothes where you bought that shirt?"

The guy spun around, looking for the voice, but never saw it. As he kept looking, the girlfriend told him to keep going since they were late, so they continued walking.

Then I said, "Hey, shit for brains. I'm talking to you," which pissed him off, and he canvassed the area, darting back and forth, and the longer he looked, the more pissed he got. Meanwhile, I'm watching from my window hoping I don't fall out of it since I'm laughing so hard.

Later, another man walked over, and he's looking around. He goes into the bushes, unzips his pants, and begins urinating. I'm thinking, "Is God setting these people up on a tee for me to slam out of the park?" I paused a beat or two, then told him, "This is the police. Come out with your zipper up."

The guy did the craziest spin move, then tried to run, but his pants weren't up all the way and he tripped and face-planted into the sidewalk. He finally got his pants up, but he had pee stains all over him as he made his getaway.

Yes, I know. I'm going to Hell...

So how is the practice going? Are you getting in any extra reps with your students? I am sure they are a tremendous help since they can keep your confidence up.

The softball team is playing well, and I'm proud of their hard work. We still have a long way to go, but it's great seeing young people finding success. I'm sure you see that in your students too.

You speak Icelandic? I have never heard that language before, so I am intrigued. You asked what language I would like to speak. I have always had a thing for French. Like you wrote about Icelandic, it's a beautiful language and smooth on the ears. I like hearing a British accent, but as far as speaking another language, I'd like to speak French.

I studied French in high school and college, but it has been a while. If we ever meet, we can speak in our adoptive languages. We won't have any idea what the other is saying, but it would be fun trying to figure it out.

Tonight's question - Who is your favorite character from an animated movie? Mine is Baloo from The Jungle Book. When he sings, "The Bare Necessities" I always get a laugh. Sometimes, when I am feeling down about things, I'll watch that on YouTube and it makes me feel better. I know I'm a grown man, but that one makes me feel like a kid again. And we all need to feel young sometimes after spending the day adulting.

Why didn't they tell us how difficult being an adult would be? We spend all this time as kids, wanting to be adults, and then we get our wish and then want to go back to being kids again. The joke's on us, huh? haha

All right, enough wasting your time. Get to practicing, Cat. You have an audition coming up that you're going to win.

We'll continue our correspondence later!

Take care!

Roy

fourteen

After a busy couple of days, I need to catch my breath.

    We beat Dawson County today, so that was an enormous victory and kept the momentum going. We don't play this weekend, so I gave the girls some time off since they looked tired. A few days off before next Wednesday's game should get them ready to play.

    The other thing I wanted to mention is Catherine. I have no idea who she is. But I can't stop thinking about her.

    Yeah, I know, that's earth-shattering news, but I figured I'd mention it since you're the only one who knows. How long will all this last?

    Catherine's words are a portal, and when I read them, she is sitting beside me. I want to reach out and touch her. Who was she, and who had she been? Who was she now, and what would she be tomorrow? What made her laugh, and what made her cry? What did her face look like when the sun's rays touched it in that perfect light that splashes over the world at sunrise? I wondered what it would feel like to hold her hand and ask what she was thinking? And waking up and seeing her lying beside me? Her sleepy face and red hair in a tussle in that morning light signifying a new day.

    You have this ideal vision of someone in your mind, the

way you want them to be, and if they are perfect for you. Nobody is perfect and I am sure there are things we don't agree on. But all that matters is not if she is perfect, but if you are perfect for each other.

If she saw me, or I saw her, would the image of the perfection we have in our minds shatter, and the magic of our words vanish? All I know is the way her words move me. It doesn't matter what she looks like.

I want to be there for her audition, but that's not likely. I hope she's not walking into disappointment, and I wish I could be there to protect her. Yet, there are times to let those you care about walk along the path destiny wants them to travel. You can't interfere when someone pulls the cosmic strings, right?

Something is alluring about not knowing what the future holds, especially with matters of the heart. You're drawn to it. It leads you where it wants you to go. You're stuck in an amorous haze, following it with the promise of your dreams, waiting at the end of the journey.

What if I never get to meet the woman behind the words?

I'm on my deck on a cool afternoon in the north Georgia mountains. The colors are changing into a tranquil pallet I wish you were here to see. What would Catherine say if she were here? She grew up in North Carolina, so I am sure she knows about the mountains this time of year.

Speaking of Catherine, I got a nice package from her today, and it put a smile on my face.

She sent me a letter and a laminated card and told me I could put it in the band inside my ball cap so I could have it during games for luck. It was a handwritten note on a white card, and the glossy lamination made sure it would stay clean.

The card read: *When they look into your eyes, they will believe.*

Her words gave me goosebumps. I put it in my wallet and when I get to the locker room tomorrow, I will put it in my hat for luck.

Is there anything else this girl can do to me?

Okay, let me get to her letter and then I will get back to you.

Dear Roy:

My goodness! You are every bit of a smartass as I am! It is nice to know I am not the only twisted soul on the planet. Since we're both going to Hell, will you save me a seat? Think about how much fun that would be!

I loved your story about the walkie-talkie. How did you not give yourself away? I would have laughed so loud and busted myself. And the guy who peed all over himself? I almost did the same thing when I read what you wrote.

We both have that silly sense of humor, bordering on being a lunatic. My mom was a prankster and had a saucy mouth, so that's where I get it from.

I remember during elementary school when the teacher asked us to talk about what mommies and daddies did for work. One person said their father was a banker. Another said their mommy was a doctor. When the teacher asked me, I said, "My mommy is a lawnmower." When the teacher asked how she could be a lawnmower, I told her, "Well, anytime I do something I shouldn't, she says my ass is grass, and she's the lawnmower." Five minutes later, I was sitting in the principal's office, waiting on my mom so we could discuss my language. And hers too.

Who came up with the lawnmower saying? I would love to meet whoever it was. Was some guy mowing his lawn, thinking of some poor dude, and thought, "Yeah, that's what that guy's ass will look like when I am through with him."

Catherine has the same silly questions about sayings too. I'm soooo digging this girl.

The Redhead and the Fountain Pen

Practice is going well. I have a coach who's been running through the numbers with me. The personnel manager from the Philharmonic sends everyone the music they want you to perform, so I have been practicing it three times a day. And yes, the kids are a big help. They don't know what it means to be under pressure, and they tell me, "What's the big deal? Go out there and play."

If we all can have that attitude, I'm sure we would be a lot more successful in everything we do. As you wrote, we all need that moment to be kids again. To them, you do it, since there's nothing to fear. The day when life smacks us in the face and shows us what we can't do, that's when we're no longer kids. And that's a sad day.

I hope your team is doing well and will make the state tournament. They have an excellent coach, so why wouldn't they? I sent you a small card for luck since I'm a big believer in luck, superstitions, and anything else that brings good karma, so I hope it helps. I'm thinking about you and the team, even if I can't watch them play.

You speak French? Ca va? That's about all the French I know. Well, that and champagne...

Favorite animated movie character? It would have to be The Little Mermaid since we both have red hair. Even though I have more freckles, we both are stubborn with the things we want.

Like Ariel, I like to make music (She sings, I play the viola) and we both sacrifice for the things we love. Ariel sacrificed everything for a handsome prince. I sacrificed my handsome prince for a chance to live my dream of playing with the New York Philharmonic.

I remember The Jungle Book and Baloo's song is hilarious. Thanks for bringing back that memory!

Question - What is the most romantic thing you have seen?

When I need peace, I'll walk over to Central Park and play my viola under the Maine Monument. One afternoon, I was playing Clare de Lune, and this elderly couple walked over and listened to me play.

They held hands, their bodies swaying to the music. During the song, the man kissed the woman on the cheek. She gave him that wonderful smile people who have been in love forever carry for each other. I was as captivated watching them as they were watching me play.

When I finished, the man walked over. "That was the first song Gracie and I danced to at our wedding fifty years ago. You played it as lovely as on our wedding day. Thank you for bringing back that wonderful memory."

He reached into his wallet, but I stopped him. "No. Thank you. Seeing the look on your faces is payment enough. I'm glad I could bring that day back for you and your beautiful wife."

The man smiled and put his wallet away. He reached for Gracie's hand, and they walked away. I watched as she said something that made him laugh, and the two kept laughing as they disappeared along the sidewalk.

I never imagined that moment would leave such a lasting impression, but it was more than that. When I first saw them, I thought it was an elderly couple, and they were taking a stroll. But it was more. It told me that no matter how old we are, or how long people have been together, love is as powerful as the first day it's born. I'll hold on to that memory for the rest of my life.

Funny, you don't recognize those kinds of moments as they happen. But later, it hits you that something magical occurred, and life will never be the same. It's things like that I appreciate since they don't happen every day.

With that, I am all written out. The ink in my fountain pen is about to run out, so I better stop writing and let you get back to your girls.

So, what will your next correspondence contain? I look forward to it, Roy!

Cat

PS - Sorry I deviated from our usual last line, but sometimes, I like to be different...But you knew that.

Wow. What did I tell you about this girl? I loved the depth

and appreciation she has for the beautiful things in the world that we sometimes overlook. I read the letter twice and loved the story of the elderly couple in Central Park. Did I write, wow, yet?

That got me thinking about what my most surprising romantic moment was. I have a few, but I guess that was the point of the question. I have to think about my experiences so we can relate to each other.

I'm not sure I can top it, but I'll give it a shot.

Dear Cat -

How is practice? I'm sure you are knocking it out of the park. I've been saying prayers for you and even lit a candle in the school chapel last week. With everyone on your side, how can you lose?

Thank you for your thoughtful gift. I will put it in my cap as soon as I get back to the office and will wear it with pride. And if it brings us luck, I'll figure out something nice to send you from me and the girls.

The team is doing well. The tournament is next month, so I hope we will be one of the teams playing. Win or lose, I am proud of them for everything they've accomplished this year, from their sacrifice to their hard work. I'm sure you feel that way when you see your students performing.

Wow, I liked your question. Seeing that couple in love and showing their affection after all these years must have been wonderful. How did it make you feel inside? I want the scoop, Cat!

The most romantic thing I've ever seen occurred when I was in college. We were studying pre-civil war architecture and our class took a field trip to the oldest church in Georgia, which is still in use today.

The stained-glass windows were original, as were some pews, and the cemetery next to the church had gravestones from before the Civil War.

I was writing notes when a family walked over. The parents were telling their little girl, who was no older than five or six, about the church.

As they spoke, an older gentleman walked past with a handful of flowers. He dabbed at the Holy Water, did the sign of the cross, then genuflected as he sat down in the pew. He placed the flowers next to him, and began praying. When he finished, he sat up and stared ahead.

After a few seconds, he reached into his jacket, pulled out a handkerchief and wiped his eyes, then exhaled and stood. As the little girl watched him, curiosity got the better of her. She waited for him to exit the pew, then walked over. "Those flowers are pretty," she told him.

The man's face brightened. "You like them?"

The little girl nodded.

"Well, I'll tell ya what. If I give them to you, will you promise to put them in water and take good care of them?"

The little girl grinned and nodded her head.

He handed her the flowers. "My wife loves wildflowers. I'm going to see her now, so I'll tell her how much you loved them."

He said goodbye to the little girl, then left the church.

I didn't think too much about it, but as I was walking to my car, I looked into the cemetery and noticed the old man. He was kneeling in front of a headstone, talking to it like it was an actual person. I thought, "Gee, the old man has lost it. Talking to a block of granite?"

Later that night, as I was going over the story in my mind, I pieced it together, and it made sense. The flowers were for the man's wife, but the little girl liked them so much he gave them to her. Then he told his wife about it at her grave. She was still alive within him. All I could do was shake my head and smile.

I went back to the cemetery a few times after that, hoping to see the man again, but never did. I guess that makes the story more magical. Do you think he might have been a ghost, and the little girl and I were the only ones who saw him? Who knows? But I saw it, and like you, I'll never forget it.

Question - Did you ever see the movie, Before Sunrise? It was about two people who met on a train, spent a day together, then fell in love. They parted the next day, vowing to meet back at the train station in six months. That got me wondering. What if you were traveling, and met someone you fell in love with, but after the time was over and you returned home, would you give the relationship a chance? Would you change your life for that person? And would you expect the person to change for you?

Whew! Wow, have we been hitting the burning question lately, or what? I promise, next time we will get back to some silly ones. I have a bunch, as I am sure you do too!

I'll light another candle for you tomorrow in our school chapel for luck.
We will continue our correspondence later, Cat.
Good night!
Roy

I'm sure Ray Charles saw what I did there. But hey, I have to know, right? Besides, I'm sure Catherine and I will never meet, so what does it matter? She will win the audition and then with her career and dreams fulfilled, she will be a superstar in the musical world. And I'll be a memorable, but peripheral figure in her mind. Nothing more than a good friend who got her through a tough time, and she'll forget about me the minute she steps on the stage.

If things should end, I'd rather it be with nothing in the mailbox. It's a lot easier than walking away, looking at those you love, and saying goodbye.

fifteen

I'm back! Things are still good with both the team and my friend in New York.

Today is the deadline for Catherine's application to the Philharmonic, so I am sure she's busy. I hope everything is good, and she remembered to breathe. Listen to me worry about someone I've never met. Am I crazy, or what?

Earlier tonight, I brought a book out to the deck to read. Pair that up with a glass of brown water, and my mind would forget things in New York.

As I sat on the deck and looked at the sunset plummeting into the mountains, Scott pulled up a chair and sat next to me, saying nothing. We both sat there, staring out into the world, taking in autumn's color. "How's it going with your dream girl?" He asked, still staring into the sunset.

"She's not my dream girl," I told him. "But she's in my thoughts from time to time."

He smiled, then reached into his jacket and pulled out a flask. He unscrewed the cap, then placed his lips over the opening and took a healthy swig. Then he raised it to me. "Here's to you, old sport. You know I'm pulling for you."

I looked at him, then raised my glass of brown water. After I took a sip, I asked, "So, what do you think?"

"What do I think?" He asked.

"Yes. I would like to know what you're thinking."

He looked over and smiled. "I think I'll have another drink." After he downed another sip, he screwed the cap back on the dull silver container that looked as if it hadn't left his coat pocket in decades. "Well, I don't think you're in love. Not yet. But maybe it's a tender curiosity."

As I thought about the words, they rolled around like balls in a Bingo tumbler, and within seconds, the winning numbers all lined up in a row. "Why did you say that?"

When he didn't answer, I looked over. He wasn't there. I shook my head, then placed the book next to me on the couch. I wanted nothing else to distract me from the last minutes of tonight's autumn beauty.

It was cool and breezy, so I started a fire in the stone fireplace. The dying light was now orange specks splashing its gooey color into the choppy clouds. As the Irish Whiskey went down, so did my worries.

I convinced myself Catherine would find what she was looking for. And one night, she would look into the same sunset that played before my eyes, and she'd be happy.

I hope she doesn't think I would abandon her as the last guy did. How do I convey that to her without bringing back painful memories? I guess all I can do is be ready with my words, and let her know she has a friend who will stick with her no matter what the outcome.

Wait. Why am I worried about that? She's going to ace her

audition, so that won't be an issue. Thanks, Mr. Bushmills. Your brown water is a tremendous help!

What I would give for her to be sitting next to me now. Maybe one day we can look at the same sunset at the same time from the same place. Maybe things will work out and maybe I'll... Aw, forget it. That's an awful lot of maybes...

To keep from getting too crazy about Catherine, there are other things to keep me occupied. A first-place rematch with our rivals, Fannin County on Tuesday, comes to mind right away. We'll see how far the girls have come, so I better get focused on that.

But before then, I have one last thing to do tonight.

"Lord, I pray for Catherine to have peace. Be with her during her time of need. Amen."

The first day of my favorite month came. Unfortunately, the sunrise was the only thing beautiful about the first day of October. Fannin Central wore us out, 13-5. I was happy with the girls as far as never giving up in the face of adversity since we got behind early and never caught up.

The loss keeps us in second place in the region. It's still good enough to qualify for the state tournament, but we have to be careful and not lose too many more before the end of the season. I guess we'll see how the girls react to adversity in our next game on Thursday.

The other news is I haven't heard from Catherine. I hope everything has gone well, and they accepted her application.

It's funny, but sometimes you want to be alone when the shit hits the fan, and other times when you need someone to tell you it's going to be okay. I wish Catherine was here to reassure me the girls would be all right. I also wish she was here so I could tell her she was going to be okay too.

The Redhead and the Fountain Pen

While I have a minute, I wanted to ask something. Who came up with the phrase, "When the shit hits the fan?" Was there an instance when someone threw shit at a fan? Why would they do this? How did they transport the shit from the bathroom to where the fan was? Or was the fan in the bathroom? Sorry, but these are questions that have plagued me for years.

At least I had the Book Club meeting tonight to take my mind off the shellacking we received earlier.

Last week, I worried the ladies would get liquored up and begin hitting on me. Now that we got our ass kicked by our biggest rival, I'm still worried they will hit on me. With bats. And canes. And walkers.

For self-preservation, I put on my best suit and bow tie, and once inside, I followed the signs to the corner wing of the bookstore. I stopped inside the doorway, straightened my bow tie, then walked inside. As I walked closer, I made sure to flood the room with charm.

"Scarlett McKeegan," I said with a grin, then looked around the room. "You didn't tell me the ladies in your book club were so enchanting."

That got awws and cute giggles from the ladies in the room.

I moved to the front, and as I did, the ladies took their seats. I heard whispers behind me. "Oh, he's so cute," and, "I can't believe he's single. I'm calling my daughter as soon as I get home."

Luckily, they must have forgotten about the score. The ladies were all pleasant, some flirtatious, and all were appreciative.

I spoke for fifteen minutes about coming to Blue Ridge, how much I loved coaching the softball team, and my passion for books. When someone asked me what my favorite book was, I replied, *"The Great Gatsby."*

An older woman who looked like she got her hair done

earlier in the day, said, "Oh, that's mine too, Coach," she assured me.

"Thanks, Mrs..."

"Please call me, Dorothy. In fact, you can call me anytime," she said with an assured grin.

I looked at Scarlett, who rolled her eyes.

After treating every one of them like Queen Elizabeth, I bid them a good night and walked over to Scarlett. I kissed her on the cheek, then turned and waved goodbye to the group.

"Please come back soon, coach," one lady said with a slight slur.

"Only for you," I told her with a wink, then turned and walked out of the room.

Yesterday was rough. Last night was fun. Today, things are much better.

After pulling into my driveway after work, waiting in my mailbox was a powder blue envelope.

Dear Roy:

Sorry, it has been a few days since I have written. Don't worry, everything is okay and progressing as it should.

I hand-delivered my application the day before the deadline, so I'm good to go. The personnel manager smiled and told me she was happy I was back and wished me luck. I take it that's an informal acceptance, right?

Thank you for lighting a candle for me. Do you think you can up the stakes to a blowtorch? Or a flame-thrower? Anything to increase my chances.

I've had a lot of time to think about what could happen in the next few months. Remember, I wrote about my parents being from Iceland? Well, I have friends there and one of them is with the Iceland Symphony Orchestra. He told me I have an open invitation to play with them full time if I ever want to. If I am rejected in New York again, I've decided to make the move.

Crazy, huh? But when you love something, it doesn't matter where you get to do it. I couldn't think of not being able to play my viola somewhere. Whether it's here or across the ocean in Iceland, that's a simple decision for me.

How are your girls doing? Is the little card bringing you luck? I'd be happy to pick up a copy of the Blue Ridge newspaper to read all about your games. But they don't carry it at the local newsstand here in New York, so we don't get the latest sports news...Sorry, I'm being silly!

I enjoyed your story about the older man at the cemetery. It brought tears to my eyes, so thank you for making me boo-hoo! I thought it was a beautiful story and wished there was more beauty like that in the world. Like my story, I will remember that one forever too.

To answer your question, when I saw the older couple holding hands in Central Park, the smile on my face grew and I couldn't control it. I thought I was having an out-of-body experience since I had all these emotions racing through me and I couldn't stop them. Nor did I want to.

I'm in awe of the love between the man and woman you wrote about. No matter the time, distance, or even death, they still love each other. That's magic.

If you have that special someone to share it with, it doesn't matter how long you've been together, it's real. With the couple in Central Park, I saw myself in the woman. I've often wished that one day when I am her age, I will have someone to hold my hand and walk with me. It was a moment of peace and gentle grace I'll treasure forever.

Sorry, I was being a little dramatic there, but, well, you asked me what it made me feel like, so I gave you my answer. Please don't tell anyone I wrote this, okay? haha

Answer to your question - I would give it a chance! I am at peace with what happened with the ex and know there is someone better out there for me. Someone with whom I can share my dreams and aspirations and not worry about what could happen if it goes bad.

It would have to be the right guy, but like the older couple holding hands in Central Park, if I could find someone like that, then why not?

And the second part of that question - When you meet someone, you both have to make changes and sacrifices, but also remain who you are. When two people love each other and want each other to be happy, they make sacrifices without it feeling like sacrifices.

Here's your question. Please don't think I'm too intrusive, and I'm asking as your friend. Have you ever had your heart broken? You know my story, but I am curious about yours.

Second question: Are you religious? I know you mentioned it earlier, but I was curious how much or how little. No judgment either way. I'm Catholic and believe in God. As far as going to mass, well, that's another story. I still pray (even more these days), say the Rosary, and wear my St. Jude medal when things get serious.

In case you aren't Catholic or don't know about the Saints, St. Jude is the Patron Saint of the Lost Cause. I can't think of any causes more lost than me wanting to play for the New York Philharmonic.

By the way, I am going to go out for the first time in a while with a good friend of mine. Her name is Clara, and she is the concierge in my building. She's been there to help me through the tough times, and after asking for months to go out and have a few drinks with her and her girlfriends, I agreed. Actually, I am looking forward to getting out and having some fun.

I better get going so I can get ready for our big night out. Whoo Hoo!

I look forward to our next correspondence, Roy!

Cat

It was a relief to hear she was okay and things were on schedule. I have to admit, I was sad about how things ended for her. To tell someone they are a dreamer, then laugh at what they love, and discount what lies in their heart is awful to do to someone.

Sure, we all have to be realists, but some of the greatest things ever created came from dreamers. Dreamers who ignored the voices telling them they couldn't do it. Where would we be without our dreams? And where would we be without the hard work, perseverance, and faith to make them come true?

After I finished the letter, I walked out to the deck and sat in front of the fireplace, my thoughts only on the redheaded girl in New York. I wondered what she was wearing on her night with the girls. The hot boots she wrote about? A dress, skirt, or jeans? And what would her face look like when that perfect light attaches itself to a girl? Or when someone made her laugh? When she listened to a friend's story? And would she think of me?

I hate to admit it, but all the courage I had last week when I thought about a future with Catherine is now gone. I understand where I am now. If she doesn't make it in New York, then she'll go to Iceland, and then she'll have her music and won't need me.

Either way, I can't win.

I guess, as long as she's happy, and she has the life she's always wanted, that's what's most important. If she's happy, I'll be happy too.

So tonight, I will picture her walking down the street. Getting out of a cab. Walking over to a table by the window, waiting for me. I fantasize about walking in, seeing her across the crowded room, our eyes locked on each other. We are the only two people in the world at that moment.

I walk over and sit at a table with her. We order drinks, laugh, and hold hands. Then we share a kiss and walk back to her apartment, not having a care in the world.

When the dream goes poof, I'm back in Blue Ridge with

the breeze and my brown water. As I swirl the brown around the ice cubes, I laugh at myself for thinking such things. For being so stupid.

No wonder I've never fallen in love. I'm sure I'd find a way to screw that up too.

sixteen

Today's game got us right back on track and we cruised to an easy victory over Fannin West to raise our record to 21-7.

Fannin Central and Holy Trinity, who were the big rivals when I was at Atlanta Catholic, are both unbeaten and sit atop the state rankings. Atlanta Catholic is seventh. Not in the state, but in their region, so as much as I am sad for the girls, I hope the AD is enjoying their season. Sorry, that was rude, but I'm sure you'd feel the same way.

Josie is my coach on the field and even in the dugout when needed. At the end of the first inning of today's game, we were behind 3-0 and the team was flat.

I gathered them together, then looked at Josie, who once again took charge. She laid down the law and told them they were better than this. Actually, the quote went along the lines of removing your head from another part of your body, but you get the point.

I should talk with that young woman about her language.

I sat back in the dugout and watched as the team rose from the dead and rolled to another victory. They are coming together and it's fun to watch the transformation.

Ivan Scott

After I got home and ate dinner, I pulled out my favorite fountain pen, the good paper, and wrote to Catherine.

> Dear Cat -
>
> How was your night with the girls? Did you consume a lot of brown water drinks? That's what I call Irish Whiskey, which is my favorite.
>
> I hope you had fun and didn't break too many hearts. I'm sure it was nice to get out and blow off some steam after being so busy the last few weeks.
>
> Speaking of breaking hearts, you have competition. My good friend, Scarlett McKeegan, who owns Blue Ridge Books, asked me to come by and speak to their book club the other night. It was a group of older ladies, and since the softball team is a big deal in this town, they loved me. Of course, I flirted and gave them my best smile. Oh, and they dug my bow tie too. I would love it if you ever got to meet Scarlett. She is a redhead too, so I'm sure you two would get along well since, as you know, redheads stick together...
>
> Glad to hear your application is in and it sounds like you are going to have another chance at your dream. Is it easier or tougher to know that you don't have to do anything, except practice, until November? I hope the wait is not too difficult, and it passes. Hey, more time to prepare, right?
>
> I checked with the music teacher at our school, and she showed me both the viola and the violin. Now I know the difference. I was glad I had time to speak with her since she's retiring at the end of the semester. She's been here for twenty-two years, so she felt it was time to say goodbye. I wish I could have gotten to know her better since I'm new here, and she's treated me like I've been at Blue Ridge Prep for years. You don't know of anyone who'd like to teach youngsters about music, would you? haha
>
> Thanks for asking about my girls. We lost to our big rival last week but bounced back to win today so I am happy with their resiliency. I have this one player, Josie Thompson, who is like a mini coach. I never have to get after the

team. She does it for me.

One day, she is going to be a heck of a coach after her playing days are over. And I mean after she finishes playing years from now, since she can play in college and past that if she wants to. Do you have any students you see as following their music after they leave school?

To answer your question, yes, I have had my heart broken. Walking out of ACS on the last day was awful. Even to this day, it's difficult to think about. That was just a shade over the time a few years ago when we lost in the bottom of the seventh inning in the state championship series to Holy Trinity. To this day, I've never gotten over either of those things.

I know I need to let go of the past, but I have this terrible way of reminding myself about coming up short. I once had a chance to win a baseball game in my senior year of high school. In the last inning, I popped out, and we ended up losing in extra innings. I still haven't gotten over that night, and it's been over twenty years ago. I haven't made peace with it yet.

Now, to your second question, I was raised Catholic, but don't go to church as much as I should. I believe in God and I pray every day.

The reason we stopped going to church, or rather, they stopped asking us to go to their church, was when we attended a late-night Christmas Eve service. My family had a little too much cheer beforehand, so I knew this would not end well.

My father and brother, Garrett, wanted to open a present before we left, which was an electric saw. Of course, in their drunken state, they thought it would be a hoot to fire it up in the dining room.

Garrett lost control of it and cut a swath through the dinner table. My father thought that was the funniest thing ever, so he took the saw and continued the cut, sawing the table in half. When mom came in to ask what was going on, dad told her, "I never liked that table, anyway."

Then we got inside the church, and Garrett stumbled into the pew. After picking up a handful of hymnals, he dropped them on the people in front of us. Then he sits down in front of the pew, brings his legs up, and passes out underneath it.

We woke him up as the monsignor walked up the aisle to begin the service. Garrett stands up, pulls out a beer, holds it out to him, and says, "Hey Rabbi. Merry Christmas. Add that to the collection plate, will ya?"

The monsignor looked at him, and with a smile said, "Bless you, my son," then shook his head and continued walking up the aisle.

That was the last time we went to the evening Christmas Eve mass. I never found out if that was a family decision or one made by the church, since mom refused to discuss that night, and we knew never to bring it up in her presence. I worry I'm on the Archdiocese "No Pew Zone," like the no-fly zone, so I hope one of these days, they will forgive me.

Okay, question for you - If someone asked your advice for finding the right person to date and fall in love with, what would you tell them?

I would tell them to find someone they can talk to and laugh with. Find someone you like. Not love. Like.

Sure, you have to be in love with the person, and that's critical. But my father told me the roses, soft music, and candlelight all fade, and there better be something to take its place.

If you can find someone you like, someone you can have long, meaningful conversations with, then you'll have a solid structure on which to build.

The other thing he told me was that with people in love, they have an invisible bond between them. No matter where one of them is, they carry the other person with them. In life and even in death. What do you think?

How are you holding up, stress-wise? If you need to write to me every day until the auditions, please do. I want to make sure I am supporting you as best I can since I'm not in New York.

We will continue this correspondence later.

Good night, Cat!

Roy

The Redhead and the Fountain Pen

Another Friday night and another week closer to the tournament. We clinched a spot a few days ago, so this season continues to be full of surprises. Hopefully, there will be a lot more.

Tara told me last year, nobody came to their games, and the players didn't admit they played for Blue Ridge Prep. She also told me Mr. Morgan, the science teacher, made waves that they should end the program and take the money and funnel it to the science department.

Pardon my French, but that guy is a dipshit.

Why do people say, "Pardon my French," when they curse in English? Those don't sound like French words to me. And why do they warn you about it beforehand? Is it supposed to be better if you ask someone to pardon you, then shower them with profanities? Why involve the French? Why not Albania or Germany? Hmmm...

Fannin Central won the regular-season championship region earlier today, but we got second. Oh, and here's more good news. Holy Trinity, the top-ranked team in the state, finished unbeaten and won their region. Fannin Central is second in the rankings. We won six of our last seven, but nobody worries about playing us.

Every day this week when I walked to the mailbox, my heartbeat accelerated, hoping to see a powder blue envelope. But there was nothing inside except bills and a postcard from AARP, which was a hoot. I know I'm no spring chicken, but come on. This preemptive advertising gives me the red ass.

But today, a powder blue envelope rested on top of a bunch of irrelevant items. I smiled and exhaled.

Why does that purple ink bring such joy?

I walked out to the deck and enjoyed the cool October air, then took a seat and opened the envelope, enjoying the anticipation of something wonderful.

Catherine's words.

Dear Roy:

How are things in Georgia? Things in New York are wonderful as they always are in October. The weather has cooled off, and I can break out the sweaters and boots. I have a pair you might like. But we'll see if they fit you... haha

I should have known I had competition. And moving up the charts to Cougar Land, I read! haha I would love to meet your friend one of these days. She sounds like someone I would get into trouble with. And yeah, it sounds like you're starting to get the redhead thing.

I was walking in the subway the other day, and I saw another redhead. I smiled as we passed each other, and she smiled back, but didn't say a word. Redheads have a secret club only we know about.

Redheads have freckles. Need to add gobs of sunscreen when we are brave enough to go to the beach. But at the end of the day, you'll never get bored with us.

I am impressed you researched the viola. I like to be different, so when my friends told me about the violin, I liked it, but the viola is my partner in crime because it's different.

The viola is a few inches larger than the violin. The frog, which is the part of the bow I grip, is chunkier and curved. Violin bows have a straight edge.

I'm glad you did your research. If you don't know the difference between the two, that is a deal-breaker for me, and we will have to end our correspondence....Just teasing.

Believe it or not, I was excited about getting out for a night. Between the breakup, and throwing myself into my work, it's been a while. When I got home, I rushed to my closet and pulled out my favorite purple and red plaid mini skirt, purple sweater and my black over the knee boots (You might like them...haha) and then saw myself in the mirror. I was like, "Wow, where have you been hiding, Catherine?" haha

Clara and I had fun, and you were right, it was nice to get out and enjoy the evening. We ordered Irish Whiskey too. I'm not sure which brand since I asked the bartender which one he liked best. Whatever it was, it was good!

Guess what? Someone asked for my phone number. I thought after all this time I had lost it, but I guess miracles happen every day. We are meeting for a drink tonight, so I'm looking forward to getting back to living again.

Clara was funny. When the guy walked over and began talking to me, she interviewed the guy and acted as my bodyguard/press agent. It's a wonder she didn't scare him off.

After the guy left with my number, I asked her why she was being so protective. She grinned and told me, "Well, that guy was a total muffin, but you shouldn't forget about your friend in Georgia. He's a lot nicer than your last boyfriend."

Mark, there's someone here who likes you. Well, it's two since I think you are a sweetie as well!

Time to take a break. She met some guy? Now I have another case of the red ass. Well, at least she thinks I'm a sweetie. And if Catherine bails on me, I guess there's always Clara. Let's continue reading…

I'm happy your team is doing well. You mentioned the tournament coming up, so I'm sure you're excited. Since you said a prayer for me, I will say two for you and the girls.

I had a strong practice session with my coach last week, so things are progressing. I wish the audition was now since the wait is a killer. However, your words are not only helping the time pass but also boosting my confidence.

I had to laugh about your church story. Did you ever find out if they banned your family from church? That would be a question I'd want to know the answer to.

I've had a few of those times in my life with my family. We had a birthday party for my sister and my parents hired a band called Platinum, and they rocked. When they found out I played the viola, they asked if I would come on stage and join them as backup for a few of their Dave Matthews Band songs. When I told them I left my viola at home, they told me there was a violin, so I hopped on stage and played backup.

Then my mom, who had a little too much wine, joined us on stage. I was thinking, "Oh no, this will be a birthday my sister will never forget," but to my surprise, she belted out the lyrics to Mustang Sally, and sounded good. I was standing next to the bass player and when the song ended, I heard him tell the drummer, "That chick has some pipes on her."

Later, one of my sister's friends got on stage and danced with the lead singer. She shimmied off the stage, then the lead singer followed her, the band followed him. Before you know it, we were all shimmying around the room in a long conga line.

Band members played their instruments, then grabbed glasses off the tables as they walked by and downed people's drinks. When they danced past the table with all the birthday cake cut into slices, some of the band members stuffed their faces, then went right on playing.

The highlight was when a woman got on top of the birthday cake table and started dancing above the saxophone player. She too had a little too much birthday cheer and, well, you know the rest.

Luckily, when the sax player saw what was happening, he stopped playing so the freak show would stop, much to the relief of drunken party goers. There are some people who dancing isn't for. She's one of them.

When she tried to get down, she slipped and fell onto the birthday cake. Talk about a photo op. Good thing most of us got a slice of cake since those who waited were out of luck.

I loved your question. As I thought about it, I remembered a wedding

I was at last summer. The way the bride and groom gazed at each other on the dance floor, that's what I would tell that person who asked about falling in love.

I'd also tell them this is the person I'm meant to be with. The one person who is my best friend in the world. But once the magic wears off, as it always does with people who have been together for decades, the hard work begins.

I agree you have to like someone first since that is the foundation for loving someone. If not, love will collapse. And lovers having that invisible bond? Sign me up! When two people love each other, they carry the other person with them wherever they go. I've always felt that way, but was too embarrassed to admit that to anyone, so when I read that in your letter, I'm relieved we see this the same way.

Thanks for asking about the stress level. I am okay now since the audition is still a month away, so there is not much to stress over. But it will rise a little each day until the auditions begin.

Despite the stress level, I love the hard work that comes with trying to achieve something. Especially when you love something you have wanted for as long as you can remember. I know it might sound strange, but for me, I like the process. The journey. The five a.m. practice sessions. I put in extra work during those sessions because I know I'm getting better.

With anything we love, it doesn't feel like work. Every person who has achieved greatness in whatever field they choose has that trait.

Okay, question for you. If your mate, God forbid, passes away and you are still at an age where you have a lot of life left to live, would you marry again?

My father passed away when he was sixty-five. Funny thing is, my father didn't want to be alone, and he said that if my mom passed before he did, he would be with someone within six months. Is it a man thing that they can't be alone? Or was that only my father? My mom passed away a few years ago, and she never remarried or dated anyone else. I've always been in awe of her over that.

For me, I don't know if I would want to marry someone else. I figure the man I marry I'll be head over heels in love with. He'll be my soulmate, my best friend. If that's the case, anyone else would be a consolation prize.

What do you think? I'm intrigued to read your answer to see if there is anything to my theory.

Your answer about having your heart broken intrigued me. Have you ever been in love? Sorry, I didn't mean to be forward. I was curious. It's okay if you haven't, and I understand some people have had their hearts broken. Not only by someone, but by falling short in the things that they want to achieve.

I've been there before, and am trying to put the memory of my past to bed so I can sleep at night. Just so you know, I understand that numbness and how you replay everything in your head over and over as if it could change it if you thought about it enough.

Roy, did you ever think this is our time? You overcoming what happened at your old school, and me making it to the stage as a member of the New York Philharmonic? Maybe we are both on a path of destiny to achieve the things we're supposed to achieve, and this is the beginning of everything. Think about it. This could be our time.

Well, time to get back to my viola. Lots of reps to take before November! I look forward to continuing our correspondence, Roy!

Cat

After reading her words, I felt like I could jog down to Blue Ridge Prep and back and not break a sweat. Why do I have all this energy after reading her letters? Every word, every sentence, every question leaves me spellbound about this woman and leaves me wanting more.

Everything except the part about the guy asking for her number. To be honest, I felt my heart sink into my stomach and that familiar heavy frown came to my lips. As I thought about it, I had no reason to be jealous or upset. And if he makes her happy, well, then I am happy, since that's all I want for her.

But that doesn't mean I can't be a little jealous. First Iceland, and now this guy. Is God trying to tell me something?

After what happened in Atlanta, I never thought I would have the strength to trust anyone again. But now, there is Scarlett, Tara and Blue Ridge, the team, and now Catherine. I have feelings again, after months of numbness. I'm leading a group of young women who have their dream and helping one woman to achieve hers. Who knows if any of our dreams will come true?

✒

I couldn't sleep because something from Catherine's letter kept flying around in my head. She asked if I thought this was our time. What did she mean by that?

I know she meant that it was time for both of us to overcome the adversity life has thrown at us. I'm sure that's it.

But there's a part of me wondering if I read between the lines. Did she mean this was our time to find each other? She wrote that this could be the beginning of everything.

Could this be the beginning of everything for me and Catherine? Or, is this just another illusion that everything I've always wanted is close, but when I reach for it, it's already gone, and I'm the last one to know it?

seventeen

Today I found a letter from my redheaded girl in the mailbox. These days, that's not an enormous surprise. But what was in the envelope was.

Her letter looked like a fourth-grade report on her summer vacation. Good thing there wasn't a field sobriety test since her sentences were way outside the lines.

I have a feeling my darling Catherine had a few beverages before she wrote this. Read on and let me know what you think.

Dear Roy -

I wanted to write after thinking about the last letter I sent me. No, wait. The last letter you sent to us. The last letter we. Wait, I think I got it. The last letter of the alphabet is Z. Wow. I'm happy I got that sorted out. And I thought you were drunk. Wait. Maybe I'm drunk. Give me a second and I'll get back to you on that.

Remember the guy who asked for my phone number? The one I met at the bar with Clara? Well, I have to confess something. Oh, and by the way, I have had a few too many Irish whiskeys, so I hope you're not too drunk to read this letter. Oh, gopher turds. Did I write that? Is this what's called drunk and dial? Wait, drink and type? Hold on a second. I'm not typing, so it's whatever you want to call it. Drink and scribble. Drunk and scribble. Scribble scrabble. Have you ever played Scrabble?

Yep, she was three sheets to the wind. By the way, why is it three sheets to the wind? Why not four sheets? Did one sheet float off in the breeze? And what about pillowcases? Not only is the person drunk, but they might not even have a blow-up mattress to pass out on. Sorry. I lost my train of thought. Where was I? I'm still not sure where I am now, so let's keep reading and see if we can get back on track.

The guy I was out with tonight was a certified, Grade A Pud knocker. All he talked about was his job as a replacement banker. Wait…That's not it. He is…was…the guy who gives people money to make more money. What's that called?

He asked what I did, and when I told him, he nodded, then said, "Oh, that's sweet," then went on with stories about how much money he makes and his new BMW. We were only a half-hour into the date, so that's when I began slamming drinks.

Thank God I got loaded. I kept nodding every so often, so it looked like he was paying attention. Wait. I was paying attention. Good thing I brought my wallet since I had lots of attention I had to pay for.

The guy was so into himself, he never knew I didn't care about what he was saying or who he was. Before I knew it, I didn't know who I was or where I was either, so that helped.

After thinking about you and what you might be doing tonight, I tuned back in and waited for him to shut the hell up so I could have some peace. He wasn't funny or told stories that made me laugh like you do.

The highlight of the night was when we were leaving. He said that this was fun, but he'd rather date someone who was more successful. Oh, and he said something about me wasting my time being in a band. That was the final straw. I'm a lady, but I'm also a redhead.

So I smiled and, as politely as I could, told him, "If you have a problem with me, write the problem on a piece of paper, fold it, and shove it up your ass." I smiled, then walked outside the bar and hopped in the first car I saw. We'll get back to that in a second.

The best part of the night was when the over thing picked me up, then dropped me off in front of my building so I could walk back to my apartment. At least I think it was an over. Or an under. You know that thing you call and they drive you around? Then again, it might not have been any of those things.

When I got into the backseat and told the driver where to go, she looked back at me like she'd seen a ghost. I wondered why there were kids in the backseat, so I must have ordered a family under. Things got kinda hazy after that, but the next thing I knew, I walked into my building.

Well, staggered is more like it. My friend Clara, who is the co-signer... consign- consignor, whatever you call the person who takes care of the people in the building, helped me inside. She took me up to my apartment and after she left, I pulled out your last letter and read it. You know what? It wiped away the stench of an awful date. I was happy again.

Roy, or Mark, or whatever you would like me to call you, please forgive me for writing all this. I'm not a psycho chick, nor do I expect anything from you other than your friendship. I'm a woman who's drunk right now, but who also has a dream, a dream that I am so grateful you support, and that means everything to me. You are such a sweetheart to do everything you do, and I hope you continue to be there for me.

I know we hardly know each other, and we have only met through our letters, but I have had this connection with you. Please don't get freaked out. It's not like I am a stalker or anything, but I'll understand if you don't want to write to me after this.

If that is the case, no hard feelings. I wish you all the success in the world

The Redhead and the Fountain Pen

with your girls and the tournament. And if you hear a woman's voice screaming in delight northeast of where you are, you'll know I won my audition. And if you hear me throwing up tonight, don't worry, I'll be okay. It's the whiskey talking. Why is it that alcohol speaks louder than words?

Can you do me a favor? If I get sick, can you write Clara and ask her to come upstairs so she can hold my hair back? Send it FedEx so it will get here quicker. You're such a sweetie for doing that.

I reread that and got a case of the teepees. Oh, wait. That's not what I got. I have plenty of teepees in the bathroom. I got the teehees. Yeah, that's what I have. I crack myself up sometimes. And other times I drink too much and write the most outrageous letters. Well, this is my first, and only, drunk and write. Hooray, I finally figured out what I was doing. Let's celebrate! I'll bring the whiskey!

What do you call it? Brown water liquid? No. Um, beige water drinks? Whatever you call it. I'm too drunk to remember, so you figure it out. I'm also too drunk to speak, so thank God we like to write letters.

This no social media idea was brilliant. You're so smart. I'm pretty smart too. Does that make us smartasses? By the way, I have a nice ass. Oh wait, I shouldn't have written that. Be a doll and take your fountain pen and cross that out when you get this letter, okay?

Whew! I hope this letter makes sense. If not, I'm sure you get the idea. And while you're getting the idea, I'll order us another whiskey.

God bless you, Mark, for being my friend. I hope our correspondence will continue. If not, please know you have made a wonderful difference in a woman's heart.

Your friend (Well, for as long as it takes you to finish reading this letter anyway). Or for as long as it takes for me to sober up, which might be March.

I hope we continue this correspondence later. Or we can dispense with the bull and keep it going right now.

Cat

Um, I need a minute to wipe the grin off my face. Where do I begin? I re-read the letter three times to get in my head what I wanted to write. I thought about sleeping on it and coming into my reply with a clear head and not confess my feelings. Or, I could be honest and write to her tonight.

I wasn't sure what to do, so I poured myself a brown water drink, then looked up at the stars and thought about what to do next. While I looked at the stars, Scott walked over and joined me.

"Well, old sport, I see someone has come back to the living."

I smiled. "It's been a long time. But I'm beginning to feel again."

He nodded, then raised his flask and said, "Glad to have you back. I was getting a little worried about you."

"Worry no more. I'm good now."

Scott took a sip, then asked, "Well? Now that you know how she feels, why are you still here? Go find her."

The thought was exhilarating, most likely brought on by sipping the liquid courage. "Aw, I don't know. She's got auditions. I have a softball team to worry about. Not now. One day."

He nodded. "You better not get the heebie jeebies on this, old sport. You'll regret not finding your redhead and seeing if this was meant to be."

I looked into the night, then nodded. "Yeah. I suppose you're right."

After a cricket serenade filled up the silence, I asked, "So, what was it like when you met Zelda?"

Scott looked at me, then grinned. "When I saw her, I knew."

"Knew what?"

"She was the girl I was supposed to be with."

"But how did you know?"

The Redhead and the Fountain Pen

He looked up at the stars and spoke. "I fell in love with her courage, her sincerity, and her flaming self-respect. And it's these things I'd believe in, even if the whole world indulged in wild suspicions that she wasn't all she should be. I loved her and it was the beginning of everything."

I listened to the words and the passion with which he delivered them. My head tingled, and a warmth surged through me. It wasn't the booze this time.

"You know, old sport, when it's right, nothing in the world can change what your heart feels. And what it wants. It's the innocence of that first glance. That first touch. That first time you hear her voice. You know it. And when you do, life is never the same."

I stared at him, then nodded. "I understand."

He smiled, then looked up at the sky. "I'll be home in a few. What? Okay, I'll tell him"

"Who was that?" I asked, not sure who he was talking to.

"That would be Zelda. I told her you were making progress, so she said congrats, but whatever you do, don't be a dumb Dora and screw it up."

"Tell her I said thanks."

"Will do. Oh, and by the way, I'd consider your next letter wisely. There's a young woman's heart at stake here. Be gentle."

I thought for a few seconds, then asked, "You know she got drunk and wrote to me?"

"I was there when she wrote it."

My eyebrows dropped into my nose. "What? You were? Wait, what are you talking about?"

"How do you think she got back to her building? Sometimes, you have to pitch in and help a damsel in distress." He paused, then smiled. "Oh, that's right. You have no idea what that means, do you?"

I shook my head. "Thanks for helping her. But I have to ask. You saw her. What did you think?"

Scott's grin almost split his face. "She's the kind of girl that if you saw her across a crowded room, you'd fall so quickly for her that nobody would hear the sound of you hitting the floor."

After Scott's final words, I sat back in an amorous haze. The tingle surging through my body as the power of his words cast a warmth I'd never felt before. And was sure I would never feel again.

I sat in silence for a few seconds, then finally exhaled and asked, "Will you help me write it?"

He shook his head. "You don't need my help. You have two choices. Write her back, or not mention it at all. But no matter what you decide, it sounds like you have that girl's heart. Take good care of it. These things don't come around every day."

And with that, he was gone.

I'm going to sleep on it, then in the morning, figure out what I would do. For now, I replayed her words in my head over and over.

After going back and forth, I decided to play it safe. I'd write her a reply, then hold on to it for a while, and if I felt the same way by Monday, I'd send it. And if not, nobody would know the difference.

My dearest Catherine -

You should hit the brown water more. What wonderful things you write when you do.

I cannot express how much I enjoyed your letter. And here's a little secret. I have the same feelings for you. It's nice to know we have this friendship, so unique, so old-fashioned. So wonderful.

Now it's time for me to be honest. I was sad when you wrote to me about the guy who asked for your number. I am sure he has his reasons for asking because of the charm and grace you must bring to any room you enter.

Cat, please do not worry about your last letter. For the record, if we ever stopped writing to each other, a part of me would hurt. This is something I've never had before. It's special. Your words healed me and made me believe there are things left in the world with charm and grace.

You have a friend who wants nothing but the best for you. I know you will achieve what you set out to do. And one day, who knows? Will our paths cross?

Catherine, you're thought of often, and no matter what happens with the audition, I will stick by your side.

Your friend and the man who looks forward to continuing this correspondence, either drunk or sober...

Roy

When I finished, I heard clapping above me, so I looked up and said, "Thanks, Scott."

I heard a female voice call down, "It's Zelda."

"Zelda?"

"Yeah. Scott's a little hungover this morning and is still sleeping, but I thought your letter was wonderful. I know you're dizzy with the dame at the moment, but take a breath before you do anything. If you still feel that way tomorrow, then airmail it, okay? Good luck, ya sweet palooka."

She was right. I read the letter a few times, then decided to hold off for now. I'll wait until Monday, then I'll have had some time to make a rational decision, instead of one made on emotion only.

Those are the ones you usually regret.

✒

When Monday came, I still wasn't sure what to do about the letter. Luckily, I had to get the girls ready for our final regular season game against Blairsville Central, so I didn't have to lose sleep about what to do. Then again, there's the old saying, "When there is doubt, then there is no doubt."

I didn't think much about hearing from Catherine, since after that last letter, she might have felt too embarrassed to write. Sure enough, I didn't see a powder blue envelope in my mailbox. Then again, unless she wrote to me on back-to-back days, I wouldn't hear from her for a while. The embarrassment could scale back her letters.

Here's where my night took a turn. After pulling out nothing from the mailbox, I walked to the front door. Waiting for me was a square FedEx envelope resting on the glass panel of the door. When I saw the return address was from New York, my heartbeat accelerated.

I ripped the tab open, then pulled out the envelope. The purple ink was back. But why was she overnighting a letter? I hadn't sent my reply to her drunk and scribbled letter, so I wondered what this could be.

Dear Roy:

By chance, did I send you a letter full of drunken nonsense?

The other night, I had a few too many and might have written you a letter. I remember stumbling to the mail room and tossing something through the outgoing mail slot, but I'm not sure what it was. For all I know it was my credit card receipt from the bar.

The next thing I knew, I woke up in the lobby next to the mail room in a chair. Someone put one of those pointed birthday hats on me and left an empty beer bottle in my hand. And they say people don't have a sense of humor...

If you got a letter and read it, please forgive me if there was anything in it that might be inappropriate. I promise I am a good person and not a crazed chick you would see on the Lifetime Network.

    I look forward to continuing our correspondence soon. That is if my last letter, which I am not sure if I sent or not, got to you.

    Your friend -

Cat

Well…Quite the predicament. But the question is, do I send my letter? Would she appreciate my honesty and the fact I am crazy about her? I remember the Latin phrase, "In vino veritas," which means, "In wine there is truth."

But when you have too much wine, sometimes the truth can get a little blurred. Along with your penmanship.

I decided that with everything going on in her life, I don't want to cloud her mind. I will write back that I didn't see a letter. This way, she will have a clear conscience going into her audition. The last thing she needs is to worry about our friendship.

Here is the revised letter I'll send tomorrow.

    Dear Cat -

    No worries my friend, I don't recall a drunken letter, so whatever it was, you are off the hook. You didn't include a check, did you? haha I wouldn't want you to lose money, as well as a phantom letter. You have more important things to worry about these days.

    I know you have your audition coming up, and the last thing I want to be is a distraction. All I want is to support you and see you achieve what you set out to do. I'm here for you, my friend.

    One of these days, you will be in the Geffen Hall and everyone will cheer you on stage. I will cheer the loudest.

    I am here as long as you want me to be, watching you move forward toward your dreams. As I wrote before, you soooo got this, Cat!

Your friend, who will continue this correspondence later - Roy

So, what do you think? Was I delicate enough? Oh well, no matter what she thinks, at least I know where I stand.

And it's a really good place...

eighteen

We play Chatsworth in the first round of the state softball tournament. They are the hottest team in Georgia, as they won their last ten games.

Great. Nothing like facing a team that has momentum. Then again, my girls are playing well and also are mentally tough. Since we are the higher seed, we are the home team in the first round, but Chatsworth is playing their best softball of the season. Not too many people outside of me, the team, and the town give us much of a chance to get past the Cougars this afternoon. Call me crazy, many already have, but I like our chances.

I never like to look ahead, but if we should beat Chatsworth, fourth-ranked Jefferson County would be next. They will be a handful, but with all due respect, we aren't too shabby either.

While I'm thinking about it, I've often wondered about the "All due respect" line. After you use it, then you insult someone. Is that a free pass to disrespect someone after you've given them your respect? Isn't that kind of insincere?

With the worry about the tournament coming up, what I would give to have Catherine here. I would take her to dinner at my favorite place in Blue Ridge, Bear Claw Farms, which is in the middle of the mountains.

We would talk a little about the tournament, then a lot about her. I want to know all about who she is and what this audition means to her. How it makes her feel and how she is preparing for it.

Then we would hold hands as we walked along the square. I would take her to the bookstore and introduce her to Scarlett. Then show her the spot where I found her book and the miracle of what brought us together.

On our walk, I would give her my jacket so she'd stay warm. We'd find a street band and I would tip them to play the Elvis song she loves. I would take her in my arms and we'd dance.

We'd sit on my deck in front of the fireplace under a blanket. And watch the way the stars float over the mountains, dropping specks of light onto the trees.

She would ask what I was thinking, and I would tell her I was thinking about seeing her on stage, watching her do what she loves.

Then she would put her head on my shoulder, and we would stare into the starry night. We wouldn't worry about the future because now was all that mattered. I'd cherish the memory of our night together, knowing it was a miracle our paths crossed.

Will there be a forever with Catherine? Who knows? Am I afraid? Nah, I can't be, since there's nothing to lose.

The Redhead and the Fountain Pen

Dear Cat:

Happy Friday! I wanted to write because my days are going to get busy since the tournament begins on Monday. Now's the calm before the storm, so I wanted to say hello while I had a free moment.

It's funny, but we are both going through our challenges. Mine with the team and you with your audition. I've racked my brain remembering all the encouragement I've learned over the years so I can help you and the team. You both are strong enough to do this on your own. I gave both of you a gentle nudge, but when you have talent, strength, and passion, you don't need my words.

Here's a little secret about me. We are alike in facing a challenge. Tough and positive on the outside, and know as long as we believe in our cause and our abilities, anything is possible. But on the inside, I worry about losing. About failing. And how I am going to live with that after the game is over.

Why do you think that is? Are you as afraid of losing as I am?

I've always feared what coming up short feels like. Sometimes it's paralyzing. But if you use it as motivation, it can strengthen you.

I would never tell the team I'm worried since I am their rock and they look to me for strength. But I'm worried, so I'm turning to you for strength. I know you have a lot, otherwise, you wouldn't be where you are today.

Do you have any words to build me back up to the rock I need to be?

I'll keep you posted on our game. Keep your fingers crossed and the prayers coming.

We will continue our correspondence later!

Roy

Tonight, I got a worried pit in my stomach. Why? Because the girls have fought so hard to get to this point. If they lose, I worry about how crushed they are going to be since that's it. Our season is over.

Remember when I wrote this was a team I could fall in love with? Well, you never want to see someone you love hurting.

Between Catherine and the team, I have a lot to worry about. Iceland. New York. The beginning of the tournament. I know I have to be the rock for everyone, but I don't know how I am going to get through this.

You must cut the cord and let life happen, no matter how much you've prepared for it. It's out of my hands now, and that's the tough part to accept. All I can do is live and let the chips fall where they may.

✒

Today is the first day of the tournament. I woke to the sounds of crickets and darkness flooding my bedroom. I looked over at the clock, and even though I had a little time before I had to get up, my stomach wouldn't let me drift back to sleep.

All the preparation and hard work culminates today. Now, we'll see how far we've come.

Making the state tournament is every team's goal at the start of a season. Well, we've made it, but my stomach is in knots. Be careful what you wish for, right? I needed something to calm me down, so I thought about a remedy.

Fountain pen at the ready.

Dear Cat:

Sorry for the early morning letter. Well, you might not read it at the exact time I wrote it, but I couldn't sleep and I wanted to say hello.

The tournament begins today. I would hate for our girls to come all this way and then fall short in the first round. All we can do is give our best effort after we arrive at 3:30 pm. Sounds easy, doesn't it?

I'm sure you've been down the same road before, right? Not sure of the outcome of something you want to achieve? Then throw in all the hours you've practiced, sacrificed, and visualized what the moment looks like. Finally, all the chips are in the middle of the table, waiting for you to scoop them up after you've won.

Pray for the girls, not for me. Pray they will be at their best, and for confidence and peace in the middle of the storm. While you do that, I will touch the card you gave me and hope for the best.

Whew. This bit of writing was a big help. I don't know how you did it, Cat, but I'm okay with whatever happens today. Can you imagine what we could do if you and I were in the same place at the same time? There wouldn't be anything we couldn't achieve...

Wish us luck today. We will continue this correspondence later.

Roy

After I got home from the game, I wrote this:

Dear Cat:

Well, so far so good. We won 10-3. As the game went on, I sensed the girl's confidence and there was no way Chatsworth was going to beat us.

How are you? It's funny, but I was thinking about how both of us are fighting the same battle. You are trying to achieve a dream and I am trying to help a group of girls do the same thing. Do you think next time we can pool our resources? I could use the extra help!

I hate to cut this letter so short, but the next round is in two days, so I need to watch a video of the next opponent, Jefferson County.

Keep the prayers coming!
Roy

. 🖋

I needed a break from preparing for the next game, so I vacated my office and drove over to see Scarlett. A gooey oatmeal cookie was the thing to recharge my batteries.

I walked over to my favorite table and exhaled, since it was vacant. For some reason, it's usually vacant, so I must be arriving at the right time. I took a seat and stared through the window at the dark outline of the mountains in the distance.

Within seconds, Scarlett appeared. "What brings you by tonight?" She asked as she placed a plate of oatmeal cookies on the table.

I reached over to pull off a chunk, feeling the heat from the cookie as the sugary goo pulled apart in my fingers. "Aw, I had to get out of the office. Good thing my table was vacant. I could use the view to relax me."

"Your table is always vacant," she said with a smile. "I know this place isn't exactly Sardis or the 21 Club, but hey, you're a celebrity in this town, so I make sure you're treated like one."

I shook my head and joked. "Why would I ever leave?"

Scarlett nodded. "Ah, you're getting the idea," she laughed, then walked over and poured hot chocolate into a cup.

She returned and placed it next to the plate. As I moved the cup, the steam serpentined into the air. "I heard it's Jefferson County in the next round. They have a lot of offense, but not a lot of pitching. If you get on them early, you'll have a chance to win," she told me.

"If I didn't know any better, I'd say you've been spying on

them," I joked.

She gave me a wry grin. "I hear things," she said with a wink. "Whipped cream too?"

I nodded.

She reached into her apron and pulled out a small can of whipped cream. She popped the cap off and swirled whipped cream around the cup, extinguishing the steam.

I took a bite of the cookie and soon forgot all about softball, the letters to Catherine, and everything else. Well, for a few seconds anyway.

She winked. "I have correspondents all over town feeding me information. Not only about softball."

"What else is there?"

"Here's some breaking news. You were the hot topic of conversation the other day."

"Oh boy. Should I ask?"

"Well, since the team is in the playoffs, I hear the ladies batted your name around, no pun intended, at the weekly Jammin' With Jesus meeting."

"Jammin' With Jesus?"

"Yeah. It's a women's group of former musicians who meet here every other Wednesday. After their meeting, they walk out to the deck and have a jam session. It's a lit rager."

"A lit rager?"

Scarlett shook her head. "You don't know what a lit rager is? And I thought this town had enough old fogies."

I shook my head.

"It means a wild party. Actually, the ladies are pretty good. They get the geriatrics rockin' sometimes. But I'm required by law to have the EMTs standing by in case someone breaks a hip, or gets ventricular fibrillation."

"That sounds kinda scary."

"Oh, it is, but I ordered an automated external defibrillator. Plus, the hospital required me to take a CPR course if I was going to have them use the bookstore for their meetings. You know, in case someone was in danger of takin' the big adios on my property. It's quite the process." As I shook my head, she told me, "They have their eye on you. Up here, they take a shine to single men, so get ready for a lot of invites to have drinks and meet a lot of single daughters."

I couldn't help but give her a grin in return. "Good to know I'm in demand. I hope they talk more about the softball team than me."

"Not with a smile like that," she said with a wink. "Aw, Coach, I can tell a good egg when I see one."

Before I could tell her I appreciated her words, I heard a familiar song playing from behind us. I saw an Alexa on the counter, and after I listened for a few seconds, it hit me. "Oh, 'September' by Daughtry. That's one of my favorites."

Scarlett turned to Alexa and stared at the speaker for a few seconds. She gave it a warm grin.

"Do you like that song too?"

She snapped out of it, then looked at me. "Never heard of it." She grabbed the can of whipped cream and placed it in her apron. "Why is it your favorite?"

Her answer didn't convince me. I squinted, then raised an

eyebrow. "I guess it reminds me of days when things weren't so complicated."

She stared at me, then said, "It's about time you told me what happened in Atlanta."

"Why do you want to know about Atlanta? I put that away months ago. Shouldn't we focus on Blue Ridge?"

"Don't sweat it, Coach, your secrets are safe with me."

I thought about it for a few seconds. Finally, I told her, "I won't bore you with the details, so I will give you the condensed version."

She smiled. "Tell ya what. I'll save you the trouble."

"What does that mean?"

Scarlett reached into her sweater and pulled out a newspaper clipping. She slid on her reading glasses from the chain around her neck and unfolded the paper. "Atlanta Catholic School Principal Lisa Madden announced on Monday that Athletic Director and former Georgia Southern All-American linebacker Mike Wilder was arrested and charged with extortion, computer fraud, and falsifying official state documents. It is alleged Wilder extorted the girls' basketball coach to get her to resign by threatening to falsify grades and adding bogus information to students' records."

The hair on the back of my neck stood up. "Where did you find that?"

She removed her glasses. "It was in the newspaper. You can find them anywhere. Even in Blue Ridge."

"Great story. But what does that have to do with me?"

She raised an eyebrow. "Sound familiar?"

I looked down, then at the cookie looking back at me. As I

picked up the crumbs from the table and dropped them on the plate, I looked up and told her, "Yes, it does. Lisa was the principal when I was there. She's a good woman. I'm glad she busted the son of a bitch."

"Is that why you had to leave Atlanta?"

I looked at her, seeing the empathy in her eyes. Finally, I nodded. "Yeah. Something like that."

"Shouldn't you have reported him?"

I shook my head. "Yeah. But I couldn't."

Scarlett squinted. "Why not? You could have had that bastard arrested. And you could have saved your job."

I nodded. "Yeah, I could have fought him. But he would have hurt the girls. I wasn't going to let that happen. I could get another job. But them? They couldn't get another scholarship. They couldn't have lies on their records, and I couldn't live with myself if I did anything to taint their future."

She nodded. "How tough was it for you to walk away?"

I looked away for a few seconds, then back to her. "It was like having my heart ripped out of my chest."

I paused and stared through the window. Images of those days were as dark as the night I looked into. "I remember," then I paused and bit my upper lip to steady myself. "I got them in the locker room and told them I was leaving. The girls all looked at each other, then our captain, Mary Bailey, stood and in tears asked, 'Coach? What are you doing? Why are you leaving us?' Being on autopilot, I gave her a rehearsed answer. To this day, I don't remember most of it. I said something about how I helped them to find their greatness, and they didn't need me any longer, or some bullshit like that. I stood strong as the only sound in the room was of sniffles. Most of the girls sat on their stools, heads down, crying. As soon as I finished, I looked at them and said, 'I love every one of you. You'll always be the champions of my heart.' And then I opened the door and left the locker room."

Scarlett stared at me. Her eyes glistened, then she looked away and wiped her cheek.

"I packed up my office, said goodbye to my closest friends, then walked out. As I left the building and walked onto the sidewalk, I looked up and saw our team in two rows of girls applauding and saying thanks. At the end was Mary, who gave me a bat signed by every player on the team. At the bottom, she wrote, 'Our hearts will never forget you.'"

Reliving the memory of that morning was too much, so I reached for a napkin. By this time, both of Scarlett's cheeks were soggy.

"I gave each of the girls a hug before I left, and as I was saying goodbye to the last girl, Wilder walked out to the parking lot. He approached me and said, 'These girls are out of the building during school hours. Unless they return to the building immediately, I will report them. You don't want them to face demerits and possible suspension. Do you?'"

Scarlett sniffled, then the fire returned to her eyes. "He did not." After I nodded, she asked, "What did you do?"

"I looked at him, and when he gave me an evil sneer, wanting to rub it in my face who was boss, I smiled, and replied, 'Tell ya what, let's leave them out of this. This is between me and you.' Then he said, 'I don't care.' So I glanced at my girls, then looked him in the eyes."

"Oh my," she gasped.

"Then I said, 'You don't?' Then I hauled off and decked him. Knocked him right on his ass. As he lay on the ground, I bent over him and said, 'Now you do.' The girls cheered and whooped it up, then walked me to my car. That's how it ended."

She nodded. "Good for you."

I raised my right hand and extended my ring finger to show her the scar and a crooked knuckle. "It cost me a broken finger, but it was worth it."

Scarlett nodded, then she shrugged. "Once they sort everything out, I'm sure one of the first things they'll do is ask that you come back."

"Me? No way. They have their coach now. They don't need me any longer."

"You don't think so?" She asked. "I know a little something about the world. You'll get a call."

"Yeah, right," I assured her. "They tossed my number the second I tossed what's his name on his ass."

Scarlett exhaled, then told me, "You wouldn't leave us, would you?" She asked as her eyes moistened a second time. "I hope this place has become home and you have family here. A family that cares about you."

When I looked at Scarlett, her eyes pleaded for me to not break her heart. "Scarlett, I'm happy to be here. I never in a million years thought things would turn out this way."

"Yeah, I guess turning the team around and making them a winner is pretty amazing."

I took a sip of hot chocolate, then wiped my mouth and

smiled. "I didn't mean that."

Scarlett shook her head. "You didn't? What do you mean?"

"Well, since you asked, I have a funny story about something that happened when I got to Blue Ridge. You're going to laugh when I tell you."

She gave me a grin with a squinted eye. "Does this have anything to do with a young lady?"

I nodded.

"Who is it?" Then she smiled. "Don't tell me it's Tara. I know she's a sweetie, but she's head over heels in love with her husband. Although, as cute as you are, I'd say she might make an exception," she joked.

"Well, I love Tara, but it's not her. It's not even the usual boy meets girl story."

"Well, you must have met somewhere. Was it the pumpkin festival we had a few weeks ago?"

"We haven't met in person."

The response stymied her. "Hmmm. Well, did you meet her online? Was it one of those dating sites? Oh, I know. It was Bow-Chicka-Bow-Wow.com."

I laughed. "Not exactly."

Scarlett's eyes squinted. Before she asked a follow-up question, I made it easy for her. "Okay, I'll explain."

I told her how I found her letter in a copy of *The Great Gatsby* in her bookstore.

Scarlett smiled. "No wonder you like that book."

"Well, it is my favorite book, so there was some destiny

involved, don't you think?"

Scarlett nodded. "I'd say so."

"The funny thing is the book belonged to her father, so she was happy I found it since she thought it was lost forever. I promised I'd return it to her."

"Nice work, my friend. Way to figure out a way for you two to meet in person. So did you set up a date for you to give the book back to her?"

I laughed. "Well, it's not that easy."

"Oh, okay. Well, mention it when you talk on the phone."

I shook my head. "We haven't spoken on the phone."

Scarlett squinted, then said, "Well, okay. Mention it the next time you email her."

"Well, we haven't emailed each other yet."

Scarlett gave me a lost stare. "Zoom?" When I shook my head again, she asked, "Smoke signals?"

I laughed. "Believe it or not, we write letters to each other."

"Write letters? Why?"

"We both aren't big social media people, so it made sense for us to communicate this way."

"Do you think you'll meet?"

"I don't know. I promised I would return her book, so our paths might cross one day."

"You know nothing about her?"

"I know a bunch from the letters we've written so far."

"Do you even know her name?"

The Redhead and the Fountain Pen

When I looked at Scarlett, and she gave me a sexy smile, it made me smile too. "Catherine. Her name is Catherine."

"Well, that's a start. Last name?"

I shook my head.

Scarlett's eyes softened, and she looked at the table. I was about to ask if something was wrong when she looked up. "Let me get this straight. No last names. You write letters. Like, actual pen and paper? Envelopes? Stamps? Writing out, haha, after silly jokes?"

"Yep." When Scarlett got quiet on me again, I asked, "Is everything okay?"

Scarlett stared at nothing for a few seconds, then looked at me. The expression from a moment ago was now a smile, but she couldn't convince me it was genuine. "Oh, yes. I'm fine. Aw, that's sweet."

"I hope my story impressed you."

"Oh," she said, raising her eyebrows. "It has. It's much more personal to see a handwritten letter. I also think it takes more effort. You have to care about the person you are writing to if you are going to go to all that trouble."

I took a sip of my drink, then wiped my mouth. "Agreed. There needs to be an interest if you are going to go to all that trouble."

"If she keeps writing, I'd say you've made a friend. But keep writing back. That's the key to this whole letter thing," she grinned. "Keep me posted on your progress."

"Off the record?"

Scarlett nodded. "Only for you."

When I reached for my wallet, she put up her hand. "I'll put it on your tab. Now get that cute arse of yours out of here so I can tend to my paying customers."

"That scares me."

"Scares you?"

"Sure. Since you've created a tab for me, I'm going to have to get a job on the side just to pay it off."

"Tell ya what. You win the state championship, and I'll see that your tab gets conveniently lost. If you know what I mean," she said with a sweet smile.

"In that case, I'll need to get two jobs," I joked.

nineteen

Hey Cat!

Today, we faced the mighty Jefferson County Rangers. I was looking for motivation since the girls seemed tight and there wasn't much said as we walked to the bus. As we left the parking lot, I stood up and told them, "Take a good look at that entrance, ladies."

They all turned and looked at the entrance to our school, then back at me. "The next time you see it, we will have beaten Jeff County's ass." Since we were heavy underdogs, I wanted to make sure the girls didn't think the same thing.

They all laughed and whooped it up. Then I sat down and the bus went silent for the next two hundred and fifty miles.

We won 12-3, to the astonishment of the home crowd. As we walked off the bus, their fans waited for us by the fence leading to the field and shouted their opinions about our ability to win on their field. (Fill in the blanks here with whatever iconic trash talk you've heard). We walked by, never saying a word, ignoring the fact they tried to intimidate us.

Instead of worrying about them, the girls focused on the task at hand. Their fans kept it up for the first few innings, but as we pulled away, the taunts and the abuse subsided. By the time the game was in the last inning, there weren't many of their fans left in the stadium. I looked at Josie and smiled. "It's kind of quiet around here. Isn't it?"

She laughed. "I'm sorry, Coach. I can't hear you over the silence."

After the girls walked onto the bus and sat, I stood and looked at them. Instead of a rousing victory speech, all I did was smile and say, "Told ya we were going to whip their ass."

They responded with groans, and someone threw a towel at me. After that, it was a riot as the bus rocked back and forth the entire four hours back to Blue Ridge.

Cat, it was amazing to see them play. And play with a bit of a swagger and a chip on their shoulder. As I sat on the bus in the darkness, thinking about the game, I have to confess, I thought about you.

I envisioned you walking down the street toward Geffen Hall. Well, striding. Striding with purpose and confidence. I know you'll vanquish whatever awaits at the end of your walk. If we can beat a team that we shouldn't have even been on the same field with, you should have no problem.

I hope what we are doing here in Georgia helps you in New York.

Well, it's on to the quarterfinals! We will continue this correspondence later!

Roy

It's been a few days since the game at Jefferson County. My overworked brain needs a rest from thinking about our next opponent. It also needs a break from worrying about Catherine.

But I'm not going to get it since the quarterfinals are this afternoon against Macon Central. Can we continue to be the Cinderella story of the tournament? We'll see in about five hours.

Hello Cat!

How are you? And how are things going in New York? Things here are good, and I am happy to report we are on to the semi-finals!

The Redhead and the Fountain Pen

The girls were a little tight early, but Anna kept us positive as she shut them down for the first three innings. In the seventh, with us leading 7-5, they had the winning run at the plate, but Anna struck her out to end the game. We all had a collective exhale as we got the last out, then got back on the bus, not sure what happened. The ride home was silent since everyone was both mentally and physically spent. But it was a good kind of tired.

Before we get too smug, guess who we get next? That's right, our old rivals, the Fannin Central Admirals, who won their quarterfinal game as well. Oh goodie.

So, you've read about our journey, now I want to know about yours. I know you're still in practice mode, but what else have you been doing? Please tell me you are getting out and taking a break. It does wonders for your creativity.

Go to the Empire State Building and spit off the top. Go to the Statue of Liberty and run around naked like Daryl Hannah did in the movie, Splash. And if those antics aren't crazy enough, go to Central Park and dive into a fountain.

Cat, when you are facing a challenge, you have to be a lunatic about it. Where's the fun of being normal? For musicians and coaches, we all have to be a little off-center to do what we do, so embrace the crazy.

Oh, speaking of being a lunatic, hang out at Bellevue and do the thing with the vanilla pudding I told you about. When someone asks you about it, tell them the mayo tastes good. But it's not near as yummy as the pickle juice you chugged for breakfast...muhaha.

In all seriousness, Cat, clear your mind and remember to breathe. Approach this as you would at the grocery store. Make a list. Then execute the plan. That's all you have to do.

Until we continue our correspondence later -
Roy

Although writing to Cat makes me feel better, I don't have a good feeling about Monday. It's not so much I worry about the team not playing well, since I know we will, but the idea of losing. Of failing. Of walking off the field for the last time this season and knowing we didn't do what we set out to do. And that is to win a championship.

I guess that's why I'm drawn to Catherine since I see the same qualities in her. That drive, that will to succeed, and that paralyzing fear of failing. I'm also drawn to her since we have parallel lives at the moment. Both of us face long odds to achieve what we aspire to do.

I'm glad we have each other to get through our adversity.

twenty

Hello, Cat. Today was a big day.

Before today's game, I sensed the girls were tight since none of them had ever beaten Fannin Central. When I walked into the dugout, the mood was tense and there wasn't much said.

My father once told me that when you lead a team, whether it be on the field or in an office, some respond to a kick in the butt, others to a pat on the back. It's your responsibility to figure out what works for each.

You also have to understand your team's mood. Are they tight? Relaxed? Whatever it is, you need to get them all going in the same direction at the same time with their best effort and attitude. You want them to believe. And once they believe, they can do anything.

I walked down the row, encouraging each player as I passed. When I got to the end of the line, I turned and looked back at the team.

"What's going on? Why so quiet? This is softball. It's a game. And games are supposed to be fun."

When nobody answered, I turned to our captain. "Josie? What's up?"

Josie rubbed her hands together, then stood. She looked at the team, then at me. "Coach. None of us have ever had a winning season before, and here we are. We've never beaten Fannin Central either. We're worried."

"What are you worried about?"

"Well," she began, looking down, then back to me, "What if we lose? None of us want this to end."

When a team is tight, yelling at them is the last thing you want to do. So, I pulled up a chair, sat down, and didn't say a word. I let the anticipation for the moment build and finally, when the players were about to ask what I was doing, I spoke. "Look at this dugout full of young women. Not girls any longer. But young women. That's what you are. I've seen you grow up in only a few months. What was once a timid group of individuals who lacked self-confidence has turned into a team that knows they cannot lose. A group of women who play for each other instead of themselves. Who knows that they will always be successful, no matter the situation."

After another pause, I continued. "No matter what happens in the next few hours, it's going to be okay. This isn't life or death. No matter the outcome, you can handle it."

I stood and told them, "Go out and play this game, like I know you can. And when it's over, I know who will be in the finals."

Before I knew it, the girls all rose to their feet, cheering, jumping up and down, shouting. I stepped back and let them have their moment. They were ready.

Cat, it had the desired effect.

Believe it or not, we finally beat Fannin Central. It was even closer than the Macon Central game, and despite our season riding on every pitch, we all were calm and focused.

In the bottom of the seventh, we led 3-2. I expected another gut-wrenching finish, but we got three straight outs and before we knew it, the girls were in the middle of the field celebrating.

However, we may be in trouble.

The last batter hit a ball up the middle. Anna tried to stop it with her leg, and it hit her ankle. The same ankle she injured earlier in the year. But this time, it was worse.

The Redhead and the Fountain Pen

Luckily, the ball bounced to our shortstop, who made the play for the third out. As the girls celebrated, Anna limped off the field. She tried to walk on it, but it was a struggle.

She came to me afterward as we were walking back to the bus. She tried to put weight on it, but lost her balance and fell onto the side of the bus. I looked at her and saw her grimace, but she covered it with a smile and laugh. "Sorry, I slipped. But I'm fine."

Her father walked over after seeing what happened. "You okay, Anna?"

"I'm fine, dad. My ankle is a little sore." She tried to walk up the steps of the bus, but hopped on one leg to the top, then looked back at me. "I'll be ready for the finals, Coach."

I watched her through the window, limping to find a seat. I told her father, "Ron, let me know what the doctor says. If she isn't a hundred percent, I will not risk hurting her by sticking her out there."

He nodded. "I'll do it. But if she can't go, who will you pitch in the championship?"

I looked him over, sizing him up. "If you took a hot bath, do you think you could fit into her uniform?"

We laughed, then I told him, "We've come this far. I'll think of something. By the way, if the doctor won't clear her, don't say anything. Let me know and I will handle it from there. I want to make sure the team doesn't lose focus."

He nodded and said he would call me later.

As if we didn't have enough to worry about, Anna's father called and told me it's a hairline fracture. If you are a position player, you might play through it, but as a pitcher, you try to adjust your delivery and end up hurting your arm. That can end a career.

Anna has scholarship offers from Clemson, Wake Forest, and Georgia, so I won't do that to her. These things happen, and when they do, you adjust.

All I can do is go with what we have left and that means having Susie pitch. I won't tell her until the night before the championship series. That way she will get a good night's sleep and not stress about it. The less time to worry, the better.

It's like going into your audition and you're using someone else's viola. In this situation, what would you do? The suggestion box is wide open.

Thanks for being there for me, Cat.

Roy

I needed to get out of the cabin after the last few incredible days we've had. Guess where?

I sipped hot chocolate and ate oatmeal cookies with Scarlett. She knew what happened with Fannin Central, and what next week's series meant.

"You've done a great job with the girls this year," she told me. "You think you have a chance in the finals?"

"As long as we step on the field, we'll always have a chance." I wiped my mouth, then told her, "I wish Catherine was here."

"Catherine? Any last names divulged yet?" She teased.

"Nah, not yet. We're good with where we are at the moment."

"So, how's the pen pal thing going?"

"Great. She's going through the same thing in New York, so we share a bond."

"She's a coach too? I thought she was auditioning to play, what was it? The oboe, or something?"

I laughed, then corrected her. "The viola. She's auditioning for the New York Philharmonic."

"Oh, that's right," she said, then grabbed my cup and walked over to refill it. After placing it on the table, she looked at me. "Wow, look at that grin."

"What about it?"

The Redhead and the Fountain Pen

"You like her, don't you?"

"Sure I do. She's a nice girl."

"Is it more than that?" She asked.

"I don't know."

Scarlett shook her head. "All I'm saying is you know nothing about each other, or what the future holds. Bi curamach, my friend."

"I'm sorry?"

"My parents used to tell me that when I was a wee lass chasin' the lads. It means be careful."

"I will," I assured her. Attempts at a poker face lacked conviction.

She gave me a hard stare. "That train left the station a while back."

twenty-one

Hey Cat:

I hope all is well with you in New York. Things are well here, so here is an update.

Believe it or not, we finally beat Fannin Central, so we are on to the finals. It was an incredible game and the girls played out of their minds. But now, we play the number one team in the state, as well as the nation, Holy Trinity.

Before I get the girls ready for that challenge, I am still in shock after beating Fannin Central. Nobody thought we could do it, but we did, so let this be a lesson. Believe in yourself and you can do amazing things. We did and look at what happened. We are playing for the state championship. And as for you? You will play in the New York Philharmonic one day soon.

I bid you farewell for now. We'll continue this correspondence later.

Roy

We had a party tonight to celebrate the victory, as well as a mini pep rally for the team. Tara found me on the field and hugged me. "Thank you, Coach."

"For what?"

"You're the one who got the girls to this point. I can't believe the transformation."

"Aw," I said, shrugging off her praise. "The girls deserve all the credit. Besides, we still have one more goal left on our pre-season list to achieve. And it's the most difficult of them all."

"Aw, you'll figure out a way," she assured me.

Later, as the crowd thinned out, Scarlett walked up to me. I practiced my Irish Gaelic over the last few weeks, so I hit her with, "Dia duit chailín alainn," which means, "Hello beautiful girl."

She stopped and gave me a sexy smile and for a moment, I thought she was going to throw me on the ground and have her way with me. She came back with, "Bhuel, nach tusa an ceann a fheictear. Cad atá á dhéanamh agat tar éis an pháirtí, fear sexy?"

I didn't know what that meant but had an idea because after she said it, her eyes looked me up and down. I was sure by the time she got to my feet, I was naked in her mind.

I smiled and told her, "That's the last time I try to be charming. I'm not sure I want to know, but what did you say?"

She grinned, then told me, "Oh, not much. Only that you are the charming one. Then I asked what you were doing after the party, sexy man?"

"Like I said, I shouldn't have asked."

"There's that crooked smile and those eyes that make me feel as if you know what color my thong is."

I winced. "Um, Scarlett, I didn't need to know that."

After she gave me a seductive wink, she asked, "How's New York?"

I thought for a few seconds, then replied, "Oh yeah. New York. She's good. She's in the middle of practicing for her audition, so she's been busy."

Scarlett's next question hit me hard. "If she makes it, what does that mean for you? Are you thinking about moving there?"

I thought about her question for a few seconds. "My, aren't we optimistic?"

Scarlett laughed. "What do the Boy Scouts say? Only you can prevent forest fires?"

"Excuse me?"

"Oh, wait. That's Smokey the Bear. Sorry, I get them confused. Who sells Tagalongs and Do-Si-Dos?"

"That'd be the Girl Scouts."

"Damn. Who tells you to be prepared?"

"That's the Boy Scouts."

She smacked her hands, then pointed at me. "Yep. That's the one."

"Now that we have that cleared up," I told her, flashing that crooked smile she loves so much. "Scarlett, we're only friends. Plus, one way or the other, I'm going to lose her."

"So much for being optimistic," she said, shaking her head.

"If she makes it, she will be in New York. And if she doesn't, she will move to Iceland and play with the orchestra there. Wherever she ends up, it's a few miles down the road from Blue Ridge."

Scarlett looked at the ground, then nodded. Finally, she looked at me. "After everything that's happened this season, how could you leave?"

"Nah, I'm not going anywhere. Tara gave me the opportunity when I didn't have a job. And after this year, it would be difficult to say goodbye to these girls." I looked into the distance, lost in thought.

Scarlett picked up on the lost look in my eyes. "I told you to be careful."

"I know."

"Do you?" She fired back.

"Yeah," I nodded.

The Redhead and the Fountain Pen

"If I were you, I'd think about getting out of this letter writing thing while you can."

"Why? I won't get hurt."

"Many ships sink in sight of the harbor. Your boat may be sinking as we speak."

"Is that some sort of Irish warning?"

She raised an eyebrow.

"Why are you so opposed to me writing to a girl in New York?"

Scarlett looked into my eyes, then shook her head. "It's not important." Before I could ask why, she changed the subject. "How bad are the girls going to tear up Holy Trinity?"

My brain shifted from one problem to the next. Oh yeah. I almost forgot. Holy Trinity. I put on a brave face and told her, "I'm sure we have them worried. Down to their number one ranking."

"No matter what happens, you've done an amazing job of turning the girls around. They will never forget you or what happened this season."

"Yeah," I told her, lacking conviction.

"Coach? What's wrong?"

I looked into the parking lot, watching the headlights of the cars move around the circle and onto the road. I was trying to buy time since I didn't want to answer the question, but had to.

"Scarlett. I went up and down both lineups. We don't match up. It's not even close. I know the final is the best of three games, but we won't play past the fifth inning in any of them. Or even the third or fourth inning. It will be two and a bar-b-que. Holy Trinity is that good."

Scarlett smiled and nodded. "I'm guessing that won't be part of your pre-game speech."

"Nah. I'll try to leave that out."

"But you've come so far with these girls. You didn't come this far to come this far."

I looked down at the gravel around the fence, then back to her. "We are playing against the number one softball team, not only in Georgia but in the nation. How does anyone expect us to compete with that?"

"Tell them it's a softball game. A game they've played all their lives. And they can do whatever they believe they can. That's the important thing."

I looked into the distance. "The important thing is, those girls know that for as long as they live, this was their time. Win or lose, they put their hearts into every game. Nobody ever promised them anything. But they took their chances and played the game for each other. They left it all on the field. With no regrets. That's the important thing."

As I exhaled, a hint of white steam fluttered into the cool mountain air. "Damn, I love those girls. I love their courage. Their perseverance. And their determination. I hope God is with them on their last journey."

Scarlett gazed at me. This time, it wasn't in lust. It was in awe.

twenty-two

As you know, things are heating up as we prepare for the championship series. Even if we lose, it still would be a remarkable year. But as much as I love to win, I hate to lose more. If we shouldn't beat Holy Trinity, it would have been a good year, but it would be a turd in the punch bowl.

Who comes up with these sayings? And are any of them true? How could someone get a turd into a punchbowl? Wouldn't someone see them do it? Wouldn't that ruin the party? And how tough would it be to climb on a table and squat over the punchbowl? I guess depending on how wide the punchbowl was. And if you deposited a turd into the punch bowl, wouldn't the punch splash on your legs? Again, these are the kinds of questions that keep me up at night.

Thank goodness for the championship series, since it has taken my mind off the fact I haven't heard from Catherine. I've sent her a few letters this week, to keep her spirits and confidence up. It would be nice to hear from her, and I hope she's okay. I guess when you care about someone, you hope they are happy, especially when you don't get to see them every day.

Between us, although I denied it to Scarlett, I'm worried

about the future. A future that's coming at me from all sides. I'm sending a group of girls out to face an unbeatable foe and there is nothing left I can do but be a spectator to their fate. If we crash and burn, I hope the pain passes quickly.

And then there's my girl in New York. I'm mobilizing every encouraging word I have and sending them into battle with her. I hope it's good enough.

Hold on a second. The doorbell rang, so let me see who's here. I'll be back in a few.

Well, this is good news. When I opened the door, waiting for me was a FedEx box. Not an envelope, but a box. The return address was New York.

I reached inside and pulled out the first thing my fingers attached to, which was a card, so I opened it and began reading. My lips curled upward.

Dear Roy:

I got every one of your letters and since I know you're playing for the championship, I wanted to send you something.

Please forgive me if I got the dates mixed up. I also wanted to apologize for the lack of letters, but I didn't write on purpose.

Remember, I told you I'm superstitious. Since your team kept winning, and I wasn't writing, I didn't want to mess with a winning streak. But the more I thought about you and the team, I couldn't stay quiet any longer.

Your previous letters about overcoming adversity, especially when nobody thinks you can move me. I know you were writing about your team, but it felt like those words were meant for me since we both face impossible odds. Win or lose, Roy, we share something magical, and I will never forget these months and what we've gone through together.

The Redhead and the Fountain Pen

I hope you accept these gifts as a gesture of my appreciation since you came to my rescue. You keep my spirits up, my confidence where it needs to be, and also you give me a kick in the pants when I need it.

The first is a tiny softball bat. When I saw it, I had to send it to you. The second is a necklace of my patron saint, St. Jude. In case you forgot, he is the Patron Saint of the lost cause, and we fit that description. You don't have to wear it, but put it in your pocket and rub it when you need strength.

I hope you're still playing and get some use out of what I sent. If not, please keep it as a gift. The next time you get into a tough spot, think of me, and know I'm praying for you.

If you're still playing, good luck. I'm thinking about you and the girls. By the way, do you think you have an extra spot on your team? If so, and that's not being too forward, I would play for you every day of the week and ten times on Sunday.

I hope your correspondence continues with good news. (Sorry to deviate, but I felt it was appropriate)

Your girl (If you allow me on the team)
Cat
P.S. - I added a small surprise

I opened the box, and inside was a tiny silver bat. I reached into my pocket for my keys and slipped it on the key ring. Next to it was the medal she referred to. It was a round, silver medal with the words, "St. Jude Thaddeus - Pray for us," around it.

Somehow, I now have a feeling we will play well in the series.

She wrote there was a small surprise, so I looked into the box to make sure I hadn't missed it. I'm glad I did. At the bottom was a thumb drive, with a yellow note stuck to it. This must have been the surprise.

I pulled it out and read the note in the familiar purple ink, a smiley face at the end of her words.

I learned how to play these songs. I hope you like them.

The first thing I did was look for my laptop. When I found it under the box, I said a quick thank you to the convenience gods, then woke up the laptop and placed the thumb drive into the port.

Listed on the drive where the files: *September.mp4* and *Can'tHelp.mp4*.

I looked at the files, not sure why she would send me the songs. Doesn't she know I have these songs downloaded already?

Then it occurred to me the files were not of the songs by the artists. They were by Catherine. I hovered over the *Can't Help.mp4* icon, then double-clicked it.

Within seconds, the sounds of a viola came through the speakers, and as the notes floated into the air, my ears and heart gathered them in. I reached for her letter, and as the song continued, I traced my finger over her name, knowing she touched the exact spot.

When the song ended, the tingling around my head subsided.

In the silence, her name on the paper was all I heard. Then I clicked on the *September.mp4* file and swooned. I finally knew what Catherine sounded like, and although it was with her viola, and not her voice, it was the sweetest sound I've ever heard.

Yes, she's my girl. For as long as I can hold on to her, I guess.

It's late, so I had to get to bed. Tomorrow, we start the championship series in Atlanta. I don't know how I'm going to sleep tonight, but knowing I have Catherine in my corner, rooting us on from New York, it gives me an optimism I wouldn't have had otherwise.

twenty-three

I woke up this morning, stared at the ceiling for a few minutes, and collected my thoughts on what lay ahead this afternoon. A small sliver of golden light sliced across the wood beams, and as I stared, I wondered what awaited us once it grew, and morning turned to afternoon.

With perfect weather expected, today would be the last games of the season. A season none of us expected. It was Championship Thursday.

I walked out to the deck to greet the sunrise. The pale morning light gained in intensity through the crisp autumn air. As the sun rose over the mountains, it illuminated a blanket of fog ambling through the colorful trees. I looked up at the cotton candy sky and exhaled. This was the most at peace I would be today, so I savored it.

As the fear of the unknown rolled in with the fog, I needed a little help to fight it off.

I drove to the school chapel to make a few special intentions. When I arrived, it took me a little longer to find a parking spot, which was unusual for the school chapel on a weekday morning. Why was the chapel crowded? No matter, I had time.

I walked inside and looked for a place to sit. There weren't many. As I looked around, Father O'Scanlon walked over. "Good morning, Father. Kind of crowded today."

"Yes, it is, my son. After all, it's a big day."

Before I could ask him what that meant, Anna's parents walked out of the pew and passed me. "Good luck today, Coach."

I nodded and said thank you. A few minutes later, Josie's parents followed the same path. "See you on the field, Coach," they said, then walked out.

I shook my head, not sure what was going on. The church was never this crowded when I came here, nor did I ever see any of the parents here the morning before a game.

I slid into the last pew and was about to pray for the girls when Tara rose from the other end of the pew, looked at me, and nodded.

What was she doing here? Trying to piece together the puzzle, I scanned the church. There were more parents, as well as shopkeepers, and members of the police and fire department. To my surprise, even the ladies from the Jammin' With Jesus Club were there. The only reason I know is I saw their shirts with their club logo on the front of them. I recognized the staff from Juniors and also the woman who sells flowers on Main Street to the tourists on Blue Ridge Drive.

What in the world was going on?

On the other side of the aisle sat Scarlett, so I got up and joined her. "Scarlett? What are all these people doing here?"

"Coach, they all came to pray for the team."

I looked around the church. Everyone was praying. As each person finished, they walked past me. They either nodded, said good luck, or touched me on the shoulder. A warm tingle surged through me. I shook my head. "Wow."

"Can you keep it down, Coach?" Scarlett asked. "I just finished praying for you and the team, so you don't get your ass kicked today. Now I'm praying they have a two-for-one sale on Bushmills at the Blue Ridge Package Store. So, if you don't mind, that one is kinda important."

She winked, then went back to silent reflection.

After finishing at the church, I walked over to my office. As I sat down and woke up my laptop, a text notification flashed on my phone, so I reached for it. The text was from Tara. It read, "You should see this," and the next bubble popped up with a link to an article on *Georgia High School Softball.com* about Holy Trinity.

The website touted them as the greatest softball team in Georgia softball history. As I wrote earlier, the Trojans were not only the number one team in Georgia but also ranked number one by USA Today.

After I read the article, I smiled and shook my head. "As if I didn't need another reminder." As a coach, you respect that, since they have the numbers to back it up. Oh, and another little tidbit. They haven't lost a game in three years.

Their starting pitcher, Kellie Gordon, hasn't lost a game since her freshman year. She signed a letter of intent to play at Oklahoma, which is a softball dynasty.

Their closest margin of victory all season was in their semi-final victory against Cartersville. The Purple Hurricanes were in the game the whole way, and the final score of 12-6 was a little closer than it looked. Cartersville trailed 8-6 until the bottom of the sixth inning, when the Trojans scored four runs to put the game away.

Holy Trinity set the all-time Georgia record for run-rule

games, run differential, team batting average, earned run average, and has the most players signed to Division One schools. No wonder we all said extra prayers this morning.

I guess if we are going to be state champs, you have to beat the best team, so nobody will ever say, "Yeah, you won, but you didn't have to play Holy Trinity."

Our girls played hard all year, did what nobody thought they could do, and arrived on Championship Thursday, two wins away from making history. The series is in Atlanta, at Georgia Tech, so it will be nice to see some familiar faces. I know the stadium well from my years working there, so that's another plus.

The director of field operations texted me and said they are giving us the Georgia Tech locker room. Although we are the visiting team since Holy Trinity is the higher seed, I appreciated the gift. I figure since I sent a few players to Tech from Atlanta Catholic, and I am an alumnus, they were gracious enough to throw me a bone.

Oh well, I guess it's time to get started with classes. Then the bus to Atlanta. I hope the day doesn't drag on, but as you know, when you look forward to an opportunity, it feels like it will never arrive.

✒

As I sit in the coach's office inside the Georgia Tech locker room, I have a little time to reflect before the game. I thought about the year we had. I also thought about the girls who busted their ass for me, their school, and each other. What would the day bring?

Then I thought about Catherine. I wished she was sitting close to the dugout so I could look at her for strength. All I could do was hold on to the St. Jude medal she sent me, rub the silver bat, and touch the top of my ball cap so her words would bleed into my fingers. Her spirit would have to do the job.

What was I going to come up with this time to motivate the team? I pulled a Houdini every time I've needed to this season, so what could I come up with next? How much magic did I have left? I figured I'd forget the magic and instead, give them a speech from the heart. That's all I could do.

When I walked into the locker room, the girls were quiet, but not like the first game of the playoffs against Chatsworth. I didn't sense the fear or anxiety. It was more of a quiet, confident focus.

I found a chair in the corner of the room and sat, saying nothing. I whistled a little, looking at the ceiling. The players looked over at me, some whispering between themselves, others staring. Finally, I spoke. "I have a question."

I continued looking at the ceiling. "Who beat Chatsworth in the first round of the playoffs?"

The players looked around. Finally, Susie spoke up. "Um. That Blue Ridge Prep school?" She asked with a mock perplexed look.

I continued looking at the ceiling. "Yeah. I read that somewhere."

I whistled a little more, then asked, "What team walked on the field and beat the hell out of that overrated bunch from Jefferson County?"

Anna balanced herself on crutches and smiled. "That was the Blue Ridge Prep Lady Lions."

"That's right. And refresh my memory. Who faced that unbeatable powerhouse from across town, smacked them in the nose, and sent them home for the season?"

Josie smiled. "It was those Lions from Blue Ridge Prep."

"Right again. Can you believe we've won twenty-six games

this year?"

Josie looked around the room, then at me. "Coach? We've won twenty-four games this year."

I raised my eyebrows. "Not after today."

The girls laughed. I paused, then looked down at the floor, collecting my thoughts. Finally, I looked at them. "You know, ladies, no matter what happens today, you are all going to do great things with your lives. You're going to be leaders. Some will travel the world and see things you'll marvel at for the rest of your life. I guarantee everyone in this room will think back to this moment as the time it all began for you."

Every girl nodded.

"After the last out, win or lose, your families will be waiting for you after the game. And they will tell you how much they love you. And for what it's worth, I love you. You've reminded me why I began coaching."

You could hear a pin drop. "And no matter what, I'll never forget this time together. It's been very special for me."

My words echoed off the walls. The silence was deafening. "You know, this is usually the time in those sappy movies when the coach stands up and gives the old David and Goliath speech."

I shook my head and smiled. "I won't recite that speech. Not today. You know why? That speech is for the underdog." I looked around at the faces all looking at me. "You aren't the underdogs."

My voice raised a little after each pause. "You will not, I repeat, will not, roll over for Holy Trinity."

When a few nodded, and others agreed, a small murmur of confidence floated into the room. I told them, "Fear doesn't exist. It's only something the unprepared create, so they have an excuse for why they lost. Once we know it isn't real, there's nothing to be afraid of. Have fun and enjoy the moment because things like this happen once in a lifetime."

I looked at the girls and asked, "Does anyone have anything they want to say before we go out to the field?"

Josie looked around, then stood. "I wanted to let you know my father texted me a link to an article he saw this morning from *Georgia High School Softball.com*. He said I should share it with the team."

Oh boy. That was the article Tara sent me. I debated if I should share it with them, since I didn't want them to be intimidated. Maybe the team would respond better if it came from their captain?

The team gave her their attention. She pulled out her phone and looked at it. "According to *Georgia High School Softball.com*, and I quote, 'Holy Trinity is the greatest softball team in the history of Georgia. And right now, the nation. They will be state and national champions by thrashing Blue Ridge Prep.'"

Josie squinted her eyes as she looked at the team. "Here's the best part," she told them, then returned to her phone. "Who is Blue Ridge Prep, anyway? Is that the school so far up in the hills its founder is Jed Clampett? Is their mascot the Hillbillies? Come Halloween night, the only trick will be if the Trojans win both games by less than twenty runs. The treat will be everyone watching this powerhouse flatten Blue Ridge Prep and become national champions. Here's a thought. After Holy Trinity finishes dragging the field with the Hillbillies, the Blue Ridge people can load up the truck and move to Beverly Hills."

She lowered her phone, then turned and placed it in her chair. Her voice was in a controlled rage. "You know what my dad says? The sun don't shine on the same dog's ass every afternoon. Make every player from Holy Trinity remember you," she snarled.

Josie paused, then shouted, "Make them remember you for the rest of their lives." She looked around the room, and in a calm voice said, "I love everyone here. Thank you for being my teammate."

I nodded, then rose from the chair. "Bring it in."

I stood in the middle of the room, the players surrounding me, their arms locked around each other. I bowed my head and began. "Lord, thank you for this opportunity. We also thank you for the ability to do the things we do on the field, and for the love we have for each other. I'd never ask for anything in a pregame prayer. Today, I'd like to change that." I paused, then looked at each girl, then bowed my head again. "Lord, these are good girls. And they work hard. Please be with them today. Amen."

I looked up, blinked back a stray tear, then put my hand in the middle and everyone brought theirs on top of mine. I looked them in the eyes, holding my stare on each player for a second before moving to the next girl. "Don't forget who you are. And where you've come from."

I paused and saw some girls nod. Others grinned.

"You have a whole town behind you. They filled up the school chapel this morning to pray for you. You are heroes to the little girls growing up who watched what you've done this season. They want to be you one day. You're everyone's hope. And no matter what happens outside that door, you'll always be the champions of my heart. Now, go out there and show the world how great you are."

Josie looked at me, and when I nodded, she yelled, "Who are we?"

"Lions," they all shouted.

"And what do lions have?"

"Courage. Pride," they shouted again.

Josie looked at her teammates, then said, "One, two, three."

The Redhead and the Fountain Pen

Everyone shouted, "Lions."

I watched them storm out of the locker room. I waited until the last player left the room so I could wipe my eyes.

Then bowed my head again. "Lord, these are good girls. And they work hard. Please be with them today. Amen."

I looked up, blinked back a stray tear, then put my hand in the middle and everyone brought theirs on top of mine. I looked them in the eyes, holding my stare on each player for a second before moving to the next girl. "Don't forget who you are. And where you've come from."

I paused and saw some girls nod. Others grinned.

"You have a whole town behind you. They filled up the school chapel this morning to pray for you. You are heroes to the little girls growing up who watched what you did this season and want to be you one day. You're everyone's hope. And no matter what happens outside that door, you'll always be champions to me. Forever. Now, go out there and show the world how great you are."

Josie looked at me, and when I nodded, she yelled, "Who are we?"

"Lions," they all shouted.

"And what do lions have?"

"Courage. Pride," they shouted again.

Josie looked at her teammates, then said, "One, two, three." Everyone shouted, "Lions."

I watched them storm out of the locker room. I waited until the last player left the room so I could wipe my eyes.

twenty-four

Hello Cat!

How is New York? Things in Georgia are going well. How well? Well, last time I checked, someone handed our team the STATE CHAMPIONSHIP TROPHY!

Believe it or not, and I am still trying to believe it, we swept the mighty Trojans of Holy Trinity! The girls played out of their minds, but what I liked most was from the moment we stepped onto the field, the Lady Lions knew they were the better team. They weren't intimidated, and when things got tight, they showed no fear.

We won the first game when Josie hit a seventh-inning grand slam to give us the lead, and then Susie got the last three outs for the 10-6 win. Holy Trinity never recovered. In the second game, they made four errors in the first three innings. We capitalized on each mistake and won, 9-1.

All the credit goes to the girls. They worked like champions, played like champions, and even after it was all over, they acted like champions.

I'm proud of them both on and off the field. I don't think I have ever felt that way about one of my teams before. Our state championship teams at Atlanta Catholic were special, but they were never the huge underdogs Blue Ridge Prep was all season. I'll always have a special place in my heart for them.

Thank you for your wonderful gift. I put the bat on my key chain and *rubbed it for luck before both games. I also kept the St. Jude medal in my pocket, and when things got tight, I held on to it. Are we on to something with these little trinkets? I hope my words will bring you as much luck as the trinkets you sent me.*

Now that the playoffs are over, I can focus a hundred percent on you. If the Blue Ridge Prep Lady Lions can achieve their dreams, you shouldn't have any problems with yours.

How are you feeling? And how are your practices going? Are you breathing and taking breaks when you need to?

It's all there for you now, my friend. I'll be with you every step of the way. Expect a few letters to arrive in your mailbox in the coming days.

We will continue our correspondence later!

Roy

The next morning, I began the first of many letters to keep Catherine's confidence up.

Dear Cat:

I'm impressed with your work ethic and your drive to get better. We either get better or worse every day, and it is up to us to determine which one. With all the work you put in, you are getting better every day. Think about where you were last year and look at yourself now.

The hard work begins when nobody is watching. And if you put in the work then, I guarantee you'll succeed when everyone's watching.

Now, get to work, my Catarina.

Roy

The next day:

Good morning, Cat!

Rise and shine!

The harder the fight, the greater the glory.

Faith don't make it easy. Faith makes it possible.

I am not phenomenally skilled, but I am phenomenally willed. I will not give up.

You are a powerful woman, Catherine. Never forget that.

And one more thing. A good friend of mine once told me, "You didn't come this far to come this far."

Roy

And the day after that:

Hello Cat:

I couldn't sleep, so I woke up early to begin our morning together. Yeah, we are in this together. A team. And since you are the one who is going to be on the stage, all I can do is watch from the sidelines and coach you up.

People see winners on the stage, the field, or the trophy stand holding up the symbol of their victory. But what people don't see are all the long hours in the training rooms, the practice fields, or in an apartment on Broadway. When they see you holding the trophy, they think winning is easy. You know it's not. The hard part comes when nobody's watching. That allows you to make it look easy.

The only place where success comes before work is in the dictionary.

All the hard work, all the hours of blood, sweat, and tears are all worth it. This is your time, Cat. Keep it up. You got this girl!

Roy

I sat down to begin my daily letter to Catherine when I heard the mail truck pull up, then zoom off. Maybe?

Yep! Waiting inside my mailbox was a gift. And in my

romantic haze, the mailbox glowed and when I opened it, angels sang. None of that happened, but it sounded good, so forgive me for being a sap...muhaha

Here is what I had the pleasure of reading:

Dear Roy:

My deepest congratulations for pulling off something I know you believed would happen from the first day! Once your players believed it, there was nothing that could stop you. I'm in awe of how you turned things around and glad you shared this with me.

I'm sure you'll lead me to my championship. I know we'll get there together because your wonderful letters give me hope. Your words inspire me, and now, I believe I can do anything.

The other day, I sat under the Maine Monument in Central Park and thought about the future. Usually, those thoughts made me shake with fear and doubt my ability to succeed. I also thought about the last audition and how the ex abandoned me and made fun of something close to my heart. Very different is the mood today. I laughed at how silly all that was. Now, there is no fear.

Thanks, Roy. I won't let you down.

We will continue this correspondence later.

Your girl -

Cat

Here is today's letter to Catherine:

Hello Cat!

Sorry I slept in today, but I figured we both needed a little extra rest since things are going to heat up soon.

How is practice going? Any worries? There's nothing to worry about. The only people who should be worried are the people who are going to be

auditioning with you. I tell my girls all the time, you should never fear an opponent or a challenge. Make them fear you.

The other thing is to have fun and enjoy the moment. Where else would you rather be at 4:00 pm on November 13th? Sometimes we get so wrapped up in what could go wrong that we forget why we're there, and who we are. If you stop, take a deep breath, and move forward, things fall into place and things go the way you want them to go.

Okay, recap -
Be fearless.
Have fun.
Enjoy the moment.
We'll continue this correspondence later.
Roy

This morning, I thought about what I was going to do for Cat, since Monday is her big day. After thinking about it, flowers and a gift will work.

I bought her a tiny, silver viola charm (not a violin, as I told the woman behind the counter since I know the difference). I hope she has a bracelet she can put it on. If not, I am sure she can have it with her for luck during the audition.

Here is the letter I wrote. It was brief since I know she has other things on her mind at the moment.

Dear Cat:

By the time you read this, it will be the 13th and your day on the big stage.

I won't bore you with any extra motivation since I've sent you a notebook full. All that's left now is to write that I believe in you, and you are going to make it. Now, go do what destiny has called you to do.

The Redhead and the Fountain Pen

It is a thing of beauty reading about you being the woman you've always wanted to be. I know I can't be there in body, but I'll be there every second in spirit, cheering you on. This is your day. Enjoy the moment. You got this!

Love -

Roy

PS - Sorry about the love thing. It's meant in friendship and to give you confidence. I love your passion, persistence, and courage. I love seeing you fight for something you love. How could anyone not love seeing the woman you are, and the fight you carry on every day as you chase down your dream?

I also sent Catherine a bouquet of roses with a good luck message, to be delivered tomorrow morning. Then I sent her the letter, and a tiny viola via my buddies at FedEx, so I hope it gets to her before the audition.

As I looked at the items heading to New York, I thought about what will happen after the audition. One way or the other, I know I am going to lose her, but it doesn't matter. I'm a sucker for a good, old-fashioned miracle.

twenty-five

It's audition day.

I woke up this morning to the clouds rolling in over the mountains. Their colors were a Crayola box full of awe as I stared at them floating before me in the damp sunrise. I had to dive right into them, so I put on a sweatshirt and tennis shoes so I could run around the trails.

I hope I'll hear something today, but I know that might be a little optimistic.

I stayed late at Blue Ridge Prep to help clean out the locker room and talk to some of the players before we officially put a cap on our miracle season. Because of that, I got back late, but it didn't keep me from wondering what happened at Geffen Hall, and when I'd hear something. It's all I thought about today, and even more on the drive home tonight.

Lo and behold, when I walked up the steps to my cabin, there was a FedEx envelope resting on my door.

I was hopeful but worried as I stared at the large envelope for a while, then finally I summoned the courage to open it. I guess I'll know in a few seconds where Catherine will be.

The Redhead and the Fountain Pen

I ripped open the envelope and pulled out the paper.

Hello Roy:

The audition went well, and they asked me to report to Geffen Hall on Friday for the semi-finals!

Believe it or not, when I began playing, there was no fear. As was the case before, there was a screen separating the judges from the candidates, so that relaxed me. They do that so the judges score the applicants on their performance, not their appearance.

I closed my eyes, took a deep breath, and when I began, it was as if I was practicing at home. It was a complete feeling of peace.

I was calm, and it was as if everything moved in slow motion. I took your advice and focused on breathing. After that, I fell into a zone. It was like I was the only one in the Hall. I focused on my fingers, then the strings and the bow moved back and forth, and the music came out without me thinking about it. Roy, you nailed it for me!

I loved the flowers and the charm! I rubbed the charm for luck, and it must have worked. Thanks to you, after all these years, I know what that feels like to have someone believe in me. I will never forget your kindness.

It's on to the semi-finals. They will be tomorrow at 4:00 pm. Say a prayer for me, okay?

As much as I would like to keep writing, I am back practicing. Being so close to my dream, I'm not going to relax now, right? Back to the viola!

Thanks again, Roy!

Love -

Cat

PS - I figure, if you can write it, I can too. I love our friendship and everything you do for me!

Since Catherine is performing today, I walked over to the school chapel to light a candle and say a few prayers. Every bit helps, right?

My watch tells me it's a little after 3:00. The audition is at 4:00, so I imagine her walking over to Geffen Hall on a breezy New York afternoon. I see her along Broadway, long coat and hat, leather-gloved hand holding to the handle of her viola case, walking to her date with destiny. As I imagine what her face looks like, I see a smile. Wait...a confident smile. She walks with all the confidence in the world. No matter if I am not there. I see it all unfolding.

As promised, I sent her two dozen roses. I sent it as a morning delivery, so I hope it got there before she had to leave. In the message, I had them write, "As beautiful as these roses are, they cannot compare with the beauty of your music. Show the world how beautiful you are."

We'll see how this afternoon goes. All I can do now is wait for tomorrow, and hope it's good news. Why didn't we do social media?

Today is a new day. I'm cleaning up around the cabin, which is something I do to take my mind off what is going on. Call it a stress reliever.

What happened in New York yesterday? How did Catherine do, and what did the judges think? What did she look like when she began, then finished?

I guess she'll let me know. How long will it take? Like I wrote yesterday, this is the only time when I wish I was doing social media since I'd appreciate knowing something now. Although, I wouldn't trade Catherine's handwritten letters for all the websites in the world.

I'm going to -

Sorry, there was a representative from FedEx at the door with an envelope with my name on it. After thanking the driver, I walked into the living room and sat on the couch. I stared at the envelope for a few minutes, and once again summoned the courage to open it.

Once I ripped it open, I shut my eyes, then opened them and found the purple ink.

Hey, Roy!

Guess who is going on to the finals of the New York Philharmonic auditions for a viola player? I'll give you a hint. The girl who is wearing this...

There was another piece of paper in the envelope. When I pulled it out, it was a printed picture of a woman's freckled wrist, wearing a bracelet with several charms on it. There was a familiar silver viola in the middle of them all. Wow, I finally saw her. Well, part of her anyway. There is an actual person who is writing these letters!

Let's continue reading...

I walked back to my apartment and had a feeling I had done as well as I could. Even though it didn't assure me of a spot in the finals, I was at peace. I stopped by my favorite coffeehouse and had hot chocolate with whipped cream, then took a seat and looked out at Broadway. The traffic going by. The people walked to wherever they were heading on this cold Friday evening.

All I could think about was being one step closer to something I've wanted for a lifetime. If luck is on my side, by this time tomorrow, I'll walk along the street, knowing I am doing something that will last forever. In this world, how many people can say that? How many people make their living doing something they love?

They told us they'd make a decision by eight o'clock tonight, so I took my time walking home. By the time I got there, it was after six, but I immediately went to my email to see if there were any messages.

I didn't think there would be anything there, but sure enough, waiting for me was an email from the personnel director. My heart leaped into my throat, seeing the email looking back at me. But as you wrote, they need to fear me, not the other way around. I clicked on the email and began reading. The first word I saw, in all caps, was CONGRATULATIONS, so I knew it was good news. The director congratulated me on my performance and looked forward to seeing me in the finals.

There are two openings. I don't know how many semi-finalists they call back, but the word is they cut the field down to double how many seats they need to fill. By this time tomorrow, my life will change. One way or the other.

Even though I'm in the finals, that doesn't mean I have the job yet. I am going to spend tonight practicing the music they want us to perform.

One thing I wanted to share was, as I was walking out, I stopped in the lobby and saw the rows of framed pictures of each performer. I stood there, gazing at everyone. I wondered if my picture would be there after tomorrow. How I hoped it would. More than anyone could ever know.

Thank you again, Roy, for everything. You'll be the first to know. Well, the second to know after me. Wait...Make that third. The judges will know. Then me. Then you. Depending on how many judges you may be the sixth or seventh to know. Oh, what the hell. You know where I'm going with this.

You told me your girls were the underdogs of the year, but they somehow made it through to become what they always wanted to be. Will your other girl be what she has always wanted to be?

I guess it's all up to me now. Say two prayers for me, will ya? We will continue this correspondence later. Pray it's good news!

Love -

Cat

As soon as I finished her letter, I drove to Blue Ridge Prep to light a candle. Then I sat in the chapel, meditating, trying to send positive vibes Catherine's way.

Remember when I wrote about Rhett Butler saying how he always had a weakness for lost causes once they're really lost? The thought of Catherine, fighting back after where she came from, a lost cause, is now on the precipice of everything she's always wanted to be. This is something she's worked hard for and put everything she is into. How can you not root for someone after seeing that? I hope God is with her.

I sat alone, staring into the silence. Eventually, I said a last prayer, then walked out.

It was a breezy evening in the mountains. I looked up to find a slice of baby blue sky looking back at me. The evening clouds would blanket the azure in a matter of seconds, but before it fell into the mountains, something told me my girl was going to be fine.

I woke up early today, and since it's Sunday, I am not sure if I will hear from Catherine. If it was bad news, she might wait to let me know. And if it's good news, thank God FedEx delivers on Sunday. Should I stick around the house, you know, in case?

I walked out to the deck, enjoying the morning breeze as the sun rose from the mountains. The smell of autumn rolled by as the smell of a distant fireplace, coupled with the crisp mountain air, brought peace. As the light cast itself onto the trees, bringing their color to life, I can't remember being this calm.

There's something about the sunrise and the way the soft light promises hope to all who believe. The slate is clean. A new day to right a wrong. To achieve the things we never thought possible. Save a soul. Tell someone you love them. All in the promise, riding in the majestic glow of the early morning light. Sometimes we overlook the simplistic beauty that arrives to begin our day.

    But not this day. At least in my eyes, I would remember how I felt this morning. And that's something I would carry forever.

✒

As of four this afternoon, nothing. I guess I need to stop worrying about things I can't control. In case things don't work out, I need to figure out how I'm going to keep her spirits up. Sometimes, when you're told no over and over, you build up resentment, and being positive is the toughest thing to do.

✒

It's after nine now, and still no word. I have to be at work early tomorrow for meetings, so I am going to go to bed. What will tomorrow bring?

✒

I woke up this morning and rushed downstairs, hoping something was lying at my door. When I looked through the glass to the porch, all that looked back at me was the wooden deck, with a few stray leaves resting on it. At least it confirmed my suspicions there was no word. Why didn't I break the rules and ask to do a Zoom?

✒

When I got home after work, there was still no word. Damn, I hate waiting. I'll go to church tonight and keep putting in a good word for Cat. I guess that's all I can do now.

It's eight o'clock and I haven't heard anything from New York. Either there is a FedEx strike I don't know about, the mail truck has a flat tire or the news isn't good.

✒

Well, it's been a few days. As the new week rolled on, I thought there would be a powder blue envelope in my mailbox, or a delivery from

The Redhead and the Fountain Pen

FedEx. But each day I walked away empty-handed.

As I drove home after a day at Blue Ridge Prep, I wondered if the mailman would deliver me from the abyss of my misery.

I stopped my car at the front of the driveway and peered at the black mailbox, now dotted with drops from the light rain that began earlier in the afternoon.

I pulled the lid down and found a stack of envelopes inside. Wanting to break my bad luck streak, I reached into the box, grasped the envelopes, but didn't look at them until I got inside the cabin. Why not try something different?

I walked inside, dropped my keys on the table, and sat on the couch. I looked out at the foggy twilight, knowing darkness was coming soon. It was time to look in my hand to see if my darkness would continue.

As I thumbed through the stack, a glow of blue lay between two long, white rectangular envelopes.

twenty-six

I stared at the envelope, wondering what the words inside would tell me. As I looked at Catherine's handwriting, the icy sting of adrenaline flowed through my veins, and I felt the dull pounding of my heart. I understood that in a few minutes, life would never be the same, whatever the letter contained. Even a brown water drink couldn't help me now.

I sat in my chair, staring straight ahead. The envelope stared back at me, neither of us blinking. I thought about the calm of autumn, and how Catherine's letters brought so much joy. But now, in the depth of winter, all I could do was hope the words in this letter would push the sun back into the sky and it would be October for one more day. There was only one way to find out.

I slid my finger under the flap, pried it open, then pulled out the folded paper. I closed my eyes, exhaled, then opened them and began reading.

Dear Mark:

It's with a heavy heart and terrible guilt I write to you today. I didn't win my audition. There are no excuses. I wasn't good enough and I have to live with that.

The Redhead and the Fountain Pen

There is nothing left for me in New York, so I am accepting the offer from my friend at the Iceland Symphony. I'm moving to Reykjavik in a few days to begin a new life.

You have my everlasting appreciation for your words and constant encouragement. You brought me through a difficult time in my life. I am sorry I failed you. I am also sorry we never got to meet.

I remember the last audition and what happened, so I won't put myself through that again. I'm sure you're a good person, and you wouldn't abandon me. But I refuse to have you see me as a failure. Or, even worse, your failure.

Mark, as much as this saddens me, I have to be honest. This will be my last letter. We both have lives to lead, and mine is across the ocean, and yours is in Georgia. You have a softball team that needs you. And their need is greater than mine. They won their championship. I didn't. Don't waste your time with me.

Strong women summon the courage to rebuild so that one day they can become great again. You'll never have to worry about me. I am strong and will survive. I've done it before, and there's no reason I can't do it again.

I'll never forget you, Mark. May God bless you for the rest of your days.
Love -
Catherine

Wow. I never expected those words. I don't...I'm going to need a minute...

The numbness I left back in Atlanta found me and was going to be my roommate for a while. Oh, and another one of my roommates joined me too. "How are you faring, old sport?"

"Not too well, Scott. Catherine's gone."

"I know. And I'm sorry." He took a sip from his flask. "No brown water tonight?"

"Aw, I gave the booze train the night off since I am going to be hungover tomorrow and I didn't want to add to it."

His mischievous schoolboy grin didn't come with him on this trip. "I hate to see you like this."

"That's what the world does to a guy." I shook my head, looking into the night, searching for answers. No matter how long I gazed into the darkness, none were there.

Scott stared into the abyss with me. I heard his voice in the darkness. "The loneliest moment in someone's life is when they are watching their entire world fall apart, and all they can do is stare."

His words sunk into me. "You're right, Scott. Damn, you've always been right. You told me to be careful. I guess I got what I deserve. How many times do I need to go down this road before I stop being so stupid?"

"What does that mean?"

I shook my head. "It means I have to stop giving my heart away to things I have no control over. It keeps getting broken and I'm too stupid to know when to quit." Scott nodded, then replied, "The ball is in your court now." "There are no more words. No more letters. The game is over. We both lost. She lost out on her dream. I lost out on my dream girl." "The game is never over for those who have hope. Gatsby carried it until his last breath. He believed in the green light. You should do the same old sport." "What's so important about the green light?"

Again, I was talking to myself.

Since there would be no more letters, I searched for one last moment of beauty before I said goodbye to Catherine forever.

I walked to the closet and pulled down the box from the top shelf. Inside was everything she had ever written or sent me. The book lay inside too. After giving it a look, or rather a stare, I removed the silver bat from my key chain. After finding my ball cap in my bedroom, the one with the good luck card tucked inside the band, I removed it and placed it in the box.

I pulled the St. Jude medal from my pocket, which I carried with me every day since she sent it, rubbed it, then dropped it inside with the rest of the items. "Well, St. Jude, you have two lost causes for the price of one. If anything, you're economical."

I gave my desk a last scan to make sure I had everything. From the corner, next to the Rae Dunn pen holder, was a thumb drive. I looked at it for a few seconds, allowing the acid pain of the past to overcome me. I stared at it for as long as I could, then looked away. With the icy blade slicing me apart, I summoned the remaining courage I had to move forward. "One last time."

I plugged the thumb drive into my laptop and was ready to press play. But then, something strange hung in the air. I heard the sounds of a viola, playing "I Can't Help Falling In Love With You." The sound in my ears soaked into my brain with such a powerful passion that I withdrew my hand from the laptop.

Catherine's music played for me, so clear and deep, I thought she was standing inches away. With every note, the damnable misery of it all overtook me. As the sound of the strings played out, my heart ached, and I had to catch my breath.

I thought I was prepared for our last dance but wasn't. I closed my eyes and saw my redheaded girl playing the viola. Her hair swaying with the music, eyes focused, every note perfect. As the music played, I reached inside and pulled out one of Catherine's letters. I unfolded it and, as I had before, traced my finger over her name. When the last note played, the only sound in the room was the tears rolling down my cheeks.

I looked into the box at all the powder blue looking back at me, pleading for me not to toss them away. I'll have to think about that.

I removed the thumb drive and made sure it was the last thing I tossed into the box. After placing the lid over it, not wanting Pandora to escape, I walked to the trash can. When I got to it, I opened it and was about to drop the box inside.

I stood over the can, looking inside, telling my hands to drop what was in them so I could close the lid and begin again. The longer I looked, the harder I couldn't let go. Finally, I gave up and closed the lid, then walked the box back to the shelf in the closet.

Maybe one day I would it let go. But it's not going to be tonight. For now, all I have the strength to do is say two words.

Goodbye, Catherine.

twenty-seven

I come to you from my deck overlooking the snowy Blue Ridge Mountains. Although it's been a few weeks since we last connected, I'm back on the road to recovery.

  I have a brown water drink in my hand, my body wrapped in a thick blanket, and I'm staring into the flickering flames of the deck fireplace. The fire sends a wall of warmth at me, so I'm not completely frozen. But I'm too numb to feel it.

  As I looked out to the night, the bare trees stripped of their colorful leaves now held clumps of white in the branches. This was Winter's death sentence.

  Only yesterday I looked at the same scene. The brilliant green leaves fluttered with life in the beauty of summer. Then in autumn, the leaves turned so many colors there was no way there were names for every one of them glowing in the sunshine.

  I thought about where I'd come from. There wasn't a day I didn't look into the beauty of the world and think how wonderful life was, and everything made perfect sense. There was an optimism floating with every sunrise. As the days passed, I was awash in anticipation. Would there be a powder blue envelope in my mailbox?

  I remembered a walk to see Scarlett one afternoon. For

whatever reason, I stopped and looked into the sky. Above was a mass of vibrant leaves as they fluttered from their branches. The glow of the cool autumn sky illuminated them in butterscotch, brown sugar, and cinnamon as they swirled in the air for the last time. They broke free from yesterday, sacrificing themselves for today to give us one last moment of enchantment. Once their time in the sun was over, they would live on only in memory.

I watched their beauty, lying in the damp street. As I looked down at their last moments on Earth, I'm convinced they deserved better. It was then I understood life moves on, and it takes everything with it. No matter how beautiful they were, or how they made me feel.

As much as I tried to relive the past, it wasn't coming back. In all the years I played and coached sports, when an umpire makes a decision, all the arguing in the world would not change the call.

Once I accepted that, the warmth of the memory gave way to an icy breeze through my hair. My hands ached as I held the frozen glass and when I looked up, the deck faded back to winter.

The only things left from the shattered remains of what was a beautiful time in my life were the memories of finding an old book. And the haunting sounds of a viola. The viola was the toughest of the two to get out of my head.

In the middle of my misery, I heard the doorbell. When I opened the door, Scarlett's face smiled back at me. "Hiya, Chuckles," she said, then brushed past me and walked inside. "I stopped by since I was out of whiskey. You wouldn't mind helping an old Irish broad out, would ya?"

I stood in the doorway and closed the door. "I don't think I have a choice."

I walked over to the bar and grabbed a glass. After filling

hers and refilling mine, I stood in front of her and handed her the glass. "What are you doing here?"

Her bright eyes and wicked smile smacked me in the face as she took the glass, then took a sip. "I haven't seen that crooked smile in a while, so I came over to check on you. Penny for your thoughts?"

I looked up. "I'm afraid they aren't even worth that."

Scarlett looked around, then walked to the couch and sat. She took a sip of her brown water, then sat back and cooed, "Damn, that's good. Is there anything the Irish can't do?"

When I continued looking down, her eyebrows rose. "So much for small talk. Let's get down to business. I have a feeling your lack of appearances has something to do with someone in New York. Call me a liar."

I couldn't meet her eyes. "You're not. Catherine left for Iceland."

Scarlett's smile vanished. "I'm sorry, Coach." We stared at each other, not sure what to say next. Scarlett broke the silence. "My face might look old. But yours looks like death."

I nodded. "Thanks. I had it redone in postmortem depression earlier this week. You wouldn't believe how difficult it was getting an appointment."

A memory of one of Catherine's letters flashed through my brain, causing a thick wave of guilt and disappointment to wash over me. I shook my head to wipe the drops of depression off my face. "Damn, I was so sure she was going to make it. I should have done more to help that girl."

"That girl faced impossible odds. You gave her the courage and optimism she never would have had if you never met."

"I guess so. But there was something else. Something I never told anyone."

"What?" Scarlett asked.

"I knew there was no chance of happiness. One way or the other, I was going to lose her. Iceland or New York. But-" I stopped, not sure about continuing.

"Aw, you can't leave me hanging now."

I took a deep breath and after exhaling, didn't care what consequences my words carried. "I held out hope that something magical would happen. Catherine would win her audition and ask me to see her first performance with the Philharmonic. Then this time, we'd fall in love in person, and figure out a way to be together."

"You believed that, didn't you?"

I looked at Scarlett and nodded. "I would have given up everything to be with her."

"You're like the lad in that book I always see you reading. You held out hope for a miracle, didn't you?"

My eyes scanned the floor, then I looked at her. "I've been told I'm a lot like Gatsby. He reached for something he'd never grasp. Damn if I didn't do the same thing. Both of us knew it wasn't meant to be, but we went anyway." I paused and then said, "That damn book. Art imitates life, huh?"

"You fought with everything you had. There was nothing else you could have done."

The words failed to make a dent in the steel wall constructed to keep out any chance of forgiveness. "We faced impossible odds to win the state championship, but we overcame them and did it. Why couldn't I have coached her to beat the odds for her championship?" I rose and walked to the window and looked into the deepening darkness. "I had some days off during the tournament. I should've figured out a way to get up there. Instead of being timid, I should have found the courage to find her."

Scarlett allowed me to continue.

"I'm such a hypocrite."

"What on Earth are you talking about?" She asked as she sat her glass on the table and walked over to me.

"Every day I preached to my girls about savoring the moment. Having courage. Standing strong in the face of fear. I wrote the same things to Catherine. And then I sat on my ass and didn't do a damn thing about it. She needed me in New York."

"We needed you here."

Scarlett's eyes bore a hole through me. When I couldn't stand the searing pain any longer, I looked away. "I could have coached her better."

"Mark, sometimes fate insists on breaking our hearts. No matter how hard you prepare, pray, light candles, or work yourself into exhaustion, there are some things we can't change."

"You believe that?"

She nodded. "I do. And always will."

"I don't. No matter how long the odds are, I'll beat them. Damn it. Why couldn't I find a way for Catherine?"

"You've played sports all your life. Once you step on the field, you play the game, and afterward, win or lose, you accept the result and move on."

"Catherine didn't win. And now she's gone. Forever. How can I move on?"

"You convinced that girl she could do it. She stepped up to the plate and took her swings. In this lifetime, she'll never have to worry about what if. Because of that, she'll remember this forever. And one day, she'll hit another wall like we all do, but because of the things you instilled in her, she will overcome it. Somehow, you'll know about it and you'll be proud of her. That's how you move on."

"What will she remember? The guy who abandoned her in Brooklyn, or the guy who screwed her over in Blue Ridge? She moved to Iceland to get away from all the assholes in the States. No wonder why men get such a bad rap. We deserve it."

"You didn't screw her over. You two were the only people who believed it could happen."

"But it didn't happen. Catherine needed a real coach. Not someone who thinks he is."

"Don't use this as an excuse to let that girl walk out of your life for good."

I threw up my hands. "It's over."

Scarlett stared at me for a few seconds. "I'm curious. Why did you come to Blue Ridge?"

"You know why I came here. What kind of question is that?"

"I know why you're here. But there was always something about this deal I couldn't put my finger on."

"Well, this should be interesting."

She paused as she walked closer. "With your resume, you had your choice of jobs anywhere in the state. Or anywhere in the country. But you chose Blue Ridge. You knew what you were getting into, and could have told Tara no. But you saw the team was in trouble. You came to their rescue. Your heart is as big as anything I've ever seen. With all that you had to do here, you still made time for that girl in New York. She was in trouble and your instinct was to help her."

"And look where it got me. And got her. Next time I try to grow a brain, smack me and tell me to move along."

"What happened in New York is over. Today, you face a new opponent. Don't let what happened yesterday beat you again today."

"What on earth are you talking about?"

"Stop wasting everyone's time and go find her."

"What possible good could come from trying to find her?"

"That girl is in love with you."

"Well, that's breaking news. While you're at it, what's the point spread going to be for the Lions game against the Packers? Now that's useful information."

Scarlett's eyes turned red and shot an angry, white-hot laser through me. "Damn it, you're such a smart ass."

I was rolling. "Yeah, I've heard that before. It's something that draws people to me," I said with a laugh. I placed my glass on the table and applauded. "Yes, let's give Coach Mark Dawson a round of applause. We have some lovely parting gifts for him in the loser's locker room."

I looked at Scarlett's glass. "Want me to top that off?" But she put her hand over it and shook her head. "Fine. More for me," I told her with a smile bordering on mean. When I walked back to my spot, I turned and stared through the window.

"Mark?" When I ignored her, she raised her voice. "Damn it. Look at me when I'm talking to you."

I turned. Scarlett's eyes changed from anger to empathy. "You take losing hard, don't you?" After a few seconds without a reply, she said, "Let me rephrase that. You take it personally."

"With the people I care about." I shook my head, then returned to looking out of the window. "I'm sorry I wasted your time telling you about the letters."

Scarlett exhaled. "Aw, I've read too many letters in my life."

When I saw her face, her eyes changed once again. This time to hurt. "What do you mean?" I asked.

She stared at the table, then looked at me. "A long time ago, there was this girl who fell in love with a boy. They met at a spring dance at an apple orchard in Blue Ridge on a cloudless spring night. The boy walked over to the girl, handed her an apple, and said, 'You're the apple of my eye. Would you like to dance?' The girl lost her heart at that exact moment and never got it back."

She swirled the brown water around in the glass, but didn't take a sip. "That first night, in the middle of the apple trees under the string lights, they shared their first dance. They went skinny dipping in the summer and carved pumpkins in autumn. Then one day, his country asked him to leave. When he said goodbye, he made a promise he'd come home. Every day there was a letter in the mailbox. His letters told the girl how much he loved her, and the longing in his heart grew every day. He promised they would spend the rest of their lives together in peace."

Before my eyes, Scarlett was now a young woman. The wrinkles around her eyes receded and her cheeks were soft and rosy, with no visible lines of time. Her hair was now deep red, and it complimented a pair of green eyes, which sparkled at the memory of life all in front of her. The optimism of youth promised happiness for the rest of her days. She was full of life. My God, she was beautiful.

"Then one September day, the letters stopped. At that moment, staring into an empty mailbox, the girl knew there would be no more letters. Well, there was one more, from someone she didn't know telling her they were sorry for the loss of her husband. He would come back, but not in the way she hoped."

When her eyes returned from the past, she was back to being the older woman I knew.

"You were the girl, weren't you?"

She looked at me, then nodded. "I crumbled at the post of the mailbox, then stared into the mountains. Those same mountains where we walked together, holding hands, discussing the future. It's funny about the future. Sometimes it becomes nothing more than a broken promise. It wasn't his fault, and I never blamed him. But it still hurts."

"That's why I never saw your wedding ring."

She smiled, then reached inside her sweater and pulled out a gold chain with two rings dangling from it. "I'd rather keep him close to my heart." I saw the smile on her face, this one genuine, as she showed me the rings. "Didn't Daughtry tell us it was all worth it in the end?"

I thought about her words, then it hit me. My eyes widened. "Hey? You said you didn't know that song?"

She smirked. "I lied. My husband died in September, so that song means something to me. I didn't admit it, since a woman holds many secrets. Since I like you, I'll give you that one for free."

My crooked smile made its first appearance in days.

Scarlett's face brightened. "When you told me about the letters, you brought back memories I put away for years. The ones dear to me. Those letters brought me back. Like the softball team, you made a difference in my life. So, as the song tells us, it was all worth it in the end." She sniffled, then continued. "I saw you as my husband, Bob, and me as Catherine. I was twenty-four again, and life was in front of us. The hazy, black-and-white memory of those days was now alive and colorful. I relived the love I lost decades ago."

I allowed the magic to live on as I sat in silence, watching Scarlett come alive before my eyes. "That was a special time in my life. All those memories. The same thoughts and feelings as you have. The same story playing itself out for me to watch as a spectator to my past."

Scarlett pulled herself back to the present. "The memories are significant, but for me, the story ends when the memory does.

But for you, there's an opportunity to keep alive those moments before they become memories. Those are the ones dear to us. You have the opportunity I wished for ever since I opened my mailbox for the last time. If you don't move forward, you'll regret it for the rest of your life."

"She's gone, Scarlett. And she's not coming back."

"She might have written the last word, but you still can rewrite the ending. Don't do this for me. Do it for Catherine." She leaned forward and pleaded, "Damn it. Do it for yourself."

Her words failed to motivate me.

Scarlett saw my resignation as I looked out of the window. "One day, you'll go to your mailbox, and you'll hope for an envelope written by that girl. All the magic, wonder, and longing for her words will come alive within you. With every step to the mailbox, you'll convince yourself miracles exist, and one is waiting for you. You'll believe it all until you open the lid, and there is nothing inside except a hollow reality of what could have been."

She reached for my hand. "That was me years ago. Mark, I'm asking you. Damn it, I'm begging you. Don't let your life come to that." She paused, then added, "Or Catherine's."

"That's a cheap shot, Scarlett."

She smiled. "Yep, I meant it to be. But it's the truth. And nobody should fear the truth. Still, not a day goes by I don't think of Bob and I guarantee a day won't go by for the rest of your life you won't think of Catherine. You'll never have peace without knowing why she wrote that last letter. We can live with hurt. But never with regret."

"I'll have to take that chance."

She shook her head. "Fine. Nobody has a right to tell anyone how to live. But you made a promise."

"Promise? What promise?"

"You promised to return her book."

I thought for a moment. "Wait. You remembered that?"

"How could I forget? What you told me doesn't happen every day."

I thought about the night, then nodded. "Yeah. I guess I did."

"No matter how things ended, you need to keep your word. A real man never breaks his word, no matter the circumstances."

I looked at the floor, unable to answer.

Scarlett rose and touched me on the shoulder. "I'm here if you need me," she said, then placed her glass on the counter and walked out of the cabin.

A few days later, with thoughts of my promise swirling around my head, I summoned the courage to walk to the closet and pull Catherine's box from the shelf. It was time to move on.

This time, the sting of the ending wasn't there, and I was ready to toss the box into the garbage can.

I pulled the box from the shelf, and walked to the garbage can. As I adjusted the box in my hands, I felt the weight shift and then I remembered Catherine's book was inside.

No matter what happened between us, the book was a different matter. I know I told her I would return it one day, but I'm sure she doesn't want to see me, so maybe it's best I just hold on to it. But I can't throw it away.

I opened the lid, winced, and peered inside. Staring back at me was a blue book cover.

I reached inside and picked it up, then examined it from all sides. I even opened it to get that old bookstore smell one last time.

As I thumbed through the book, I noticed handwriting on

one of the blank pages.

>*My Dearest Catherine:*
>
>*The road has ended for us, but it's nobody's fault. Time marches on.*
>
>*I made a promise to your mother, and now I make it to you. I will live the best I can with what time is left.*
>
>*When a person grows old, you hope your spirit will live on in the people you love. Please accept this book because it means a lot to me, and I want you to have it. Whenever you look at it, you'll remember me.*
>
>*Fear not, my beautiful daughter, for death can never take away a man's spirit. It will live on forever within you.*
>
>*Love - Dad*

I was lost in a haze of pride fighting with guilt. I sat in the floor, the book in my hands, just staring at her father's words, knowing I wasn't entitled to witness his final message to her.

The ache of regret surged through me. I winced.

Finally, I closed the book, shook my head and exhaled.

I don't have a choice now.

twenty-eight

I'm sitting on an airplane headed for Reykjavik to fulfill a promise made months ago. Who would have thought when I walked into Blue Ridge Books, I'd end up thirty thousand feet in the air heading to Iceland in December?

As I wrote before, someone has to be pulling the cosmic strings for this to happen. But why? And why was I the one pulled across the Atlantic Ocean?

The string pullers had something different in mind than what I envisioned happening. I thought we'd meet, I'd give Catherine her book, and then we'd see where it went from there.

Today, I have no such plans. Once I give her the book, my duties are complete. Catherine will begin a new life in Iceland with her music. I will continue my life in Georgia with softball and spend my spare time wondering how things slipped away.

After landing, I walked into the terminal and scanned the surroundings. The people looked the same, although I didn't understand some of the conversations. In an attempt to impress Catherine, I learned a little Icelandic. But I was in way over my head here. Luckily, the signs were in both English and Icelandic, so getting around might not be as tough as I imagined.

My watch read 10:50 am, so I wondered why I saw the sunrise. It was a little unnerving since I felt as if I were in an alternative universe, then it hit me where I was.

The first order of business was to figure out how to get to Reykjavik. It was going to be the first of many hurdles I would have to overcome today. Oh, and throw in the fact I was looking for a girl who I have never met before. Yeah, this was going to be a piece of cake.

In the morning haze were massive piles of snow covering the ground, airport vehicles, and a ticket booth next to the parking deck. I hope whoever was taking tickets got out before the Abominable Snowman attacked. Thick plumes of steam floated into the air around the buildings, then disappeared into the grayish backdrop of the mountains in the distance.

Iceland was indeed ice land.

The lines to the rental car agencies were not encouraging. With all the snow outside, I had a feeling traveling might be difficult.

I walked to the end of the shortest of all the lines. A few minutes later, a representative greeted me in Icelandic. Fortunately, I knew what she said, so I replied, then asked if she understood English. She nodded. "Good morning. My name is Inga. May I assist you?"

"Yes. I need a car to get to Reykjavik."

"A storm came through last night. Since the roads are being plowed as we speak, there is a bit of a delay. Let me get your information, and when we get word the roads are clear, I will text you and then I can get you headed in that direction."

I gave her my information, and being a smartass, asked if she had a convertible. She laughed, so I told her to reserve it for me the next time I was in Reykjavik.

"I'll do that," she assured me with a grin. "By chance have you ever traveled by dogsled?"

Wanting to get in and out, I didn't care if she told me she'd let me borrow Wile E. Coyote's Acme Rocket Powered Roller Skates. "No, but I'll try anything at this point."

Inga gave me a suspicious smile. "So, who's the Frau waiting for you in Reykjavik?"

I shook my head. "Wait. How did you know?"

"I saw it in your face."

Good thing Catherine moved to Iceland instead of Vegas. I'd never make it at the World Series of Poker. I nodded. "There is a girl. But I'm not sure she wants to see me."

"Well, whatever happens, if you've come all the way from America, I'm sure she'll give you a few minutes to state your case."

"I hope you're right."

She smiled, then said, "Let me see what I can do to speed along the process. And I was serious about the dog sled. My cousin Olaf runs a dog sled company and can get anyone where they need to be, no matter how much snow there is. I'll text him and he'll have the sled here whenever you need it."

After an hour of nothing but sipping hot chocolate and looking at my phone, someone touched me on the shoulder. I turned to see Inga. "Mr. Dawson? Olaf is outside waiting if you want to go with the dogs."

I smiled, knowing I'd solved the first of many obstacles to getting out of this situation in one piece. Ignoring what the ride might be like, I told her, "Okay. I'll do it."

Inga looked me up and down. "I'll let Olaf know you need to change clothes first."

"A change of clothes?"

"Yes, Mr. Dawson. You'll need heavy layers to protect your body from head to toe, and also protection for your eyes and face. Don't worry, Olaf has what you need."

That's a comforting thought.

A few minutes later, I turned and shuddered when a behemoth of a man walked over, stopped in front of me, then squinted and sized me up. He looked like the mascot for the Minnesota Vikings with his bushy red beard, thick fur hat, and furry coat that looked as if he were wearing a bear. I figured he must have flown in after an open audition for *Game of Thrones*. "I sure hope you're not looking for me," I told him.

"Is this the boy?" He asked as Inga appeared. When she nodded, he extended his hand, and we shook. I looked down, but my hand was completely within his. "Olaf Sigurdsson," he said in a thick brogue. "I hear ya need a ride, boy?"

I nodded. "Yes. I have to get to Reykjavik."

"My dogs will get ya there. I imagine ya in a hurry, so put these on and we'll go."

He handed me a thick coat and pants. "Ya gonna need 'em since it's colder than a well digger's arse out there."

Who exactly is the poor sap who has to go down into the well to gauge the well digger's temperature? Is there a thermometer involved? And is the hole big enough to have room to conduct this procedure? How cold does the well digger's ass get? Will the well digger need special clothing to avoid frostbite? Is this where the term chapped ass comes from?

After changing clothes, I walked out of the restroom looking like Ralphie's brother, in *A Christmas Story*, as I stiff-legged it over to where Olaf waited.

The Redhead and the Fountain Pen

He led me outside to his dog sled. Before me were several dogs lined up, waiting to pull us through the ice and snow. When the dogs saw Olaf, they all jumped up and down and began howling. "Are they okay?" I asked.

"Oh, sure. They get excited when we are about to mush."

"Mush?"

Olaf gave me a squint of one of his dark eyes. "Ya never been on a dog sled before, boy?"

I worried I touched a nerve. "No, Mr. Olaf. They closed the only dog sled company we had back home, but I'm sure this will be fun." I smiled, trying to lighten the mood.

"You are in for the ride of your life. They talk about the joy of sex, but it don't last near as long as the thrill of outrunning an elk who's missed dinner."

Great. This adventure keeps getting better and better. Next time I get the bright idea to do the right thing, shoot me, okay?

Olaf strapped my small suitcase into the sled. I took a seat, buckled myself in, then looked ahead. The dogs howled, barked, and sprang up and down like jumping beans. If they kept that kind of energy, I suspect we'd be in Reykjavik within minutes.

He walked to the back of the sled, then called out in a high-pitched howl of his own, "Time to run, ya mutts. Mush," he yelled.

Within seconds, the dogs jerked forward, and the sled moved. I felt like I was in the convertible I wanted, only I was on the ground, moving through the snow instead of it being under me. I will say the first few miles on a dog sled were an experience I'll never forget. Ice chips flew around me, as my breath came out like a fire extinguisher. Oh, and the scent of one dog who must have had chili for breakfast was a bonus too. Will Olaf give me a first timers discount for that?

A few minutes into the trip, I was thankful Olaf dressed me for the occasion. The extra layers for my legs and torso were a necessity. The goggles and thick hat protected me from the wind, snow, and plummeting temperature, along with several blankets. I should have asked if Olaf carried a bottle of Irish Whiskey in his sled for dumbasses like me.

After an hour on the trail, the shadows behind the mountains grew longer and the valley in front of us looked dark and forbidding. I didn't think we'd been out that long.

"Olaf, why is it getting dark? Did I fall asleep or something?"

"Ya crazy American. Ya arse is in Iceland in December. Blink once and the day's over."

With us completely in the shadows now, it was colder, if that was possible. We had been on the trail for a while, and when I asked Olaf how much further, he said we were almost at a stopping point, so the dogs could rest and refuel. Reykjavik, he added, wasn't too far away.

As we pressed on, I focused on the gentle sound of the dogs panting and the sled slashing through the thick snow. Through the icy winds and numb cheeks, my brain was warm enough to ponder what lay ahead to pass the time since I needed a game plan. How would I find Catherine? And if I did, what would I say once I found her?

True to Olaf's word, the sled slowed to a stop at a large cabin in the middle of...Well...Middle of nowhere. And when I say cabin, I mean a real cabin. Not the kind they have in Blue Ridge. This one was a fortress. The massive entrance featured floor-to-ceiling windows and massive logs stacked on both sides of the wide double doors. "What is this place?"

Olaf hopped off the sled and walked around to help me

unstrap. "It's a resort where people come to see the Northern Lights. They are beautiful this time of the year."

I stood and stretched my legs. "I'll take your word for it."

"You've never seen the Northern Lights, boy? It's what Heaven must look like."

The words were familiar. Then I remembered. Catherine wrote the same thing to me in one of her letters. I shook my head. "Yeah. I've heard of them."

As I looked up at the sky, seeing it ease into darkness, I told him, "I won't be here long enough to enjoy them."

After looking around the picturesque landscape, I saw a row of dogs that wanted my attention. They had enough energy to give a few kisses, but what they wanted more were belly rubs, so I obliged.

"Let's go inside and get ya warmed up, boy."

"What about the dogs?"

"They'll be fine. They could use the rest."

I looked down. Some dogs rolled in the snow. Others sat still. A few had their tongues hanging out of their mouths, white puffs of steam coming from their snouts. "Yeah," Olaf said as he walked beside me. "Some like to roll in the snow to cool off. They work up a sweat in those thick coats."

We walked inside the lobby, the warm air a welcomed sensation. Olaf pointed to his right. "Ya get something to eat there. Order whatever you want. Tell 'em to put it on my tab. Grab a table and I'll join you in a minute. I'm going to get the dogs lunch."

I nodded, then headed to the dining room. When I found a menu on top of the table, I sat, picked it up, and looked it over. I didn't see oatmeal cookies, so it confirmed I was a long way away from Blue Ridge.

After ordering a hot chocolate and bagel, I placed the menu

back on the table and waited for Olaf to return. As I looked around, watching everyone either working or playing, I pulled out a copy of Catherine's book. I wrapped it in white paper and tied off the blue ribbon with a large bow. I figured it was close to Christmas, and since this would be a gift she'd appreciate, I should dress it up a bit.

I looked at it and said, "Thanks for bringing me out here. Merry friggin' Christmas."

I heard heavy steps coming in my direction, so I put the book away. "Did ya order, boy?" He asked, one hand holding a cup of something steaming, and the other holding a white sack. He placed the sack on the floor next to the chair, then sat down.

"Yes. A bagel and hot chocolate are on the way."

"Good." Olaf took a sip, then asked, "I don't get to travel with too many Americans. Whatcha doin' way out here, boy? Ya lost?"

"Something like that."

"Aw, there has to be a girl in this somewhere. Am I wrong?"

First Inga, and now Olaf. "Do Icelandic people read minds?"

Olaf smiled, then belly laughed. "Icelandic people have superpowers ya Americans don't know about. So, I was right, wasn't I?"

I nodded. "Yeah, Olaf. You got me."

"Ya crazy Americans. Ya got a screw loose?"

I smiled and nodded. "I must. To be honest, I have a promise to keep. Then I'm going home."

Olaf took another sip of his coffee. "Well, I guess ya have your reasons. She must be something for you to come all this way. Especially on a dog sled."

"Yeah," I told him. "She was once."

Olaf's eyes found mine. He gave me a sympathetic nod. "You're a good man."

The Redhead and the Fountain Pen

"Thank you, Olaf." Before the mood got too heavy, I asked, "Aren't the dogs getting hungry?"

Olaf smiled. "Yeah, I suppose ya right." He reached down and pulled up the large bag on the floor.

I looked at it. "That's a lot of food. What's inside?"

"Raw meat."

"Is all that for the dogs?"

Olaf smiled, "Nah. Some of it's for me since I gotta eat too." He got up and patted me on the shoulder. "Enjoy your bagel."

I wasn't ready to get back out in the cold yet. After eating half of a bagel and sipped hot chocolate, I wasn't quite warm enough yet, so I decided to hang out a little longer.

From down the hall, I swore I heard a viola, which made sense since I had been hearing strings everywhere I went the last few months. Even in the most remote outposts in Iceland, my brain couldn't shut them off.

I rose and dropped my plate and cup in a bin on my way to find where the imaginary music came from. As I walked along the wide hallway, the sound grew, so I knew I was getting close to something. When I turned the corner, I found what I was looking for. In a large room was a group of string performers. Whew. I wasn't crazy after all.

I listened for a few minutes, and as I scanned the stage, my eyes locked on a sign behind them. "Iceland Symphony Orchestra."

Does someone know Catherine?

After they finished the song, the woman at the front of the stage told the small crowd, "Thank you. We all hope you will join us for the full show at the Harpa Concert Hall beginning tomorrow night and running through the new year. Besides your Christmas favorites, we have a few other songs we like to play to keep things fresh. In fact, for our last song, today is one we've been working on and wanted to play it for you. This is one of the new ones we've added to our performance, so forgive us if we miss a note or two," she laughed.

As I watched the woman on stage, I examined the instrument she brought to her neck. Sure enough, it was a viola, since it was larger than a violin.

As the music played, I stared at the woman as she swayed to the music, eyes closed, her hand dragging the bow across the strings. My eyes locked on her, studying every move. As I walked closer, I saw her hair, pulled back in a bun, glow in the lights above. When she turned, it glowed red. As the moment unfolded before me, the wheels turned in my mind. Could it be?

She finished the song, and as the crowd applauded, the woman, and the performers bowed. They waved goodbye and packed up their instruments.

I walked to the stage and waited for whatever destiny had for me. With my heart pounding, I felt beads of sweat forming on my brow. As I steadied my legs, I faced the woman, then summoned up every ounce of courage I had. "Excuse me." When she turned and located my voice, a warm smile came to her face. My eyes locked on hers. The light blue sparkled as she stared back at me. The wrinkles around her face told me she was older, but not old, and her hair was an elegant shade of cinnamon. "Yes?"

I wasn't sure how to begin the conversation, although my brain shuffled around several appropriate responses. I went with the first thing that came to me. "That was beautiful."

The woman smiled, and a blush of red came to her freckled cheeks. "Thank you. Judging from that wide grin on your face, we accomplished what we set out to do."

My grin grew wider. She sounded like she was American, so I checked off another box. With that information, it allowed me to continue. "By chance, do you know who I am?"

The woman's grin grew to match mine. "Yes, I do."

This wasn't as difficult as I thought it was going to be.

Another performer walked over, grasping the handle on her black instrument case in one hand, and a stack of sheet music in the other. "I'll load these in the van."

The woman looked at her. "Sure. Let me get packed up and we can go." Then she turned back to me. "You're a charming man who enjoys beautiful music. Thank you for taking time to let me know how much you enjoyed our performance."

After hesitating, I said, "I'm Mark." I paused, making sure I had the words in the right order, then asked, "Are you Catherine?"

The woman's grin faded, and she furrowed her brow. The sparkle dimmed. "No. I'm afraid I'm not. My name is Julia."

All my momentum crashed to the ground with a dull thud. I looked at her and smiled. "Oh, sorry. I...Oh, it's nothing. Thank you, Julia. I enjoyed the performance."

Julia smiled, then asked, "Are you looking for Catherine?"

Her question smacked me between the eyes. As I attempted to respond, something to the left of Julia's shoulder caught my attention when a woman opened her instrument case.

twenty-nine

Taped to the inside cover was something familiar. The card featured a red heart drawn in crayon with the words courage, perseverance, and peace around it. Musical notes rested in the corners.

As I watched, the woman turned in my direction. The charms jingled as her arm moved to place her bow inside the case. I had a hunch there was a silver viola on the bracelet somewhere.

I took the woman in. Her silky red hair surrounded a freckled face, and when she smiled, the world moved in slow motion. From behind, Julia said, "Catherine? Someone was asking for you."

She looked at Julia, then at me.

My eyes never left Catherine's face. After months of wondering who this woman was, she stood before me, just a heartbeat away. An ocean once separated us, but now the only distance was the uncertainty of the next moment.

All the wonder, and the power and the allure of the surging wave of the unknown unfolded before me in a panorama of clarity.

I no longer chased the purple inked ghost. Catherine was real and as full of life as breathing in a distant fireplace floating on the first breeze of October, bringing a peace we all long for.

Her silky hair lay in long seductive curls over her shoulders, guarding a set of azure eyes. It was blue I wanted to dive into, knowing I'd never come up for air. But oh, it was such a sweet demise.

Freckles dotted her rosy cheeks, leaving me in breathless awe. The brown specks were placed so perfectly around her face, I couldn't wait to ask God how he was able to create such a masterpiece.

When her lips curled upward in a curious grin, that was the final, fatal blow. As I gazed at her, I could have sworn this was Heaven, and she was my angel.

But as the glow dimmed and the clouds darkened, I was back to reality. Catherine didn't love me. The magic of autumn was now replaced by the darkness of winter.

I accepted my fate with stoic calmness, knowing I needed strength to do what I came to Iceland to do. I'd allow myself to fall apart later.

Catherine's curious grin remained, not knowing what was about to happen. "You're here to see me?"

The first time I heard her voice after hearing it in her letters for months left my head spinning. A tingle ricocheted through my knees, and I had to remind myself to shift the weight in my legs so I didn't lose my balance. I adjusted, making sure both legs were under me, then I took a breath and exhaled. The moment of truth I thought about for months arrived.

I pointed to her case, then looked at her. "I once made a card for someone with a heart drawn in crayon when she was preparing for an audition."

Catherine squinted her eyes and looked at me. "I'm sorry?"

"I also gave her a silver viola charm."

She squinted, then brought her wrist to her face. After a few seconds, her face turned to stone. She was about to speak, but when her mouth opened, nothing came out. She stared at me for a few seconds, a wave of wonder overcoming her. The silence between us spoke volumes.

Whatever was about to happen, I was going to face it with courage because I had come this far, so the hard part was over. Not wanting the silence to be deafening, I said, "Ég fann þig, Cat."

Her eyes softened. She replied, "I...I...Um...I forgot the words in French." She shook her head, then asked, "You're Mark? Mark from Blue Ridge?"

"Yes, I am. And you are Catherine from New York."

Our eyes locked in a mystical dance. I saw inside her soul. The fear, the guilt, the passion, and all the good. I saw the things I loved about her, and the things I came to depend on when I was in trouble. After all this time, I was standing across from the woman who dazzled me with her words. Who made me fall in love with everything about her, even though this was the first time we'd ever met.

"What are you doing here?" She asked, as her face remained blank.

Her words weren't exactly what I hoped for, so it took a moment to absorb the blow. I swallowed hard, then went numb to ignore the pain so I could focus, knowing I had only a minute to speak my peace. Whatever I was about to say, I had better make it memorable. "I'm here since I made a promise, and I'm a man of my word."

She shook her head. "Promise? What promise?"

I reached into my coat and pulled out the book. "This is for you."

Catherine gave me a puzzled look, then looked down at the

wrapping. "What's this?"

"I know it's not Christmas yet, but…" I said as my words trailed off. Finally, I told her, "Actually, that's not a Christmas present."

She took the package from my hand, looked it over, then pulled the ribbon out of its bow. She unwrapped it, and when she saw it was her book, she gasped, then covered her mouth. Tears formed in her eyes, and she held the book to her chest. "My God. You remembered."

My eyebrows rose. "Yes, I did."

"I thought I'd never see it again."

"Well, they say Christmas is a time for miracles." I gave her a half hearted smile, and added, "I didn't want to be the last guy, so I wanted to make sure your father's book got back to you."

Catherine looked at the book, then at me. "Thank you for doing this, Mark." She got quiet and looked at the floor. An uneasy silence hovered over us. That was my cue.

She had her music and finally, her book. There was nothing more she needed from me. Now it was time for me to leave her alone.

The game was over. I lost to an all-powerful foe who didn't walk, talk, or write beautiful words. I lost to a passion, and that's a game that you cannot win. Ever. When there is passion, nothing can change what lies in the heart. I felt foolish for even trying.

"Well, that's the reason I came here. I…um…Wish you the best with your career. I am sure the Iceland Symphony Orchestra has the best viola player in the world now. Congratulations, Catherine. One day, you will change the world with your music."

Catherine continued looking at the floor, then her eyes found mine. "Thank you for the words. How long are you in town for?"

"I'm going back to the airport now. I have a late flight back to Atlanta." Her face gave away nothing as she stared at me. I gave her a questionable smile. "Well, I better get going. God bless you, Catherine. Merry Christmas." I nodded, then turned to walk away.

As I walked, I didn't hear her say stop, or my name, so I continued walking until I reached the door. After pushing it open, and receiving a frosty rush of air greeting me, I continued down the stairs. Funny. I didn't button my coat or put my hands in my pockets. I was too numb to feel anything.

The landscape greeted me in complete darkness. The azure sky was now navy, with blinking lights hovering over everything. I smelled a fireplace and heard the crunching of snow under my feet. Funny things you notice when you want to forget the previous few minutes of your life.

As I stepped down the icy stairs, a razor wind caught me flush in the face. The numbness intensified, but there was nothing the outside could throw at me that was colder than the frozen daze I became. I was a dead man walking.

I found Olaf checking the harnesses of a few of the dogs, so I approached. "Change of plans. Take me back to the airport."

Olaf gave me a confused stare. "The airport? What about Reykjavik? And your dream girl?"

I looked over his wide shoulders to the mountains in the distance. "She'll have to remain a dream."

Olaf rubbed his frozen whiskers with a thick leather glove. As he rubbed, some icicles dropped from his beard. He gave me a sad stare, then nodded. "Well, ya must know what ya doing. Give me a minute while I check the harnesses. I'll have you back at the airport in no time. Before you know it, you'll be home."

As another gust of winter slapped me in the face, thoughts of home never looked so good.

While I waited, I looked down at one of the dogs. It looked up at me, its tail wagging. I crouched down and took its thick neck in my hands, and rubbed it. Then I moved my hands up and rubbed the back of its ears. The dog's eyes were slits and its tongue popped in and out of its mouth. When he growled in spurts, letting me know I was hitting all the right spots, I knew I'd made a friend.

After a few more rubs and growls, the eyes opened, and it looked to the side. Its tail fluttered back and forth as someone approached. At this rate, its tail could clear a path for the people walking up the snowy sidewalk.

I guess it wanted someone else and didn't need me any longer. Funny how that recurring theme kept popping up wherever I had the misfortune of going.

The dog moved its snout into the leg of someone standing next to me, so I stopped rubbing and looked up. "This is a sweet dog."

"Yes. I'm sure it is," the voice replied.

thirty

"You have a way of making everyone feel special, don't you?" Catherine said, looking down at me.

Before I answered, Olaf shouted over, "We'll be on our way soon, boy."

I waved to him, then rose and faced Catherine. My heart pounded as her face paralyzed me. What did she want now? I let her speak since I couldn't.

"Mark, I—" she stopped, then looked at the row of dogs. "What's this?"

I looked down at the dogs, then back at her. My power of speech returned. "Um, this is my transportation."

"Transportation?"

"Yeah. Because of the snow and the blocked roads, this was all I could find to get me to Reykjavik."

Her face lit up, and her mouth emitted a puff of white breath. "A dogsled?"

I stared into her eyes. Her freckles glistened in the artificial light, and the combination drenched me in a calm I could swim into forever. Even though she wasn't going to be mine, sometimes it's okay to admire something so beautiful. "I promised to deliver your book. I wouldn't let a little thing like thirty-three hundred miles, a snowstorm, and a flatulent dog keep me from doing what I said I would do."

Her cheeks, pink from the cold, became crimson.

I smiled, which was difficult since my frozen cheeks didn't want to comply. Then again, my heart wasn't in it anyway.

There was a hint of happiness on her lips as they went horizontal. "I wanted to ask you something."

"What's on your mind?" I asked.

"You said something about not being the last guy. What did you mean by that?"

I watched as Olaf packed the sled with supplies, then looked back at her. "I wanted you to know I wasn't the last guy. No matter what, I wouldn't have abandoned you."

The smile went from horizontal to exposing two rows of straight teeth.

"But that doesn't matter now," I told her. "You have your music, so I read between the lines of your last letter."

"Mark, about that—"

"It's okay. I know you took the audition hard and I'm sorry it didn't work out. I want you to be happy. You're here performing your music now and that's what you've always wanted. I won't stand in the way."

"Mark. Let me explain."

No matter how hard this was going to hurt, I had to let her have her moment. I kept my big mouth shut and allowed her to break my heart a second time.

"First, I am blown away by your kindness. Your perseverance in returning my father's book amazes me. It's a lot better than having it dumped in a used bookstore. You really are special."

I nodded. Her words flattered me, but I didn't need flattery. I needed this to end so I could retreat to Georgia to begin the healing process.

She looked at her gloved hands, the book still clasped between them. "Mark, I made a fool of myself in New York. After the last time, I swore I wouldn't do it again. I wouldn't involve anyone else in my dreams, since it was too painful if they didn't come true. Why feel guilty by involving you, and then not succeeding? But silly me, or rather, stupid me, I allowed you to come into my life, and for that, I am sorry. You'd think I would learn by now, but I haven't. I worried you'd ghost me like the last guy did." She paused and looked down.

I let her continue.

She looked up. "I felt a severe jolt of guilt since I let you down, especially after everything you did for me. Then the memories of what happened last time came back, and I guess that's what spooked me. I couldn't bear not seeing another one of your letters in my mailbox. I decided it was best to cut the cord and start fresh. But it was okay. I had nobody but myself to blame. I could live with that. Not well, mind you, but it was something I felt I had to do."

I nodded, then asked, "Are you happy?"

"I wasn't until a few minutes ago."

I furrowed my brow. "What? I thought playing your viola makes you happy?"

"Me too. Then you walked back into my life."

"Catherine, I don't understand."

She looked away, then back at me. "When I sent the letter, I was in an awful place. All those feelings from the Brooklyn Bridge came back, and I let them take over. I was wrong."

"Look, Cat, this is my fault. I should have done a better job coaching you. I'm the one who should say I'm sorry."

"What do you have to be sorry about? Don't you understand what you did for me? I never played the viola better in my life. Instead of playing the music, for the first time in my life, I was the music. I felt the passion of the moment. I don't know if I'll ever feel that way again. Don't you see? I reached a level with my performance I never would have ever known, thanks to you believing in me."

"Cat, I—"

"Mark, there are people blessed with the talent to create beautiful things the world will remember forever. With some, they have the tools but need someone to give them the heart. You did that for me."

"But you didn't win."

Catherine gave me a sly smile. "Didn't I?"

"You told me you didn't win the audition."

"I wasn't talking about the audition."

As I thought about her words, the small, familiar tingle found its way around my frozen body.

Catherine continued. "When I lost the audition, I thought I'd never see you again. That's why I told you goodbye. I couldn't bear the thought of abandonment again. But the moment I saw you tonight, especially given the circumstances of how you got here, and returning the book, I'm not going to make the same mistake twice. You're the miracle I've waited for all my life. Since miracles don't happen every day, and since the days in Iceland aren't very long, don't you think we should get started on ours?"

"I would love to. But can we back up for a moment?"

She nodded. "What's wrong?"

"Catherine, in your last letter, why didn't you say anything about the book? I was sure you wanted it back."

She didn't speak for a few seconds. Finally, she said, "Yeah, I know. The book is special to me. My father gave it to me before he died."

"Yeah. I saw what he wrote."

"You did?" She asked in amazement. After I nodded, she looked at the snow underneath her feet. She moved it with her foot to one side, then back again. With white steam flowing from her mouth, she looked up and said, "Mark, the book was one of the most important things in the world to me. But knowing you had it was okay."

"Okay? How?"

"I wanted you to keep the book because it was the thing that brought us together." As I stared at her, she continued. "It was the only thing of me you had left." After she finished speaking, tears leaked down her cheeks and glowed in the light coming from the cabin.

Before I could stop the words coming out of my mouth, they fluttered into the frosty air. "I love you, Catherine."

I paused and looked at her in fear. She gasped, then gave me a long stare. As she looked at me, I said, "I know it's not possible for you to feel the same way." I paused, then told her, "When I'm back in Georgia, I'll embrace this moment, knowing I'll never regret not saying it."

I didn't feel the cold, hear the dogs, or see anything past her face. She wiped her eyes, then stared at me. "I can't believe you said that."

"Yeah. Me either."

As I waited for what would happen next, she grinned, then leaped into my arms, holding me as if she would never let go. I heard her sobbing and felt the wetness of her cheek. "I love you too, Mark."

Knowing my words were perfect for the moment, I closed my eyes and exhaled as I held her tighter.

"I thought I lost you forever," she said through the tears.

"Amazing what you find in the lost and found these days."

When we released, we looked at each other, then shared our first kiss. As with everything I thought about with Catherine, reality was so much better than the dream.

When the kiss ended, I looked at her. Something was missing, but I couldn't put my finger on it. Then it hit me. I reached for her leather-gloved hand, and when she grasped mine, I said, "I don't even know your last name. Isn't that the craziest thing you've ever heard? I'm in love with you and don't even know your last name."

She laughed as she wiped her cheeks. "It's Jensson," she said, then sniffled.

"Well, Catherine Jensson, you think those three words might be the best way to fix your broken heart?"

She nodded. "They might do the trick," she said with a grin.

From behind, I saw a van pull up in the parking lot. Julia got out and walked over to us. "There you are, Catherine. I thought you were only going to be a minute?"

"Um, sorry, Julia. I got a little distracted," she giggled, then looked at me.

"Well, we're getting ready to head back to town. Are you ready?"

Catherine looked at me with uncertainty in her eyes.

"It's okay. Go," I told her. "I have a dog sled to catch."

Her face lost its glow. "What? No, Mark. You can't leave now."

"I don't want to hold you up."

"It's okay," she said. "Wait here."

I watched as she walked over to Julia. After Catherine finished speaking, Julia nodded. "Fine. I can do that."

Catherine walked over to me.

"What's going on?" I asked.

"Watch."

Julia went back to the van and came back with her viola. She looked at us, winked, then brought the instrument to her neck. She began playing, "Can't Help Falling in Love," and within the first few notes, I felt a warmth I never thought I'd feel again.

Catherine looked at me with an innocent glow. "May I have this dance?"

"Shouldn't I ask that question?"

She shook her head. "You silly boy. Don't you remember anything from my letters? I like to be different."

I brought her to me, and we shared our long-awaited dance. Unlike the last time I heard this song back in Blue Ridge, thinking I lost everything, I knew now I had found my redheaded girl. I looked at her, and when she returned the gaze and threw her arms around my neck, we shared a second kiss.

After the kiss ended, I picked her up and we twirled. When I brought her feet back to the snowy sidewalk, everyone who gathered in the freezing darkness to watch us dancing cheered. Since it was so cold, our cheeks were already crimson, so nobody saw us blushing. As I looked around, I whispered, "What should we do?"

Catherine smiled at the crowd. Out of the side of her mouth, she said, "I got this. When the crowd cheers, you bow."

We held hands as we took a couple's bow, which got an even larger ovation.

After the crowd left, Catherine looked over and asked, "Mark, do you think there's room for one more on your sled?"

I raised my eyebrows and smiled. "Let me check," then we held hands as I walked her to the dog sled. "Hey Olaf? You think we have room for one more?"

Olaf nodded, the grin splitting his face. "I have space in the dream girl section. Does she qualify?"

Catherine's eyes sparkled. "Dream girl section?" She asked with an amorous grin.

I grinned. "I'll explain that later."

I looked at Olaf and managed a frozen smile, made more difficult by my numb cheeks. "After tonight, I'd say so."

The numbness of the breeze throwing snow on us turned into warm joy. Catherine smiled. "A dear friend of mine once wrote that we didn't come this far to only come this far. What do we do now?" She asked, gazing into my eyes, the sparkle almost blinding me.

"I don't know. But I wouldn't worry. It will come to us."

Catherine gave me a sexy smile and nodded.

As we waited for Olaf to clear a space, she wiped her face and sniffled. "All those times I imagined what it would be like when we met for the first time. I'm sorry you have to see me like this. I was hoping you'd think I was beautiful."

I looked at her again. The freckles blended into her frozen cheeks. Above her left eyebrow was a scar I would ask her about one day. Her hair was pulled underneath a purple wool cap. None of that mattered. "Catherine, I knew you were beautiful."

"You knew I was beautiful? How?"

I wiped away a strand of thick red hair that escaped her cap. "Cat, my love, beauty isn't something you see. It's something you feel."

She gasped. "Wow. I knew you could write. But you can also

talk a pretty good game too."

As we gazed at each other, Julia walked over. "Catherine? Would you like me to take your viola back with us?"

Catherine sniffled and wiped her cheeks dry. "Sure. I'll walk it over." Then she looked at me. "Give me a second?"

"Of course."

I watched Catherine walk over to the van. As I followed her path, a greenish hue engulfed her. As I looked around, we all bathed in the same light. Where was it coming from?

From my right, I heard a familiar voice. "You know, Gatsby believed in the green light, the orgiastic future that year by year recedes before us. It eluded us then, but that's no matter. It hasn't eluded you tonight, old sport."

Standing by the stairs was Scott, adorned in a thick fur coat.

I looked at him, but all he did was smile back at me. "What? No flask tonight?"

He smiled. "Don't need it. I wanted to see this sober."

I looked at him, wondering why he was a shade of green. "Where are all these green lights come from?"

"It's the Northern Lights, ya rube. Don't you remember I told you to keep looking for the green light? Well, here's your shot."

I looked at the sky, which was no longer navy but adored in a swirling panorama of Kelly. As I bathed in the glow, Scott's words came back to me. And as they did, it all made sense now. I looked at him and shook my head. "You did this."

He smiled, then replied, "No, Mark. It was you. You dared to fight for something you loved. And now you get to bask in the greenish glow of love that Gatsby would have given anything to have. This is a moment that will last forever. Take good care of it. Promise?"

"Promise," I assured him.

As we shared a meaningful gaze, I said, "Before you vanish like you usually do when things get good, I wanted to say something."

"What?"

"Your words have made a difference in many lives. I'm living proof. I know it might be a little late, but thank you."

I thought I'd be talking to myself as usual, but this time, he stuck around. He stared at me, then a small smile crept onto his lips. "No. Thank you, old sport. I thought Gatsby was nothing until I saw what a difference it made in your life. Thanks for giving this old ghost a moment of validation."

He smiled and waved goodbye. Within seconds, he vanished into the greenish hue. As I thought about his words, it was then I understood what the green light meant. I exhaled, knowing we both found what we came for.

As I looked at the sky, marveling at the heavenly light casting its beauty on us, Catherine walked up behind and put her arm around my waist. "I'm glad we got to see the Northern Lights together. I remember mentioning it in one of my letters, but I never thought we'd be together to see them." Then she put her head on my shoulder.

After staring at the sky for a few minutes, I asked, "Would you like me to take you home?"

In puffs of white steam, she told me, "I'd like that."

After walking back to the sled, Olaf strapped us in. He looked at us and said, "Well, this was the raisin at the end of the hot dog."

I looked at Catherine and squinted.

She grinned. "My grandparents used that phrase. It means a pleasant surprise at the end of the day."

"And you think Americans have a screw loose?" I asked Olaf, who threw his head back and roared with laughter.

Catherine's body rested in front of me. I wrapped my arms around her, and her hands found mine. Her scent waffled through the crisp air, causing me to breathe her in. All I could do was utter a contented sigh.

The dogs heard the command to mush, and off we went into the green light. It was the green light that eluded Gatsby, but somehow, destiny allowed us to capture it.

Catherine looked at me and asked, "So, how does it feel to be in a RomCom?"

Her words brought back the memory of an old friend in Blue Ridge "You'll end up in your own little RomCom," Scarlett predicted. Damn if she didn't nail that one. I smiled, then told Catherine, "You know. It feels pretty damn good."

When the sled passed by the onlookers watching us, they cheered as if we had won first place in the Iditarod. We waved to them as they shouted their best wishes.

As the dogs pulled us through the snow, I held my redheaded girl, never wanting to let go. When she looked up and smiled, my mind drifted back to Scarlett's bookstore, where this all began.

Miracles happen every day, usually when you least expect them. As long as we keep our eyes, and our hearts, open to the possibilities. What were the odds of me being in Blue Ridge? Then going to the bookstore, finding her book? Oh, and by the way, what were the odds of a letter averting several attempts at ending up in the trash, or buried under a pile of papers? Then falling in love. That's the biggest miracle of them all.

I don't know how I am going to explain this to Tara, and of course, Scarlett. I don't know where I will be living once Catherine and I sort everything out.

And, of course, I don't know how long Catherine is going to love me. But none of that matters.

Now she's in my arms, so I'm going to appreciate the moment with no fear. Tonight is all that matters.

Tomorrow, I'm going to wake up and then figure out what the future holds. But as we sled through the snow, and bask in the green light, there's one thing I am sure of. Catherine is mine, and nothing can take that away.

thirty-one

After months of reading about what Catherine was doing, I now got to see it firsthand. The way her smile lit up the room. The way she brushed her hair. The way her cinnamon hair fell over her purple scarf. How she couldn't begin her day without Diet Coke. The way she looked at me when I said something she liked.

Our first official date was a night at the Harpa Concert Hall, where the Iceland Symphony Orchestra played a holiday concert. Catherine didn't tell me, but as a new member of the orchestra, they have the rookies perform a solo so the Orchestra could introduce them to the audience.

As she walked to the front of the stage, she looked at me, winked, then played our song. As the sound floated to me, and I focused on the stage, we were the only two people in the world at that moment.

I gushed at the way her red hair snapped around her shoulders as she moved to the music. Her eyes closed and head locked in on the viola. The way the bow glided over the strings, producing a sound that would forever live in my heart. I would take it wherever I went, no matter how far apart we were.

After the performance, we held hands as we walked around

the snowy streets of Reykjavik. We stopped at a small cafe, where she told me the performers liked to go after performances. As we sat sipping hot chocolate, she asked, "So, what do you think of Iceland so far?"

I knew Reykjavik was going to be freezing, and it felt like Atlanta in January, so it wasn't that big of a shock. What amazed me was how beautiful and clean it was. It reminded me of Seattle, the way the town was next to the water with a long row of snow-capped mountains in the distance. I smiled, then wiped my mouth. "It's cold," I told her with a grin. After she winked, I added, "Actually," I said, then paused. "It's perfect."

When a warm grin pushed her freckled cheeks upward into her rosy cheeks, I didn't say a word for fear it would bring a halt to a beautiful moment.

The next day, Catherine showed me the sights and sounds of her new city. The rows of multicolored homes and buildings added a splash of excitement to what was unfolding before my eyes. As the sun sunk into the horizon, she looked over and asked, "Do you think you'd be up for one last spot on the tour?"

I nodded. "Where are you taking me?"

"You'll see. I hope you're not afraid of heights."

As we turned the corner and continued along the street, I looked around for the tallest building I could find. In seconds, I had my answer.

In the distance was a large tower ascending into the frosty sky like a shaved pyramid. At the top of the curved structure was a golden cross shining in the twilight. "A church, huh? And it's not even Sunday."

Catherine giggled. "Well, we should say a few prayers of

gratitude for finding each other a second time."

"Yeah. I suppose you're right." As we walked closer, the tower grew larger as it scraped the sky. "What kind of church is this?"

"One of Iceland's most popular attractions. The Hallgrímskirkja church."

Catherine led me inside, past the pews to the elevator. After feeling the floor lift us, the doors opened to a wide lobby area. On all four sides of the lobby were large clocks, looking out to the sky like Big Ben in London.

After looking out from all four sides, Catherine took my hand and led me up a set of stairs. "Where are we going?"

She smiled. "You'll like it."

We got to the top of the stairs, then walked to the left through a door that opened into a viewing area. From there was an unobstructed view of the city below. The stiff breeze brought the scent of honeysuckle, coming from Catherine's perfume, into my face as she stood next to me. We held hands as we looked out to the city below.

"It's beautiful up here, isn't it?" I asked as I looked at her.

She nodded, then looked at me. "It's my favorite place in Reykjavik. I've been coming here ever since I was a little girl. I'm happy I got to share it with you."

Catherine put her head on my shoulder, and when she did, I leaned back and kissed her on the top of her knit cap. She leaned back and smiled. "How long do you think you'll be in Reykjavik?"

Her question brought a halt to the magical moment. "You know, Cat, I haven't thought about it." When a look of resignation came over her, I added, "But we can work something out."

As resignation morphed into happiness, she said, "Yeah. We can work something out."

The Redhead and the Fountain Pen

Catherine and I returned to her apartment, had dinner, then fell asleep together on her couch watching *Casablanca*. I found a copy of it in her DVD collection, so it was a no-brainer when I suggested it. It was an even better surprise when she smiled and said, "Wow, Roy. Good choice. That's one of my favorite movies."

I guess you can say that was the 40s version of one of those RomComs I was now in the middle of. Although there weren't as many laughs as you'd see in a Tom Hanks/Meg Ryan movie, it served its purpose of throwing a blanket of amorousness over the room.

After we watched Rick say goodbye to Ilsa's airplane, we decided to call it a night. Catherine walked us back to her room, then stopped at the foot of the bed. She turned and looked at me. "Mark, I know you slept on the couch last night, and that's cool. I was...well, I wasn't sure about, you know. I'm not the kind of girl that..." she stopped as the words filled her mouth and got stuck trying to come out. "What I'm trying to say is, after months of waking up to your letters, and wondering what you were all about, I would love it if we could wake up to each other." She paused, then pushed a strand of cinnamon over her ear. "I would like it if we slept together."

When I raised an eyebrow, her eyes became saucers. Then she covered her mouth and blushed. She removed her hand and tried to get the words out, but they got stuck as they tried to escape her ruby-red lips. She took a breath, then got them in the right order. "Oh my God. I didn't mean it that way. I meant literally, to sleep together. You know. Like us holding each other. Both of us in our PJs, you know..." she said with a smile and nod, hoping I understood where she was going with her words.

I put up my hand and grinned to relax her. "Cat, I get it. I know this has been a whirlwind the last few days, especially after all the letters. Just so you know, I've wondered for months what that might feel like."

Her face glowed. "Me too."

"Good to know," I replied, then winked. After a pause, I asked, "You don't snore, do you?"

She laughed. "You silly boy. How would I know that?"

I brought her to me and we laughed harder. When we released, Catherine exhaled. "Whew. I hoped you would see it like I do. Chalk it up to another thing we agree on."

"That's why I kinda have a thing for you," I said with a smile.

Her grin dwarfed mine. "Yeah. I kinda have a thing for you too."

✒

After she fell asleep, which I was sure of when I heard a gentle snore from her mouth, I walked out of the bedroom since I couldn't sleep. I had something on my mind. Something heavy I had to address.

I found my backpack, pulled out a piece of paper and my fountain pen, then walked over to the kitchen table and sat. I stared at the paper for a few minutes, knowing the ink I was about to apply to the paper would change my life forever.

Once I finished, I leaned back and read what I wrote. "Am I sure this is what I want?" I asked as I looked at the paper.

No matter, I walked back to the bedroom, got back into the warm bed with Catherine, and nestled in close to her. I laid my head on the pillow, then looked out at the blinking lights of Reykjavik through the window. It was no use worrying about it now, since it would be waiting for me to deal with in the morning. I closed my eyes, and drifted off to sleep.

Oh, and by the way, her gentle snore. It was more charming than annoying...

The Redhead and the Fountain Pen

When I woke up, Catherine lay next to me. I rolled over and saw her sleepy face inches away. Her red hair and sweet smile made my heart beat faster, and as I gazed at her, there was no way I was going back to sleep.

As stealth-like as possible, I slipped out of bed. When I looked back, Catherine hadn't moved, so I was off to make breakfast. I know she had been in Iceland a short time, but I figured I could whip something up. As I looked through the refrigerator, I found eggs, bacon, butter, shredded cheese and orange juice. Oh, and a rectangular carton with the words Coke Light in red on the side. "Hmm, I wonder if Iceland doesn't sell Diet Coke? That might be sore subject," I thought.

There was bread in the cabinet next to it, so this was a slam dunk.

As I placed the plate full of scrambled cheese eggs on the table, I heard footsteps approaching. Within seconds, Catherine's smiling face filled up the kitchen. "Hey, Roy. Sorry, I was so sleepy."

"No worries," I assured her. "It gave me time to make us breakfast. I hope you like bacon and eggs."

"Sounds good to me," she replied, then asked, "So, did I snore last night?"

I pondered her question for a second, then shook my head. "Nah, I didn't hear a peep." I smiled then asked, "Um, please don't shoot the messenger, but I looked for a Diet Coke for you. I saw a carton of Coke Light, but I didn't–"

"Oh please," she said with a wave of her hand. "Cat needs her Diet Coke in the morning. And no matter how they try to spin it, Coke Light is not Diet Coke." Then she growled.

I saw the look in her eyes, and shuddered. *Change the subject,*

Mark. Change the subject. "Um, yeah. So, how about those cheese eggs?"

Her scowl faded into a smile. "They were delicious."

I sensed I had moved out of danger, so I changed the subject, Quickly. "So, how did you get that scar over your eye?"

Catherine wiped her mouth with a napkin, then shook her head. "Aw, the scar. You noticed."

I nodded.

"Well, that was a funny one. I was playing in an intramural basketball game in college. It was my sorority, the AD Pi's, against our rivals, the Tri-Delts. We were in the third overtime and with the score tied, and only a few seconds to play, I was running down the court. Out of nowhere, I got laid out by an elbow."

"No way," I told her with a concerned voice. "What happened? Did the ref throw the girl out of the game?"

Catherine shook her head. "Well, not exactly. When the game went into the third overtime, I told our captain I had to leave for a performance with the campus orchestra, so she told me to head out. I rushed off the bench to leave, and when I got to the end of the bench, I didn't see another player from the adjacent court stumble into my path. She never saw me either, and we both laid each other out. I got nine stitches. She got a concussion."

"Wow, I never saw that coming," I told her.

"Neither did she," Catherine laughed. "We ended up winning the game, so all's well that ends well, I guess."

"Remind me never to play one-on-one with you," I joked.

After breakfast, I rinsed off the plates and placed them in the dishwasher. After I closed the dishwasher door and turned the machine on, I walked into the living room. Catherine sat on the couch, waiting for me. "So yesterday, you mentioned sticking around," she said as I sat next to her. After I nodded, she smiled. "You know, Roy, you can stay here as long as you like."

I looked at her for a few seconds. Then I told her, "I'd like that."

Catherine smiled and nodded. Her grin faded.

"What's wrong?"

"The last guy said the same thing, and when things went south, he bailed on me. I...well, I'd hate it if something like that happened to us."

"I've had a lot of time to think about this, Cat. I'd give it all up to be with you. To give us a chance to see where this thing could go."

She squinted. "You would? But after what you've accomplished with your softball team, how could you?"

"Well–" I began, but she continued her thought.

"I'd understand if you wanted to go back to Georgia," she said, her eyes staring into mine. Her voice was soft as it drifted into the air. "It would be difficult for you, or anyone for that matter, to give up everything and roll the dice on a girl across the ocean. I'd understand if you didn't want to take your chances with me. Besides, you have something wonderful back home. You have a team that loves you and you've cemented your legacy after one year. That would be difficult to walk away from."

I thought about what Scarlett said about having a family in Blue Ridge, and having a place to call home. "It would. But we'd always wonder what might have happened if we had given this a shot."

"I know." She paused, then said, "I'll still have your letters, so no matter what happens, there will still be a part of you with me."

I leaned over and kissed her on the top of the head. "It's funny you mentioned that."

"Mentioned what?"

"Letters. I'll be right back."

"Where are you going?" She asked.

I grinned. "You think we need something in writing?"

She squinted. "Well, I don't think we have to go that far," she said with a giggle.

"Wait here," I told her.

A few minutes later, I returned and handed her an envelope. "Open it."

She took the envelope, then turned it over and saw her name written on the front. "What's this?"

I laughed. "It's a letter. I figured if anyone would know what it was, it'd be you."

Catherine looked at me in an amorous wonder, then turned the envelope over and pulled out the flap. She reached inside, pulled out the folded white piece of paper, and began reading.

I watched her face as she wondered what the letter contained. Within seconds, it lit up. Then she brought her hand to her mouth, and tears formed in her eyes. "You can't-" she said, then stopped as the emotion of the moment overcame her. After a few seconds, and a couple of deep breaths, she shook her head. "Are you serious? This is a resignation letter. You can't mean-"

I nodded. "Yeah, every word of it. When I get back to Blue Ridge, I'm giving that letter to the head of the school. Her name is Tara, and she'll understand why I'm doing it."

"But why? You love Blue Ridge and you love your softball team."

"Yeah. But I love you more."

Catherine gasped, then rose and threw her arms around me as we shared a long, meaningful kiss. Once the kiss ended, she looked up at me with those beautiful blue eyes that left me weak in the knees. "You know, Mark Dawson, the feeling is mutual."

An hour later, I exited the shower and got dressed so Catherine and I could spend the day together. I looked forward to our future together, starting with the next heartbeat.

After I finished dressing, I walked out of the bedroom and was about to ask if she was ready, but I heard her voice in the kitchen, so I veered in that direction. When I got there, I saw she was on the phone, so we waved at each other, then I retreated to the living room since I wanted to give her privacy.

I walked to the window and stared out at the snow descending on the buildings. With the snow piled high on the streets, and with more snow falling, I wondered if we'd be snowed in. Then it hit me. This was Iceland, not Blue Ridge, so the chances of that were minimal. I figured Iceland knew how to handle winter much better than we do in Georgia. As I thought about the snow, a warm feeling washed over me. "I'm okay with this."

The real test would be when I got back to Blue Ridge. That's when my resolve would be tested. What would I say to Tara? And to Scarlett? And most of all, what would I say to those young ladies who I was fortunate to coach through a championship season?

As I looked out the window, watching the boats in the distance making their way across the icy water, I heard footsteps. I turned to see Catherine walk into the room. Her face was as frosty as what lay outside the window, so I stood and walked to her. "What's wrong?"

She hugged me. "Can we sit for a minute?"

The look on her face and the tone of her voice sent an icy knife slicing up my spine. We sat, and once I found her eyes, I asked,

"Cat? Are you okay?"

Catherine reached for my hands, and when they clasped together, she looked at them. As I waited for her to speak, she looked up and our eyes met. "Mark," she began. She didn't start by calling me Roy, so I knew this was serious. "I got off the phone with the head of the Orchestra. There's a slight change in plans."

The look on her face dropped a dose of adrenaline into my stomach. "Cat? What happened?"

"She told me they've created a touring orchestra that they want to send to Europe." Catherine looked past me to the window, then down at her hands, and continued. "I have to be at the concert hall to catch the bus to Kópavogur this afternoon."

"Where is the tour going?"

"After the show tomorrow night in Kópavogur, we travel to England. We'll play in London, Canterbury, Southampton, then Paris, Munich, Berlin, then a few cities in Italy. She told me to get everything in order since we won't be back until May."

Adrenaline splashed around my stomach and sent icicles throughout every corner of my body. "I see. Well, if you gave me a spare key, I could hang out here until you get back," I joked. When Catherine didn't laugh, I stopped smiling.

"You were going to give up everything to be with me. And where am I? I'm going to be traveling around Europe. Without you. You sacrificed everything for me. And now I have to leave you. Again. I promised myself I'd never let that happen."

"But this is your dream. Being able to play your music around the world. It has come true."

"But, Mark. What about us?"

Her question hit me between the eyes. Being caught up in feeling happy for her made me forget what all this meant. After everything I did to find her, I would lose her just as quickly.

I sat back on the couch and gave her a smile to mask my hurt. "You told me in one of your letters that not making it to the New York Philharmonic had something to do with this not being your time. As much as we thought otherwise, could it be that it's not our time? Is this what destiny has in store for you?"

"You didn't answer my question. What does this mean for us?"

"It means you need to find your place in the world. Make your mark and never look back. One day, you'll be happy that you've contributed a verse to the powerful play. Have you ever heard of the powerful play?"

Catherine nodded. "Walt Whitman," she replied in an almost resigned whisper.

"Catherine, this is your opportunity." As she stared at me, digesting my response, I saw the hurt in her eyes. "What this means for us is I love you. And when you love someone, you want them to be happy, and to live their dreams. Last night, Rick had to let Ilsa go, since it was the right thing to do. So let me quote him. If that bus leaves Reykjavik, and you're not on it, you'll regret it. Look, Cat, I'd never forgive myself for holding you back. For denying you the one thing you've always wanted."

Tears formed in her eyes. "Mark, I can't do it."

"Yes, you can. Now, get packed. You have a bus to catch."

She leaned forward and collapsed into my chest. I let her turn my shirt into a soggy mess.

🖋

At four o'clock, Catherine appeared in the living room, bundled up in her winter coat with her suitcase in one hand, and viola case in the other. I looked at her, then rose and walked over to give her a hug.

"Are you ready to go?"

Catherine looked at the floor and nodded. Then she looked up. "Yeah, I guess so. Did you call an Uber?"

I shook my head. "Sort of."

"Sort of?" She asked, squinting her eyes.

"You'll see."

When we walked out of her apartment, Catherine locked the door, and we moved to the sidewalk. Her eyes widened, and she managed a smile. "Olaf? What are you doing here?"

"We started this thing together. And after speaking with your boy about why you needed a ride, I guess we're going to finish it together. I thought I'd give you both a freebie. It will be my goodbye present."

Catherine looked at me, then nodded. "I can't think of a better way to get to the Harpa."

Olaf loaded us into the sled and the dogs mushed us to the Harpa Concert Hall. I paid him a little over the asking price to take the longer route, so Catherine and I would have extra time to be together. Final, precious seconds.

I held her, inhaling the scent of her hair and perfume. I wanted to memorize every smell and feeling, knowing there was no guarantee I would ever see her again.

When we arrived at the concert hall, Olaf helped me unload Catherine's bags. After placing them on the icy cement, he stood in front of her. "The boy here told me where you were going."

"He did?"

"Yeah. I'm sorry you have to leave. Öruggar ferðir vinur," he told her in Icelandic. "Friður sé með þér."

"Þakka þér fyrir, Olaf." She smiled, then leaned up and kissed him on his bearded cheek. Olaf turned, then walked over to the dogs.

The Redhead and the Fountain Pen

I walked to Catherine and reached for her hand. "What was that about?" I asked.

"He told me to have safe travels. Then he said, 'Peace be with you.'"

I looked at Olaf, and when our eyes met, I smiled and nodded at him. He nodded back.

As if on cue, snow descended on us, which I'm sure Scott was responsible for so we'd have a memorable finish. Then again, once I get back to Georgia, I'll try to forget much of what was about to happen anyway.

We walked through the flurry of ivory to the bus. Once we got there, we saw people standing around talking, and a few others loading instrument cases and equipment underneath the bus. Catherine saw this, then looked at me. "I guess I need to get going."

"Yeah, I guess so," I said as white puffs of breath came out of my mouth.

We hugged, then she broke into tears. "I thought once we found each other, we'd never have to say goodbye."

"It's okay, Cat. You need to go. Don't worry about me. Or us."

"I can't help but worry. What if we lose each other?"

"Then we'll lose each other," I told her. "If that happens, then it wasn't meant to be. But what's meant to be is you getting on that bus. And once you finish up doing what you need to do, you know where I am."

I reached inside my coat pocket and pulled out a navy blue fountain pen. I showed it to her, then said, "Take this. One day, I hope I'll find a letter in my mailbox from you. No matter what happens, Cat, nothing will ever take away how we feel about each other. It was magic, and it will live forever."

Catherine leaned in and we embraced. I held her, then waited for her to raise her head. When she did, I brushed away her tears. "You have to go. Safe travels, my love."

We kissed, then I let her go. I watched as she walked to the bus, then gave her bags and her viola case to the driver. She walked to the stairs, gave me a last look, then turned and climbed aboard.

I stood in the snow, and as the bus pulled out, I saw Catherine in the window. She waved goodbye, and when the bus disappeared into a blanket of ivory, I felt the icy reality of what lay before me. It was going to be a long, cold ride back to the airport.

When I got back to the dog sled, I shook my head, then looked at Olaf. "Well, close the chapter on that story."

He nodded. "You never know, boy. This could be the start of the sequel."

"Yeah. But if it ever does, it will be a long time from now. And when that time comes, who knows if she'll have given me a second thought? She has her music now. And she has her lifelong dream. Kind of hard to go up against that."

"Are you going to call her?"

I thought about it, then it hit me…I never asked for her number. Instinctively, I looked at the road, but all I saw were cars swallowed up by the descending snow. "I guess I got so wrapped up in us finding each other, then getting her on the bus, I didn't think about it."

I looked again at the road, then shook my head. "Serves me right for trying to fight for something I knew I couldn't beat. I guess David only gets to be Goliath once in a lifetime."

Olaf's eyes squinted. "What does that mean?"

I exhaled, watching the mist roll out of my mouth. "Aw, it was something that happened a while ago. Funny how it doesn't seem real anymore."

He looked at me for a few seconds, then continued getting the dogs ready to mush. "Keep the faith, boy. You never know."

"I will, Olaf. But I have a feeling I know this time."

thirty-two

I arrived in Atlanta, bleary-eyed, zombie-brained, and brokenhearted. All the great elements for a fun drive home.

At this moment, I had no idea where Catherine was, but I was sure she was happy. And for that, I found a small piece of life to be happy about.

As I drove north, the familiar sting of seeing Atlanta in the rear view mirror returned. This time, the hurt came from thinking Catherine would see it with me one day. Once again, I was forced into exile, beaten and alone, to face what waited for me in the days to come.

I drove north in the foggy, semi-darkness of a rainy afternoon. The windshield wipers and satellite radio were my only companions, but I wasn't listening anyway.

When the music stopped, I instinctively peered at the dashboard because I had an incoming call. As I looked at the name, I thought, This is going to be an interesting conversation. I pressed answer, then said, "Hello, Lisa. How are things at Atlanta Catholic?"

"They are great," her cheerful voice boomed through my car. "I don't know if you've heard the news, but things have gotten better in the last month."

"Yeah, I heard something about that," I told her as I changed lanes along the rain-soaked interstate. As I veered into the right lane, I heard the tires splash through the water.

We exchanged small talk for a few miles, including her congratulating me on our state championship. After that, she got down to business.

"Look, Mark. You've always been one of my favorites. I loved you and what you did for the team and our school. I wish you would have come to me and told me what was going on. We could have done something about it."

I shrugged. "Yeah, but I didn't want anyone to mess with the girls. As much power as Wilder held over the school and around the city, I worried about collateral damage. When someone throws out a rumor of impropriety, everyone thinks guilty before proven innocent. Especially with all the success we had, I'm sure he would have spun it as nobody can be that good unless they are cheating." I paused, then added, "The more I thought about it, the more I thought it was best to walk away and save the team."

"Well, the team didn't fare too well this year," she told me, then asked the million-dollar question. "Would you consider coming back?"

I heard Scarlett's voice flowing into my ears. "Once they clean house, they will ask you to come back." I shook my head. That old Irish board was right again. "I don't know what to say, Lisa. This is a surprise."

Then I thought about the current team at ACS. "What about Coach Murphy? Are you going to boot her out of the head job after one season?"

"I spoke with Coach Murphy. She said she would love for you to come back and coach with you again as your assistant. Plus, you can hire whoever you want to fill out your staff. Another assistant, a batting coach, a pitching coach, whatever you like. And I got approval to break ground on an addition to the stadium. We're going to have new dugouts, a larger grandstand, indoor batting cages, and an expanded weight room. The best part is we're constructing tunnels leading back under the stands to the locker rooms. We hired the same construction company who built the Braves stadium, so our field will be the envy of every school in the country."

As I digested that news, she force-fed me more tasty nuggets to whet my appetite. "The parents and boosters agreed to help with your salary. I guarantee it would be more than they are paying you in Blue Ridge." Before I could reply, she added, "Being transparent, it would be more than you made when you were here. I want to make things right for you to come back. We want you to come home."

I have to admit, her offer was intriguing. It was more money. And since Blue Ridge couldn't afford even one assistant, I would have as many assistants as I wanted. The best part would be coming back to the school where I had so much success.

But the numbness of Iceland clouded my mind, and I couldn't process what Lisa laid out for me. "I'm intrigued," I told her. "But with the holidays coming up, can you give me until the first of the year to decide? It's only a couple of weeks, and you know not a lot goes on in December."

Lisa told me she was good with it. "Since it was the end of the year, nobody was thinking about anything school-related until January. I can wait until then." She wished me a Merry Christmas and said she looked forward to speaking with me after the holiday.

I ended the call and drove the rest of the way to Blue Ridge in a haze, as I added another piece of gut wrenching drama to the long list of things I had to deal with.

The Redhead and the Fountain Pen

When I pulled into my driveway, seeing the Christmas lights I strung up before leaving for Iceland left me in a bitter tug of war. Sure, I was home. But most of me was still in Iceland.

I wasn't sure what I would encounter in Iceland when I walked off my porch a few days ago. Little did I know how things would play out the way they did. I went from desolation to euphoria back to desolation all in a few days. I almost got the break that would make everything okay. But in the end, like I told Catherine, it wasn't meant to be.

I exited my car, then instinctively walked toward the mailbox. As I got to it, and looked at the black box dotted by a row of snowflakes on top of it, I couldn't take another step. I stared at the mailbox, an invisible wall of loss preventing me from walking further.

Before me was the resting place of so many memories of Catherine's letters and gifts. I saw autumn's hue casting a heavenly light upon it, and inside was a glow of powder blue that greeted me when I opened the lid. I was happy again.

I reached out to touch it, hoping for the magic of October to swirl around me, and pull me out of the frozen despair I encountered in Iceland. But as my hand came closer, I heard Scarlett's voice telling me, "One day you'll open the mailbox, hoping for a miracle. But it won't be there."

My hand stopped, and I drew it back.

I stood in the cold night, my eyes lost in the haze of what once was. Finally, I summoned the courage for one last stand. I knew there wasn't a letter inside, but it was enough for me to reach out, and put my hand on the mailbox.

As I hoped, I felt October again, and I heard the sounds of a viola. When I thought about what happened in Iceland, finally meeting Catherine for the first time, and ensuring that we would never part as strangers, I was grateful for the few days we had together. That was something winter could never take away.

When the last image of Catherine faded, I gave the mailbox a final rub, then brought my hand back and walked to the porch.

Tonight, I would lick my wounds. Tomorrow, I would dig graves for all that died within me.

I spent the night on the deck, covered by a blanket, with a glass of brown water not too far away from me on the table. I stoked the burning logs in the fireplace, allowing the molten orange to shoot warmth into my face. After dodging the sparks escaping into the icy December evening, I returned to the couch.

I looked into the sky. Gone was the glowing green of the Northern Lights, replaced by the navy blue of a southern sky. I was back in Georgia. I was home. There was no better place to let the healing begin.

As my mind rifled through every one of her letters, one of them stood out over the others.

She asked if I ever had my heart broken. I wrote back that the only time it ever happened was when we lost in the state championship. As I look back on it, I know how silly that was. And how silly my life was before I met Catherine. Now I know what real heartbreak feels like. Losing the girl you fell in love with is the worst pain I've ever felt. There's no next season when that happens.

Since it was December, school was out, which for me was both good and bad. I had a few days to compartmentalize what happened in Iceland, which was good since I could sleep in and do whatever I wanted. The bad news was I could sleep in and do whatever I wanted. I had a lot of free time on my hands to think about things I shouldn't have gotten myself into.

When in trouble, go to where you feel safe. Where you're loved.

✒

I pulled up a chair at Blue Ridge Books. I figured it was the first stop on the healing tour. Scarlett walked over with my usual. I looked at the plate but left the cookies where they rested.

"I got your text," she told me. "I'd ask how you are, but I see it in your face, so I won't ask a stupid question."

"Thanks. I'm too tired to want to conceal it."

"She's in London?"

"I'm not sure where she is now."

"How long will she be gone?"

"May." I looked at the plate and said without thinking, "A lot can happen between now and then. I'm sure by then, she won't even remember my name."

"Come on, Mark. Stop feeling sorry for yourself."

I looked at Scarlett. She was not mincing words. "You experienced something millions of people dream about, but never experience. In this lifetime, you'll never have to wonder what the mystical feeling of being in love feels like. She was with you every second of the day, even though she wasn't standing next to you. Once those letters began, you were never alone."

"But I'm alone now. With her busy schedule, I'm sure she won't have time to write. Then again, she has her music. Like moving away from a best friend, the letters will continue for a while, then trickle away until they dry up."

"Are you going to use that as an excuse when you move back to Atlanta?"

I squinted. "Atlanta? What are you talking about?"

She raised one eyebrow. "We've been over this before."

"Oh right. The Irish thing." I nodded. "My compliments."

Scarlett wasn't having any of my charms today. "Your sexy smile won't get you out of this one. Are you going back to Atlanta?"

"I haven't thought about it. I've been thinking about a redhead."

"I'm sure you have. But remember this: once a place touches you, friends become family in the blink of an eye. When you find a home, there's no need to search for a home ever again." As I let the words sink in, she rose. "This is home, Mark Dawson. And it will be for the rest of your life. No matter where you go from this day forward."

Within seconds, she vanished behind a row of books.

thirty-three

I woke the next morning to an inch of snow that fell overnight. I looked out of the window, and found more snow descended during the night, and it joined the white blanket that fell yesterday.

As I lay in bed, I thought about Scarlett's words. I know she's right. Home is something everyone longs for, and when you have it, there's nothing more you need. Blue Ridge is where I found peace. And also found a new family of people who came into my life as friends.

But would the memory of the magical months Catherine and I shared make me want to run away again? Right now, I doubt my ability to make the right decisions, so the flood of dread about the future only deepens.

Go and I leave everything behind in a place where I had the best time of my life. I would leave behind a team of girls who believed they could do something they weren't good enough to do. And I would leave behind a strong leader who has supported me in everything I did at Blue Ridge Prep. Throw in a sassy Irish redhead, who has become one of my closest friends, and you can see it would be difficult to say goodbye.

If I stay, I have to live with the memory of letters in my mailbox. And then the reality of not having any letters in my mailbox. Everywhere I go, Catherine's ghost would be lurking. Could I live with that?

Scarlett was right. Every time I'd walk to the mailbox, the memory of a powder blue envelope, the autumn colors and the gentle breeze of peace would be waiting. And the hurt would renew with greater force each day when the mailbox was empty.

There was no hope of coming out of this alive. One way or the other, the day will come when I'll have to dig graves for everything that died within me.

I needed something to fill the cavities of dread entrenched in my mind, so I got out of the cabin and drove over to Blue Ridge Prep. As I pulled into the parking lot, I wondered if this was the last time I'd be there as head coach of the girl's softball team. I should have a last look around, you know, in case?

When I arrived at my office, I turned on the lights and took note of the setup. It was time for a change, so I began moving the furniture around to get a fresh start.

I moved my desk to the side of the window so I could see the softball field with the mountains behind it. As I looked out the window, I saw they were bare and brown with touches of white around them. I knew when spring came they would come back to life, and turn into a bounty of green, signifying life had returned to the world. It would take time, but it would come one day.

After moving a bookcase to the other side of the office, I returned the pictures and trinkets to the shelves. I reached for the last frame resting on the chair, and before placing it on the top shelf, I looked at it. It was a picture of the last state championship team I coached at ACS.

I stared at the smiles on the girl's faces. Then I thought about how I walked away without a fight. As the guilt from the past cast its shadow, it reminded me I performed the same feat in Iceland. I should have fought for my redheaded girl.

I know I did the right thing in both cases. But that doesn't glue together what's left of my broken heart.

The memories of both came at me so thick and in vivid color that I never heard the footsteps coming up the hallway and stopping at my door.

"Knock, knock," a woman's voice called out. I turned and saw Tara standing in the doorway.

"Hey, you. What are you doing here?"

She wiggled her fingers at me and made spooky noises. "I'm the Ghost of Christmas Past." She walked into my office and folded her arms across her chest. "I hear your ex-girlfriend wants you back."

I gulped, then thought, how does she know about Catherine? Then I realized she was talking about Atlanta Catholic. "Yeah, I was going to mention that to you. I got a call a few days ago."

"Yeah, I know all about it."

"Scarlett?" I asked.

She shook her head, "Nah. Lisa called to ask permission to speak to you about coming back. I told her it was okay." She paused, then raised her eyebrows. "How did it go?"

"Fine. I told her I was going to take the holiday to think about it."

"Are you leaving us? The only reason I asked is if you are, I need to get moving on hiring a new coach."

I looked at Tara. Behind a self-assured smile lay a sadness in her eyes. It was the same sadness I saw in Scarlett's eyes. I'm sure it was the same sadness in my eyes too.

It didn't seem right that sadness was all around us since the holidays were coming up. I told her, "We won't worry about it now. It will be there when January comes."

"Okay. I'll follow up in January. But just so you know, I–"

"I love you too, Tara," I told her, not wanting her to have to say it. "Lisa and I will talk about it after the holiday." I paused, then admitted, "Just so you know, it would be difficult to say goodbye."

Tara smiled. "Yeah, it would be."

As the weight of having to deal with things I would rather not evaporated, I changed the subject and looked around the office. "I thought I'd have the place all to myself."

"Almost," she said with a grin. "I am here to meet the new teachers we hired for the spring semester. We had a few spots to fill because of retirement and teachers who took other jobs."

"By chance, did that Morgan guy retire?" I asked with raised eyebrows.

Tara shook her head, then giggled. "Sorry. I know that was on your Christmas list, but I don't think his retirement will be in your stocking," she joked. "Maybe Santa will deliver it next year."

After we laughed, she continued. "This was the only day I could get all the new teachers together before the holiday. I'm giving them a lay of the land so they will know where to go when school gets going again in a few weeks."

"How are the newbies looking?"

"Impressive," she said. "I finished with a couple of them a few minutes ago. I showed them their classrooms and got them settled in. A few asked if they could get their classrooms set up today."

"A tad eager, especially since the semester doesn't get started for a few more weeks."

"I told you I hired some good ones."

"You've been lucky with your hires," I told her with a grin. "Except for the softball coach. He turned out to be a real turd," I joked.

Tara nodded. "Yeah, but I'll give him one more year. You know, to see if he can turn things around," then she winked. We laughed, then she told me, "Before you head out for the day, drop by the classrooms and introduce yourself."

I nodded. "Will do. When I was a rookie last summer, I appreciated the other teachers coming by to say hello and welcome me to Blue Ridge. I'd be happy to return the favor."

"So, when you tell them who you are, will you mention you'll be the softball coach next season?" She asked with a wink.

I walked over, and we hugged. "Merry Christmas, my friend."

✒

It was twilight when I moved the last piece of furniture and the last framed picture onto a different shelf on a different bookcase in a different corner of my office.

When everything was moved where I wanted it, I was ready to leave. I slid on my jacket, dropped a thumb drive containing videos of last year's finals in my coat pocket, then left my office.

I walked down a long, shadowy hallway, passing a row of lonely lockers that wouldn't have anyone to greet until the new year. I turned right and continued along until I came upon the first classroom.

I looked at the nameplate next to the window, which was blank, since Tara was in the middle of getting the nameplates replaced. But I knew what classroom it was since there were musical notes taped to the walls and photos of musicians of different genres hanging next to them. A set of chairs adorned the tiered stage.

I walked inside and saw a woman with her back to me, writing on a whiteboard. "Hello. Welcome to Blue Ridge."

The woman turned and smiled. "Hello there," she said in a welcoming voice. She walked over and extended her hand. "I'm Becky Sharp. And you are?"

"I'm Mark Dawson. I'm the softball coach," I told her as we shook hands.

After we exchanged small talk, I looked at the instruments. I found a violin and a viola sitting next to each other, so I walked over and looked at both without speaking.

"Are you a music fan?" She asked.

"A friend of mine is. She taught me the difference between the viola and the violin."

"That's impressive.."

"Thanks. She taught me well."

"Does your friend live in Blue Ridge?"

I thought for a few seconds, then replied, "Nah. She's

traveling the world. Living her dream."

I told Becky goodbye, then walked out of the classroom and back down the hallway. I patted my pockets for my car keys, and when I felt nothing but my legs, I knew I left them in my office. As I walked back to retrieve them, I passed by the open door of the softball locker room. "Might as well get a look, you know, in case," I told myself.

I pushed the door open, turned on the lights, and looked around at the empty lockers. Sitting in front of each locker were the ghosts of what once was.

I looked over and sure enough, the same chair I sat in all season to speak to the team waited for me in the same place I left it in October.

As I looked at the empty lockers, all I saw were a bunch of girls jumping up and down. They threw towels, slammed their lockers, and savored what it meant to be alive. The sound was deafening. When the images faded, another silence came. This time, it was the silence of reality.

After grabbing my keys, I left the athletic building and walked to the chapel. I peered into the window, seeing Father O'Scanlon, leading mass. I looked at the pews, remembering how they once swelled with the hopes of the parents and townies who spent their morning praying for our girls.

From behind, I felt the December chill rolling in off the mountains, causing me to pull the collar of my winter coat up. As I felt the spikes jabbing at my neck, the colorful, breezy autumn days seemed as if they never happened.

I remember the mornings I spent praying for Catherine so she would have peace as she fought through her audition. Even though she didn't win, I guess God granted me what I asked for. She's at peace now, achieving something nobody can take away.

    I left the chapel and walked across campus to the softball field. I entered the dugout and took a seat inside. It was a bitter afternoon, with snow flurries tumbling in the breeze. I shivered, which was in contrast to the brutal pre-season practices in the summer when I had to remind everyone to hydrate.

    I thought about the times Josie took over the team when we needed a kick in the pants. My talk with Anna after the first game when she cried after the loss. And all those days in the sun, where I saw a ragtag group of girls, turned into a team of champions right before my eyes.

    With a howl of ivory slicing through the fence, adding to the row of snow piled on the cement dugout floor, I stood and looked out at the field. Gone were the green grass and cocoa dirt I remembered. Replacing them was nothing but a blanket of white, over a sheet of ice that signified my days in the sun were long gone.

    I left the field and walked to the parking lot. With the specks of icy snow blowing into my face by another strong breeze, I turned and gave the field a last look. As the memory of our day in the sun evaporated into the reality of today, I savored the irony.

    Once I started the car, cool air blew from the vents, but within a few seconds, warm air tumbled out. As I waited for the warmth to take hold, I put thoughts of the gray December day aside and focused on tonight. It would be nice to not have to do anything, be anywhere, or see anyone. I can order takeout and lock myself up in my fortress so I can begin to heal.

✒

As I contemplated picking up Juniors, pizza, or Chinese, my phone

The Redhead and the Fountain Pen

lit up. Within seconds, a familiar number flashed on the screen over the radio. "Hello, Scarlett. How are you?"

"Great," she replied. Her voice was cheerful, which was in contrast to how we left each other yesterday. "I wanted to let you know we have book club tonight. I'd love it if you stopped by."

I raised an eyebrow and frowned. "I don't think I'm up for it. It's been a tough few days."

"Yeah, I know. But just now, someone requested we discuss The Great Gatsby. Since that's your favorite book, who's better to talk about it than you? Besides, the ladies would love for you to come over and charm their support hose off."

"Come on, Scarlett. Support hose?"

"Well, some of them have moved on to compression socks with rubber grips on the bottom so they don't fall and break a hip. Is today's technology a bitch or what?"

Before I could come up with a reason to say no, Scarlett added, "There are free oatmeal cookies and hot chocolate."

"Scarlett, you always give me free cookies and hot chocolate."

"Fine," she said. "I'll start charging you if that's what you want."

Her comment made me laugh, so I figured it might be good to be out and have the chance to smile for the first time in a while. "Okay," I told her. "You talked me into it."

"Whoo hoo," she yelled into the phone. "Can you wear that blue bow tie everyone likes?"

"I'll see what I can do."

As I walked into the bookstore, I saw a table surrounded by lights and copies of *The Great Gatsby*. A sign above featured an old photograph of Scott, and a sign reading, "Tonight - Blue Ridge Book Club discussion of Fitzgerald's, *The Great Gatsby*. Fiction room, back of the store."

"Gee, Scarlett has gone all out for this one."

I made my way to the back and saw the usual group milling around. There were a few people I didn't know. An older lady wearing a shawl, flowered dress and pushing around a walker stood by the coffee machine.

As I scanned the room, I exhaled. At least this time, there were a few people my age there. Some sat, some looked at their phones, and by the podium Scarlett spoke with someone I didn't recognize. No matter. We were going to be talking about my favorite book, so I could lose myself in the words at least for an hour.

A few minutes later, Scarlett came to the podium and welcomed everyone. "I'd like to change things up tonight. Instead of a speaker, let's all put our chairs in a circle, and everyone can recite what the book means to you. You can even read a few of your favorite lines to the group. And if you're not comfortable doing that, no problem. Sit back and enjoy the discussion."

Everyone took their chair and placed it around the room. I took mine and placed it by the entrance, so I could exit once the book club ended. I didn't feel much like being social or putting on the charm tonight.

A woman wearing glasses stood with a paperback copy of the book in her hands. She greeted everyone with a smile, introduced herself as Jennifer Adams, a professor at North

The Redhead and the Fountain Pen

Georgia College, then opened the book. "My favorite quote is, 'His hand took hold of hers, and as she said something low in his ear, he turned toward her with a rush of emotion.' I know Gatsby's love for Daisy was doomed, but I've always loved that line and the imagery."

Scarlett rose. "I like that, Professor," she said. "Anyone else?"

I mentally checked out for a few seconds and stared at the floor. People stood and talked about their favorite quotes. Most of the ones they mentioned I recited to myself for years, so it was nice to hear. But tonight, it was only white noise since the words made me think about a redheaded girl and the book I returned to her.

I heard laughter, so I woke up and watched Scarlett smile and lean forward. "Does anyone have anything to add?"

I don't know what compelled me to do it, but I shifted into auto-pilot, then rose. I looked around the room, then at Professor Adams. "I agree about the imagery. My favorite line was at the end when Scott wrote that Gatsby was so close to his dream and he couldn't have possibly failed to grasp it. But he didn't know it was already past him."

I paused, then looked at the floor and shook my head. I gathered myself, then looked around the room. "The ironic thing is Scott wrote those lines, not knowing the same thing would happen to someone a century later. Just like that, someone's dream was right there in front of him, and somehow, it slipped out of his grasp. Poof. Already past him, and he wasn't smart enough to realize it. I'm sure he felt the same pain as Gatsby. Art imitates life, huh?"

When I woke up and looked around the room, stone faces

greeted me as the silence washed over everyone. Finally someone asked, "Did this happen to you?"

I looked at the woman, then at Scarlett, who gave me an empathetic smile. I looked back at the woman and told her, "Nah. It was someone I used to know. He lives in Atlanta now."

I glanced at Scarlett, whose face went from empathetic to worried as her eyebrows dropped into her nose.

After I returned to my seat, the room fell silent. Scarlett asked if there were any others, and when there were no takers, she stood. "Thanks for stopping by. Next month, we will review *69 Summers* by Elin Hilderbrand."

After the room cleared, Scarlett found me by the exit. I didn't want to leave without saying goodbye, so I hung out and said hello to the ladies I remembered from the last book club.

"Wonderful event," I told Scarlett as she walked over.

"I thought so. Well, it sounds like you've already made your decision."

I nodded. "I think so. But I'll wait until the first of the year to tell Lisa I'm going to accept her offer. When Scarlett gave me a resigned nod, I told her, "I had to say goodbye to Catherine. I might as well say goodbye to you too. But it won't be official until the beginning of the year so keep this between us."

"Good. I still have a little time to talk you out of it."

I saw the look of determination in Scarlett's eyes and shuddered. "I figured you would."

After saying goodbye to the last of the ladies, I figured I'd walk back to the classics section and dig the final grave of what lay within me. Once that was done, all my obligations were over.

The Redhead and the Fountain Pen

With the last spade of dirt, I would bid farewell to the past, and begin again. With no regrets, no ties to the past, and most of all, no guilt about the way things ended. I looked forward to my rebirth.

I walked to the corner of the classic section and sure enough, the bookshelf which started this madness stood before me. Instinctively, I looked at the fourth shelf, fourth book over and saw the gap that remained from that July day when I pulled the book from the shelf. How I remember the exact location I have no idea.

While *Tender is the Night* and *This Side of Paradise* wondered where *The Great Gatsby* went, I walked up to the shelf. *So this is where it all began*, I thought. All the incredible events that happened between then and now are over, and it's time to stop living in the past.

I exhaled, then gave the shelf a last look. In the silence, I heard a voice. "There I was, way off my ambitions, getting deeper in love every minute, and all of the sudden, I didn't care."

Funny, I thought. I've heard those words before. I know they are in my favorite book, but the way the woman delivered them was hauntingly familiar. My eyes focused, trying to solve the mystery. Where have I heard that voice before?

Then it hit me. Without turning, I smiled, and said, "Thanks, Scarlett. That's one of my favorite lines from my favorite book.

The voice replied, "You're welcome, Roy."

I squinted. Why did Scarlett call me that? Then I turned to ask her.

thirty-four

"I've always called you Roy," Catherine said with a smile.

My legs buckled, so I had to find the strength to steady myself. I reached out to the bookcase to keep from falling into it.

As my vision blurred, I fought through it so I could attempt to form a sentence. "Yes, you have," I told her, hoping I said the words in the right order.

I worried this was a dream, so I didn't move or speak. If I did, she would dissolve and I'd wake up alone in my cabin, and the miracle would be a mirage.

I continued staring as she smiled and said, "Remember, I wrote that quote in one of our letters. I thought it was appropriate for the moment."

I thought about the words, then asked, "What are you doing here? You should be in London. Or Paris. Or...anywhere but here."

Catherine shrugged her shoulders. "I heard your school was looking for a music teacher."

I thought for a second, then told her, "Yeah, but they filled it. I met the music teacher today."

"Becky?" Catherine asked.

"How did you know that?"

She smiled. "Becky is my assistant."

"Your assistant? I...I..."

Scarlett walked over, laughed, then looked at Catherine. "We're working on that stammer."

Catherine smiled at Scarlett, then looked at me. "Tara hired me a few days ago. I wanted it to be a surprise."

"Tara? How do you know about Tara?" I asked as my worlds collided.

Scarlett shook her head. "Cat, sweetie, give the boy a few seconds to compose himself. He's a little cray-cray at the moment."

I gulped, then asked, "You know Catherine?"

Scarlett smiled. "We met earlier. She came in here looking for you and when I saw her, I knew who she was before she said a word."

"You did?" I asked.

Catherine nodded. "I went by your cabin. When you weren't there, I thought about where you could be. I drove over to the school to get settled, hoping I'd run into you there, but they told me you had already left."

"Yeah. Um, sorry about that."

"So last on my list was the bookstore since I remembered it from your letters. I figured someone here would know you, so when I ran into Scarlett, I knew who she was. And she knew who I was even before I introduced myself."

When I looked at Scarlett, she smiled and nodded. "Never underestimate the intelligence of the Irish."

I laughed. "Yeah. I won't." Then I looked at Catherine and exhaled. As our eyes locked on each other, Scarlett cleared her throat. "He's looking at her the way all women want to be looked at by a man."

Her words broke the amorous dance our eyes played with each other. Catherine looked at Scarlett. "That's from *The Great Gatsby*."

Scarlett nodded. "Yeah, it is. I figured you two wouldn't mind if I followed your lead."

As we all shared a laugh, Scarlett told us, "Well, as I am about to be an afterthought, I have some books to shelve." She looked at Catherine, then hugged her. "Welcome to Blue Ridge. I'm sure I'll be seeing you around here soon."

"You will. So much, you'll get sick of me."

"I hope so," she said, then looked at me and smiled. "I'll have some cookies out for you two in a few."

Scarlett walked over and hugged me. Then she leaned in and whispered, "Don't screw this up. A cat only has so many lives. And that Cat there is a special one. Take good care of her."

After Scarlett walked away, I looked at Catherine. "I know you don't like oatmeal, but Scarlett can find you some Oreos."

"Oatmeal is fine."

I walked closer. "I hate to rain on our parade, but I have to ask about the Orchestra. Why did you leave Iceland?"

"Would you believe it if I told you I needed a real Diet Coke?"

I nodded. "That I can believe."

Catherine smiled, then told me, "The first night I walked on stage, I thought about you being in the crowd. Then when I looked at the faces, and you weren't there, being where I thought I wanted to be wasn't as magical as I imagined."

The image of Catherine's rosy face and freckles stopped me in my tracks. I tried to speak, but no words came out. Finally, I said, "Someone once told me that anyone who comes to Blue Ridge is running from something. You have nothing to run from."

Catherine told me, "I'm running toward something. I remember reading a letter a friend of mine sent me a while ago. He wrote I should never be afraid of anything. Well, there is one thing I am afraid of," she told me.

"What's that?"

She looked down, then locked on my eyes. "How I'd feel if I couldn't be with you."

As it had on the stage in Iceland, everything around Catherine's face blurred. Then she took a step closer. "There are thousands of orchestras throughout the world. But there is only one Mark Dawson."

I reached for her hand. When she reached for it, I told her, "I only wanted you to be happy. Letting you go was something I had to do because I love you."

"Well, I'm happy now. Why do you think I came here? I love teaching children, like I did in New York."

"You'd give up your dream to come here?"

"Which dream?"

"What do you mean?" I asked.

"There are a few dreams I have. But the one I wanted more than anything I didn't realize until we were an ocean apart."

"You didn't?"

"No. The dream I wanted turned out not to be in New York, Iceland, or even touring Europe. It was in Blue Ridge. It took me a while to figure that out, but I did. And that's why I am here."

"Are you sure this is what you want?"

"Well," Catherine said with a raise of her eyebrow. "All I've ever wanted was to make sure children know the difference between a viola and the violin. And since you're here, there's nothing more in the world I could ever want."

"But what about the orchestra? Won't you miss it?"

"Yeah. But I have a plan."

"Plan?"

"I'll make a deal with you. I'll be your assistant coach for the softball team in the fall. And when school's out, you'll be my travel guide and secretary for the summer."

"I don't know if I have the legs to be your secretary, but I'll try anything once. Do you have a pair of boots that might fit me?" I joked.

"I might," she said with a laugh. "I told my manager at the Iceland Symphony Orchestra I wanted to take a leave of absence, then return for our summer concerts in Reykjavik that begin in May and continue through August. Do you think you might be able to get away from Blue Ridge and go with me?"

A warm feeling of calm washed over me. "I could ask Tara for a little time off before school begins," I told her with a wry grin.

As silence took over, neither of us needed to say another word. We rushed to each other and shared a long kiss.

From behind, I heard someone approach. "Okay you two," Scarlett said. "Knock it off. This is a family bookstore, not some damn Hallmark Channel RomCom," she joked.

We turned and saw her holding a tray with oatmeal and Oreo cookies, and two cups of hot chocolate. "So, does this mean you'll be sticking around Blue Ridge?" She asked me.

I looked at Catherine, who gave me a tilt of her head and a questioning smile. Then I looked at Scarlett and replied, "Yeah. I could stick around for at least another season."

Scarlett shook her head, then smiled. "That's the smart move. If you keep making moves like that, this pretty girl standing next to you might stick around too. At least for another season. Right?" She laughed.

Catherine nodded. "I'll give him at least one season, then we can reevaluate," she said with a sparkle in her eye.

Scarlett squinted at Catherine. As she stared, Catherine asked, "Is everything alright?"

After a few more seconds of scrutiny, she asked, "By chance, are you from Ireland?"

Catherine shook her head. "With my red hair, people think I could be. But my parents were from a tad northwest of there. Iceland, to be exact. Can we still be friends?" She giggled.

Scarlett nodded. "Ireland. Iceland. It's one letter off, so that's good enough for me." She smiled at Catherine, then asked, "Can I interest you in a Bushmills sometime? Your friend here calls it a brown water drink."

Catherine looked at me, then back to Scarlett. "Well, the last time I did that, it didn't end well. But I'll give it another shot I suppose."

"Leave everything to me," Scarlett assured us. "Give me a week, and I'll have her wearing a kilt."

I swooned. "Ooh, I like that visual," I told her.

Scarlett laughed, then told Catherine, "It was wonderful meeting you. See you soon." Then she looked at me. "Mo ghrá thú," she said, then walked over and kissed me on the cheek.

"Grá duit freisin," I replied. Scarlett never suspected I knew what "I love you" in Irish meant. When I replied I loved her too, it was worth seeing the joy on her face.

Scarlett's eyebrows shot upward. I smiled and said, "I learned a little Irish too."

She winked, then said, "Love you, Mark Dawson."

"I love you too, Scarlett McKeegan."

After Scarlett walked away, Catherine asked, "What was that about?"

I shook my head and smiled. "Aw, it was nothing. It appears Scarlett has taken a shine to you."

Catherine looked over my shoulder, watching Scarlett walk away, then nodded. "I like her too. But what was that about you sticking around Blue Ridge for one more season? You aren't leaving me after all we've been through. Are you?"

I wasn't sure what she meant. Then the light bulb went off. I shook my head and smiled. "Aw, that was nothing. It was a bad idea that I'm not going to follow up on."

"Whew," she said. "So, does this mean you'll take me up on my offer?"

I grinned, and with a sparkle in my eye, I told her, "Yeah. After careful consideration, I think we can make that work."

Catherine screamed in joy, then jumped into my arms. After our embrace ended, she backed up and smiled. "By the way. Nice bow tie. Is that the same one you wrote about before?"

I looked down, then back to her. "Yep. The ladies seem to like it."

"Add me to the list," she said with a smile. "Although, I think you'd look great in a purple bow tie. You know how I am with that color."

"I know of some places we can go," I assured her.

She straightened my tie, then looked at me with a sparkled in her deep blue eyes. "I know we asked each other the same question in Iceland, but," she paused, then raised her eyebrows. "What do we do now?"

I smiled. "Like I said before, it will come to us."

We left Blue Ridge Books holding hands as the snow

descended upon us. I stopped and turned to look at the bookstore's glowing window.

"What are you looking at?" Catherine asked.

Through the snowflakes, I saw a man and woman grinning at me. The man tipped his flask, the woman blew me a kiss, then the pair vanished into the snowflakes.

"Ah, just a good friend. I have him to thank for helping get us together."

"You do? How?" She asked, then wrapped her arms around mine as we walked.

I smiled and shook my head. "Aw, it's a long story. But we have all the time in the world to talk about it now."

As we walked into the descending ivory, I looked over and asked, "What do you say we walk back to my cabin, I'll start a fire on the back deck and we can spend tonight getting reacquainted. I want to hear all about your European tour."

"I'd rather tell you all about me leaving the European tour to find you."

I grinned. "Hmm. Sounds like fun, Cat."

She kissed me on the cheek. "Lead the way, Roy."

After thousands of miles, stacks of letters, and months wondering who Catherine was, she was now here beside me.

I've used words all my life. Lately, to inspire a group of underdog girls to find greatness. Then I wrote them on paper to another underdog girl who needed someone to believe in her.

Words can inspire those to do the impossible. Move a person to tears. Take a moment buried under years of gray amnesia and splash it with vivid color so it comes back to life. Glue together a shattered heart.

Words can change the world.

Ivan Scott

When Catherine looked over at me and smiled, you'll never be able to convince me otherwise.

I could not have written this book without the help of some very special people: Kathy LeNoir, Colleen Fernandez, Michele Packard, Elaine Sapp, Katie Cunningham and Ella Piazzi. My thanks for all of your help, guidance and suggestions. They made the book what it is!

And to Shaye Strager, thanks for your kindness, support, and belief in this book when so many others did not.

Please visit me on social media @AuthorIvanScott on Instagram, Facebook, X, Pinterest, Goodreads and YouTube

If you'd like to see the inspirations for who I saw as the characters and locations in this book, as well as my other books, visit my Pinterest page.

Printed in Great Britain
by Amazon